Praise for the Fa

FRA   ...... (#4)

"A snappy, clever mystery that hooked me on page one and didn't let go until the perfectly crafted and very satisfying end. Faith Hunter is a delightful amateur sleuth and the quirky characters that inhabit the town of Eden are the perfect complement to her overly inquisitive ways. A terrific read!"

— Jenn McKinlay,
New York Times Bestselling Author of *Copy Cap Murder*

"Christina's characters shine, her knowledge of scrapbooking is spot on, and she weaves a mystery that simply cries out to be read in one delicious sitting!"

— Pam Hanson,
Author of *Faith, Fireworks, and Fir*

EMBELLISHED TO DEATH (#3)

"A fast-paced crafting cozy that will keep you turning pages as you try to figure out which one of the attendees is an identity thief and which one is a murderer."

— Lois Winston,
Author of the Anastasia Pollack Crafting Mystery Series

"A little town, a little romance, a little intrigue and a little murder. Join heroine Faith and find out exactly who is doing the embellishing—the kind that doesn't involve scrapbooking."

— Leann Sweeney,
Author of the Bestselling Cats in Trouble Mysteries

DESIGNED TO DEATH (#2)

"Battling scrapbook divas, secrets, jealousy, murder, and lots of glitter make *Designed to Death* a charming and heartfelt mystery."
–Ellen Byerrum,
Author of the Crime of Fashion Mysteries

"Freeburn's second installment in her scrapbooking mystery series is full of small-town intrigue, twists and turns, and plenty of heart."
– Mollie Cox Bryan,
Agatha Award Finalist, *Scrapbook of Secrets*

CROPPED TO DEATH (#1)

"A great read that had me reading non-stop from the moment I turned the first page...kept me in suspense with plenty of twists and turns and every time I thought I had it figured out, the author changed the direction in which the story was headed...and I liked the cast of characters in this charming whodunit!"
–*Dru's Book Musings*

"Witty, entertaining and fun with a side of murder...When murder hits Eden, WV, Faith Hunter will stop at nothing to clear the name of her employee who has been accused of murder. Will she find the killer before it is too late? Read this sensational read to find out!"
– *Shelley's Book Case*

"A cozy mystery that exceeds expectations...Freeburn has crafted a mystery that does not feel clichéd or cookie-cutter...it's her sense of humor that shows up in the book, helping the story flow, making the characters real and keeping the reader interested."
– *Scrapbooking is Heart Work*

MASKED
to death

The Faith Hunter Scrap This Mystery Series
by Christina Freeburn

CROPPED TO DEATH (#1)
DESIGNED TO DEATH (#2)
EMBELLISHED TO DEATH (#3)
FRAMED TO DEATH (#4)
MASKED TO DEATH (#5)

MASKED
to death

A Faith Hunter Scrap This Mystery

CHRISTINA
FREEBURN

HENERY PRESS

MASKED TO DEATH
A Faith Hunter Scrap This Mystery
Part of the Henery Press Mystery Collection

First Edition | January 2017

Henery Press
www.henerypress.com

Copyright © 2016 by Christina Freeburn
Author photograph by Kristi Downey

Trade Paperback ISBN-13: 978-1-63511-137-8
Digital epub ISBN-13: 978-1-63511-138-5
Kindle ISBN-13: 978-1-63511-139-2
Hardcover Paperback ISBN-13: 978-1-63511-140-8

Printed in the United States of America

To my "big sister" Pam.

You are one of the bright lights and soft places in my life. I adore and love you to the moon and back, and infinity and beyond. I didn't always have a big sister in my life and am so grateful you came along later, even though I was in my thirties when I finally had a big sister of my own. I will forever be grateful to Terry for asking, "Have you meet Pam?" I don't think he realized he was creating a family with that question...or maybe he did. Thank you for being my big sister. Love you.

xoxoxoxoxo

ACKNOWLEDGMENTS

Another book is finished and ready to go out into the world, and I know I couldn't have accomplished this without the help of some wonderful and talented people. I owe a ton of thanks to my wonderful editors Erin and Rachel who helped to make sure my characters didn't randomly move places, change names, and that I was accurately getting across my point to my beloved readers.

Much love to my cover designer who makes such lovely and beautiful "faces" for my stories.

Teresa...girl, you know I couldn't have written this book without you. Thanks for keeping me sane and reeling me in when I needed to focus and keep the story grounded, and encouraging me to get crazy when I needed to stretch the plot. I can always count on you to be my better half—or worse—depending on my need at the moment.

And last, and never least, a huge thanks to my husband who was willing to agree that of course we needed to go on another cruise to experience a different line as a Disney Cruise isn't like other cruises. Thanks for putting up with me and all the fictional people that come along with me. I love you.

ONE

Shoving the keycard into the slot on the cabin room door, I hoisted the straps of my carry-on and camera bag onto my shoulder. For seven days, this room would be my home away from home. Away from my grandmothers. My friends. My community. Sadness bubbled up in me. Stop it. I was a grown-up. There was no need to feel homesick. I was going on a cruise. Sun. Sand. Relaxation. I had traveled away from home before, so why was I feeling out of sorts this time?

Ted. Or more precisely his family. I adored his brother, Bob, who I sleuthed with over a year ago, and loved hanging out with Bob's betrothed, Garrison, but I hadn't met his mother, nor had Ted formally introduced me to his ex-wife or daughter, Claire. I had seen the pair around town a few times a month when Elizabeth dropped Claire off for visitation. Ted and I hadn't been dating long, so we agreed it was best to wait as we were still navigating our relationship. This trip was a huge step in our romance, even with him rooming with his mom and daughter.

I slipped into the stateroom and pressed the door closed. Sweat coated my hand. This cruise practically counted as our first date. The last ninety days had both of us helping put Scrap This, and Eden, West Virginia, back together after a member of our community decided arson was a profitable business—basically making Ted and I have a long-distance relationship even though we lived ten minutes apart. So far, our romance was less exciting than our friendship. Now, we had seven promising days where we could explore our new relationship without having to worry about interference from my grandmothers, his job, or my ability to find a wayward soul to help.

My heart pitter-pattered at the thought of being able to have a face-to-face conversation with Ted and a real first kiss. Quick pecks didn't count. It was hard to even hold hands when we couldn't be in the same area for more than ten seconds. I had thought our flight from Baltimore to Orlando would be perfect for quality time, but Ted had slept from the minute the tires lifted to the moment the pilot brought them down.

The curtains covering the veranda were drawn back, giving me a glimpse of my window to the world for the next week. Right now, all I saw was the cruise ship next to us, a huge one that dwarfed our ship, the *Serenade*. After we left Port Canaveral, I knew I'd be treated to sights I'd once only dreamed of. I'd have coffee out on the small balcony and watch the sunrise, a glass of wine in the evening to watch the sunset. A fantastic week lay before me.

I dropped my carry-on onto the queen bed. There was enough space under the bed for me to tuck my suitcases underneath. End tables bracketed the bed. The sleeping area took up half the cabin space. Not a problem, since I wasn't planning on spending much time in the room. My schedule was pretty filled with wedding events. The remainder of my free time I was using to take advantage of the amenities on the ship, not hole up in my room.

This was a special trip. In a few hours, Bob and Garrison would say "I do" as the ship sailed away from Port Canaveral and sailed to the Eastern Caribbean. Odessa, Ted and Bob's mom, had arranged the wedding on the liner she worked on, and I was here to join in their joyous event and indulge in my own romance.

I sat on the bed and drew out my brand new travel journal, running my hand across the smooth leather. The first page was a list of the events I'd been invited to attend: wedding, family dinner, portrait session tomorrow during formal night, the Mardi Gras ball the following evening. Odessa Roget hadn't just arranged for one night to celebrate Bob and Garrison's nuptials but a whole week. Of course, it helped when she convinced the grooms the Mardi Gras cruise was the perfect one for holding a wedding.

There was a light rap on my door. I cracked it open.

A good-looking man in dress whites held a bedazzled black garment bag and a small hat box. The extra weight in his midsection stretched his coat to its maximum ability. "Odessa Roget asked me to deliver your wedding attire. The rest of your luggage is here as well." He made a small sound, a cross between a snort and a cough as he focused on the coworker next to him. "Make it quick. I have a fitting to conduct."

I held the door open and stepped aside. The steward wheeled in my large bag, the other hand holding up my own lackluster fabric garment bag. For one person, I sure brought a lot of luggage. I'd never been on a cruise before and had watched *An Affair to Remember* as research. The women and men were dressed impeccably. I wanted to look like a world-class traveler, not like a— well, not like I had lived in a small town all my life. I packed enough dressy clothes so I wouldn't be wearing the same outfit every night for dinner. A whole new wardrobe. My stomach did its little flip flop again. I wasn't sure if I was more excited about Ted seeing me in the sexy dresses or just wearing the new-to-me fabulous clothes.

"Where would you like your luggage?" the steward asked.

"On the bed," I said.

"Goodness, can't you see I'm waiting?" The other man had entered the room and tapped his foot on the carpet. "Odessa is expecting this wedding attendant to be perfection. I must start her fitting now."

I wasn't sure if the strain in the man's voice was at having to turn me into perfection or pleasing Odessa. I had heard mutterings from Ted and Bob about their mother turning the wedding into a Broadway show, including having the ship's costume designer make the outfits the women would wear to the ceremony. I wasn't too happy about not choosing my own outfit, but I kept quiet. One, I didn't want my first interaction with Odessa to be a fight over a dress I'd wear for two events. Two, I had enough trouble finding dresses for the formal and semi-formal dinners scheduled on the cruise.

The steward placed my quilted garment bag onto the bed.

I dug around in my carry-on and pulled out some dollar bills. "Thanks for your help."

He discreetly pocketed the tip and scurried out of the room, fixing an evil eye on the other man's back.

"Let's get this started." The other man whirled me around and yanked my jacket off.

I swatted at his hands. "What are you doing?"

"Did you hear me? Odessa sent your dress. Dress patterns are never a good match for a woman's body. One size does not fit all."

"I can dress myself."

"I can't let anything happen to my creation."

"What can happen between here and the bathroom?" I pointed to the room that was six feet away from us.

Delicately, he placed the bag on the bed and unzipped it. He scooped the dress up and placed it in my arms as if the garment was a newborn. It was made from a gauzy off-white fabric with a sheer fabric underneath. Tiny rhinestones on the hem and straps of the dress made it sparkle. "Don't. Ruin. The. Dress."

I stepped into the bathroom and flipped on the light. The door slammed closed behind me. A hand slapped over my mouth and I was pressed into the corner between the wall and sink. The dress squished tightly against my body. My heart pounded, draining all thoughts from my head.

"Quiet," a voice whispered in my ear.

Help. I needed help. The scream I tried letting loose was muffled by my attacker's hand. Doing my best to keep the dress protected—I wasn't sure whose wrath I feared most: the designer, Odessa, or whoever was holding me captive—I rescued myself. I flung my body to the side, throwing the attacker against the sink. There was something to be said for small bathrooms. I ground the tip of my heel into his foot, then brought my foot up to kick him, letting out another muffled scream.

"Stop," the man said. "He can't know I'm in here."

He can't know? What about the fact a man shouldn't be in my bathroom?

"You sound like an elephant charging through the jungle, not a lady getting ready. You better not be ruining the dress," the designer said.

Now I wanted to kick another man.

"Odessa found a male version of herself," my captor whispered.

I broke free and spun around, finding myself looking into a familiar pair of green eyes. I blinked. Once. Twice. The third time was a charm and the image clicked. The man before me was Ted in about thirty years. His hair was a faded red, worry lines around his mouth and eyes. Why was John Roget hiding in my bathroom?

His face relaxed and he drew closer. "We don't have much time. Pay attention."

No wonder Ted was so bossy; it was in his mother and father's genes. The poor guy hadn't stood a chance. Did I want to know what John had to say? Of course I did. It wasn't every day you found your boyfriend's father skulking in the bathroom of your stateroom.

John pulled out a grainy photograph of an attractive man. "I have reason to believe this man, William Hastings, is involved in a diamond scam."

"And that made you hide in my bathroom?"

The look he centered on me was a cross between annoyance and thinking I was an idiot. I asked a reasonable question. It wasn't my fault his explanation was lacking critical details.

"I've heard about your helpful nature when it comes to Ted's cases, and I thought you might be interested in doing the same for me."

Was Ted's dad serious? He was hired for a job and waited to pick a partner for the mission once he was onboard? The man had been an FBI agent, he should plan better. Then again, maybe that was the reason he *had been* an agent and wasn't now, and not from reaching retirement age. "You should've worked it out before today. I'm not getting involved."

"Hastings's sister, Ronnie, is Garrison's best friend. She has a delicate nature. If she's wrapped up in this or Garrison sees me, he'll explode. If he does, I won't have a chance of making amends with Bob. And I might lose Ted."

John looked so forlorn. It plucked at my sympathy. I bit my lip. This was a celebration for Garrison and Bob. I didn't want their wedding and honeymoon ruined, nor could I stand by while a deeper wedge was driven between John and his sons. I knew Ted hoped for reconciliation between his dad and Bob, though I didn't know why they were estranged.

"The captain and cruise line want this done quietly. If the public knew a jewel thief was targeting passengers, it would bankrupt the line," John said.

"People are going to find out."

"It wouldn't linger as long in the news if it's solved."

True. "Why don't you ask one of your sons?"

A loud rap startled me. "What are you doing in there? The muster drill starts soon. I need time."

"You said be careful," I shouted back, pulling back the curtain of the small shower. "It takes time to change."

"Hurry up, and treat the dress delicately," the bossy designer said.

I pointed at the shower. "Get in."

"We're not done," John said.

"I need privacy to change."

"Ted and Bob can't know what I'm doing."

"Why?"

He stepped into the shower. "I was banned from the wedding, and their mother is one of the suspects." With those words, he drew the curtain closed.

"I've called for reinforcements. You're in for it now."

Please not Odessa. The last thing I wanted was for her to find her ex-husband, who she didn't invite to the wedding, hiding in my room. I had tons of questions for John, but first I needed to show the designer the dress before he beat the door down.

I shimmied into the dress. The fabric skimmed my body; the hem was irregular, like small scarves had been added to the skirt. It flowed around my calves in some places, grazing the bottom of my knees in others. The tiny mirror in the bathroom didn't allow me to see how I looked in the dress. I slipped out of the bathroom and caught my reflection in the full-length mirror beside the couch.

The dress hugged my body perfectly. It showed my shape without being skintight, and the gauzy material gave the dress an elegant feel. I twisted. The fabric danced with me, swishing and gliding, the rhinestones winking when the light hit them. If Odessa wanted me to look like I stepped out of a fairy tale, she nailed it.

"Quinn, Quinn, Quinn." He waltzed around me, delight making his eyes glow. "You have outdone yourself this time. The lines are beautiful. Fabric choice exquisite. This is a masterpiece. And to think it's wasted..."

I shot him a glare. "Thanks a lot."

"Just a small adjustment here..." Quinn pinched a centimeter of fabric at my waist.

I scooted away from him, feeling very protective of my dress and wanting Quinn gone so John could leave my room. "If you take the dress in, I might not be able to move freely."

"Odessa has a look she is going after."

"I doubt a smidgen of loose fabric will ruin her look."

Quinn crossed his arms and gave me a haughty look. "I am the designer. I am the one whose head will roll if your appearance isn't perfect. I expect you to cooperate while I make adjustments to the wedding outfit." Quinn tugged out a small box of pins from his coat pocket. "No more arguments from you, Missy."

"That's not my name." I edged toward the middle of the room, not wanting to box myself into a corner. From the look in Quinn's eyes, I knew the only thing stopping him from wrestling me to the ground to complete the alternations was fear of ruining the dress—and Odessa.

"Get over here so I can finish. I need time to make the corrections. The muster drill will be announced soon. You need to know where were lifeboat station is located."

I kind of hoped I wouldn't need to know where it was, though I knew the ship wouldn't leave port until every passenger checked into their muster station. "There's nothing to fix."

"You have given me no choice." He pulled out a cell phone, fingers flying over the virtual keyboard.

I needed him out of my room. I was sure he was tattling to Odessa that I was an unreasonable wedding guest. "You made a perfect dress. Beautiful."

There was a knock on the door. Quinn yanked it open. "Your attendant is not cooperating with me."

Garrison stepped into the room, sending me an apologetic smile. Relief flowed through me. He was better than Odessa or Bob showing up.

"I'm sure Faith is just overwhelmed. She's meeting Odessa Roget for the first time, a woman who could potentially be her own future mother-in-law. That has to be nerve-racking."

Quinn's expression softened. "Odessa is a force to be reckoned with."

Garrison took hold of my hand and twirled me. "Faith looks absolutely beautiful. I must concede, Odessa was right insisting you make the dresses, Quinn. We'd never have found something off the rack with this quality and attention to detail."

Quinn blushed. "I am known for my beading. With the fairy wings I designed, this lovely gown will transform instantly into a costume for the ball."

Fairy wings. I pressed my lips together. Starting an argument wouldn't get either man out of my room. There was plenty of time to plead my case on why an almost thirty-year-old woman was too old for wings.

"The tiara," Garrison said. "I want to see the whole look."

Quinn let out a shocked gasp. "How could I have forgotten the crowning touch?"

A tiara. And fairy wings. What in the world had Odessa created and the grooms gone along with?

Quinn rushed over to the bed, took off the lid of the black box, and reverently reached inside and pulled out a sparkling tiara fit for a seven-year-old. Rainbow-colored crystals trimmed the headpiece, and sticking up an inch from the base of the tiara was a very large gold filigree heart with three round crystals. I liked bling. I liked glitter. But more than that, I wanted to look like a grown-up, not a little girl playing dress-up. A fairy princess outfit didn't bring out the temptress in a woman. When Ted saw me, he should want to secret me away, not hand me a lollipop.

"Speechless. I know. It's magnificent. Odessa wants everyone in the wedding party to wear one." Quinn's voice told me he was getting miffed with me. His phone buzzed. He looked down and blanched. He thrust the tiara at Garrison. "Odessa wants me. Now."

"Go on." Garrison shooed him out of my room. "We all know Odessa comes first."

A frazzled Quinn scurried out of my room.

Garrison gave me a one-armed hug. "A little tip for you, honey. It's easier to go along with Odessa. She's a great lady, but doesn't understand the word no when it's used on her."

"Wonderful." And the man she banned from the wedding was hiding in my bathroom.

Garrison squeezed me tighter. "I didn't mean to worry you."

"I'm not worried."

"You can't fool me. I didn't mean to give you the wrong impression of Ted's mom. She's an opinionated lady. Had to be considering she was married to an unyielding man." A darkness crossed Garrison's face. "When Bob told his parents he was gay, his dad disowned him. Immediately. They haven't talked to each other for fifteen years."

"That's horrible." What a louse. How could a parent turn away their child just because of who they loved? I definitely had no interest in helping the man.

"He refused to allow Bob in his house. Odessa told John either he accepted and loved Bob or she'd leave. John pointed at the door and said, 'There's the exit,' so she left."

Their mother is a suspect. John's words took center stage in my brain. I had been married to a scheming, deceiving man who knew how to manipulate the legal system. Adam had known just enough about the law to make my life miserable and almost got me sent to prison for his crime. John Roget knew the legal system backwards and forwards from having been a FBI agent for over thirty years. He knew exactly the scenario to create so Odessa ended up in prison for the rest of her life.

John Roget was going to have my help—or so he'd believe.

TWO

A bolt-you-out-of-bed alarm filled the room, followed by an announcement from the captain.

"Muster drill," Garrison said.

I hustled us both out of the room, hoping no one saw John sneaking out. "If I get the dress dirty, Quinn will have a fit."

Garrison slipped off his decorated windbreaker-style jacket and draped it over my shoulders. "Here you go."

On the right-hand side, there was an embroidered cruise ship with wedding bells floating over the ship and the word "groom" underneath in a cursive font. I zipped it up. "Let me guess, a gift from Odessa."

"Ronnie, my best friend. She's eccentric. She also had jackets made for Bob and Ted."

A crew member wearing an orange vest waved a sign with an arrow and the word "exit" toward the stairs. "Everyone to the stairs. Have your room key out."

Crew members looked at the cards and directed us to the floor where our lifeboat stations were. Garrison was on the sixth deck, while I had to go up to the eighth. I followed the dwindling group to my destination. I walked out of the lobby and onto the deck. It was chilly. It looked like most of the cruise goers had already made it to the station. There were large groups lined up in rows at the end of the deck.

"How many in your party?" a crew member asked. He ran a handheld scanner over the back of my room key.

Wasn't it obvious? "One."

A security guard directed me to the last row.

I walked toward a blonde woman who was draping a pale pink scarf over her wide-brimmed hat. She knotted it under her chin. The silk material matched the scarf she wore as a belt.

"The wind wants to snatch my hat right off," she said.

I adjusted the tiara on my head and took a selfie, the first picture for my travel journal. "Hopefully we won't be out here too long. My legs will turn into an ice pop."

"That wouldn't be good considering you have a wedding to attend." She smiled at me.

How did she know?

"I was worried about the whole tiara thing, but it looks quite lovely. I would've gone with all pastel stones as the clear one seems out of place. You were smart to get ready early. Once this is over, I won't have much time to put on my matching dress and fix my face. I look a mess." Her makeup was artfully applied, and her navy-blue pants paired with a white blouse decorated with tiny red anchors were the perfect outfit for the cruise. Her hair was pulled into a messy bun with honey blonde tendrils curling beside her ears and down her neck. I found it hard to believe this woman ever looked a mess.

"You look wonderful. You must be Ronnie." I hid my annoyance behind a bright smile. John and the captain had already plotted out my help in the matter. It was not a coincidence I was in the same muster station as Ronnie.

"The one and only. I was so excited when Garrison called me and told me he and Bob were finally getting married. If any couple deserves to tie the knot, it's those two. I just hope Odessa doesn't forget this event is about them and not her."

"You know Bob and Ted's mom?"

"Yep." Ronnie let out a long sigh. "I work with her. Or used to. I've taken a sabbatical from entertaining on the ship. We can be cruise partners." Ronnie linked her arm through mine. "Garrison will be spending all his time with Bob, and since I'm not working this cruise, I'll have plenty of free time."

Why did John leave out the tidbit about Ronnie working on the ship?

"I'm not by myself," I said. "I am right now because Ted is in a different room, so he's at another station, but we're together on the cruise."

"I'm sure your man plans on spending time with you."

For some reason, I had the impression Ronnie was humoring me. I wasn't sure if it was the half-sad smile or the sympathetic look in her eyes.

A woman squealed from the line beside us, a mix between shock and alarm. She shoved her fingers through her gray curls, ruffling them into a chaotic halo around her head. The lines on her face deepened and her mouth quivered. She lifted her arm, the sleeve of her oversized Hawaiian print shirt decorated with cavorting dolphins bunched around her underarm. "My diamond bracelet is gone."

"It'll be all right, my love." The gentleman next to her wore a matching outfit, except his was paired with white knee socks and sneakers instead of sandals. A straw sun hat was tugged low over his forehead. "I can always buy you a new one."

"The clasp must've broken, Glenda. It's probably by your feet." An elderly woman with a cane attempted to lean down. Her movements were awkward and jerky.

"I hope so." The woman shuffled her sandaled feet from left to right, then forward and back as she studied the ground. "It's not here. It's not here." Panic grew in her voice.

"We'll help you look." I elbowed Ronnie gently. We couldn't stand around doing nothing.

Ronnie pressed her lips together. She was not pleased by my suggestion. Her attitude surprised me until I spotted the young guy at the end of the line—William Hastings, the man from the picture. I might be able to prove John's case before we even left port.

"We'll be fine." The woman with the cane smiled at me. "I wouldn't want you to get your lovely dress dirty. William will help us. Won't you, dear one?"

"Of course, Ruth." William had a distinct voice, a southern drawl with the ending of words clipped off. Gathering the fabric of his trousers near the pockets, he hiked them up and squatted down. William duck-walked to the railing. The cruisers around us stayed in their line, watching with curiosity.

Hunching over, I scanned the deck around me. Nothing. I took a step forward, repeating the process.

"Didn't I tell you he was a dear?" Happiness rushed through Ruth's voice.

"That you did. It's such a shame your son-in-law and daughter canceled at the last minute," Paul said.

William backed up inch by inch from the rail.

"I've chosen to see the rainbows, not the storm. If they hadn't backed out, you and Glenda wouldn't have been able to travel on this cruise. We've always wanted to cruise together." Ruth's smile slipped for a moment. "One can't cruise forever."

"Do you see it?" Glenda worried her hands together.

"I see it." Ronnie pointed toward the deck near the rail where William had been. Half hidden behind a white column, a bracelet sparkled.

"I was leaning over the railing earlier," Glenda said. "It must've snagged on something."

"I'll get it." I reached for it at the same time William lunged to pick it up. Our heads knocked together. Pain blinded me and I fell onto my backside. My tiara slipped off, clattering to the deck.

It hit Ruth's cane. The tiara skittered toward the edge of the deck.

I couldn't lose it. I crawled toward it.

"What is going on?" The security guard glared down at me. "Get back in line. We're still having the drill."

"I dropped something." I continued forward, hoping everyone remained calm until I retrieved my prize. The tiara was half on, half off the deck.

"Let me get that." William lost his balance as he reached for it. His fingers nudged the tiara.

It was the final push needed. The tiara plunged from the deck, doing somersaults in the air. The stones caught the sunlight, casting tiny sparkles around it. It stopped its descent when it landed on the lifeboat below us.

"No," I wailed. I collapsed onto the deck. The finishing touch for Odessa's masterpiece wedding was only eight feet below me. I had helped bring four murderers to justice—five if I counted my ex-husband. That was harder than climbing down the side of a ship and getting a tiara. Right? I eyed the distance and the railings. It would be doable, except for the fact there was no ladder and I wasn't Spiderman.

Ronnie rushed over. "Are you hurt?"

"My tiara is down there," I said.

"Sorry about that," William said, the apology not ringing true to my ears.

Ronnie stared at him for a long moment before she leaned over the railing. "It's on the lifeboat. No problem."

No problem? She was a woman, not a trained spider monkey. "I don't think the captain will lower the rafts for a crew member to get it."

"The raft is fine where it's at." Ronnie untied the scarf belted around her waist and the one keeping her hat on her head. "I always come prepared."

"Don't you dare," the security guard said.

"You know I love a good dare." With that, Ronnie attached the scarves together. She slung her right leg over the safety rail.

"Stop." Even though the security guy repeated the warning, he made no move to back the words with actions. "I forbid you to rappel down."

Ronnie looped the scarf around the rail. She wrapped the ends around her body, leaving two feet of the scarf to trail down in a rippling wave.

"The last time you did that you had to take a sabbatical," the guard said.

Ronnie's laugh sounded like the tinkling of bells at Christmas time. "If I do it for a show in the atrium, I'm a sane cruise performer. Do it off a railing from a deck and I'm a lunatic. Never could figure that one out."

"Please don't." I placed a hand on Ronnie's arm. I glared at William. Why wasn't he doing more to stop his sister from doing something so dangerous? "I don't want you getting hurt. It's just a silly tiara. I'm sure Odessa will understand."

"Then you don't know Odessa." Ronnie lifted her other leg over the railing and sat on it. With a cheerful wave, she pushed herself off and used the scarf to twirl herself down. The cruisers crowded the railing.

Her feet touched the lifeboat. Keeping hold of the end of the scarf, she tiptoed her way over to the tiara and picked it up. She pulled out the left side of her sweater, exposing her lacy red bra. She tugged the strap away from her skin, weaving the tiara through the strap like it was a crochet hook. "I'm coming back up."

We all watched with bated breath. Ronnie held her legs straight out, turning herself into a letter L, and hand over hand she climbed back up. The woman had some incredible muscles. When Ronnie's hand touched the top of the rail, William pulled her over.

Ruth clapped her hands. A large diamond on her left ring finger sparkled. "Marvelous. Didn't I tell you the shows on the *Serenade* were breathtaking?"

"Will you be performing in other aerial acts?" Glenda asked. "You're amazing."

"Not on this sailing. I'm here as a guest for a wedding." Ronnie's face glowed with happiness and exertion. She unlooped the scarf from the rail and secured it back around her waist, the knotted ends nestled against her belly button. "I told you it was no problem."

"You're about to have one." The annoyed guard's gaze shifted away from Ronnie and toward the wall where a phone was located.

"If you tattle, the cruise will be delayed." Ronnie said. "No one wants to miss a port because a performer did an impromptu performance. No harm came to anyone."

The other cruisers voiced their agreement with Ronnie.

"I'm sure you don't want to explain to the captain why you allowed me to do it."

"I told you to stop."

Ronnie grinned at him. "I didn't hear you say it. Did anyone else?"

I let out a syllable then shut my mouth, not wanting to make enemies of the rest of my muster station group. Everyone else was willing to forget what he said.

"Let's finish the drill. We keep the life jackets at the station rather than requiring passengers to return to the cabin if there's an emergency." He showed us where the life jackets were kept before demonstrating how to put them on. "Are there any questions?"

The group shook their head in unison.

A loud buzz echoed through the air. "Good afternoon," the captain said through the speakers. "The muster drill is now over. We'll be pulling away soon. Everyone please join us by the pool for the sail away party to start off our Mardi Gras celebration." The captain continued speaking, but I couldn't hear him over the dull roar of my station buddies leaving.

William held out his arm to Ruth. She rested her hand in the crock of his arm and walked away, chatting away about some jewelry pieces on her buying list. "I told my friends you were just the man to help them. Paul wants to find a unique piece for his wife. Their fiftieth anniversary is coming up."

"Gemology is only a hobby of mine. I'm not an expert."

"Glenda loves the pieces you picked out for me, and that's what matters."

Gems were a hobby. I filed away the information.

Ronnie unlinked my tiara from her bra strap and placed it on my head. "I'll see you at the wedding. I must have a chat with my brother." She tilted her head in William's direction.

Her earlier words about being alone buzzed around in my head, annoying me so much I had to release them. "I thought you didn't know anyone on this sailing."

"My brother being here is a surprise."

From the expression on her face and her icy tone, I knew this surprise fell into the same category as finding your spouse in bed with someone else or your husband killing someone and blaming you.

THREE

John was spying on us—me—from behind a column halfway down the eighth deck. He motioned for me. I hesitated. His gestures became a little more frantic. Instead of going back to my stateroom and freshening up for the ceremony, I headed toward John. He pivoted away, strolling toward the end of the deck and away from me. What was that about?

I glanced over my shoulder. Bob and Garrison, debonair in their matching white tuxedos, were walking toward the stern of the ship where the wedding was taking place. I hurried and caught up with John, making sure the couple didn't witness my dash.

"There's a problem." John placed a hand on the small of my back and directed me toward some deck chairs situated behind a group on a family reunion. He released me and pointed at the chair.

I dropped into it. "Besides the grooms almost spotting you?"

John sat in the lounger beside me. "Yes. The captain sent word that he knows Bob is a private investigator and Ted's a homicide detective. He wants me to ask them to help."

"What did you say?"

"The captain is occupied at the moment, so I haven't spoken with him. I'm going to let him know I have acquired assistance that's adequate for this job."

I had a feeling I was the adequate assistant. "What if the captain disagrees with your help's qualifications?"

"I'll remind him I was a FBI agent for almost four decades and am now a consultant for them, and I agreed to do this for free, so he shouldn't ask either of my sons to investigate the matter."

"Why don't you want your sons helping?"

John heaved out a sigh and looked heavenward. The mannerism reminded me so much of Ted. "Bob and Garrison are on their honeymoon."

That was a good reason. If I was on my honeymoon, I wouldn't want Ted solving a crime during it. Not that Ted and I were anywhere close to planning a wedding. "Why not Ted? He's not honeymooning." Since John asked me to get involved, the man wasn't worried about interfering in Ted's romantic vacation.

"I don't want to take him away from Claire. She misses her dad."

Heat skittered along my cheeks. I wasn't the only one on the ship this week who'd like some of Ted's attention. I was sure his little girl was looking forward to enjoying a vacation with her daddy.

The family standing by the railings leaned over halfway as they waved and cheered.

John moved his chair closer and whispered something. All I heard was mumbling.

The boisterous family made it hard for me to hear anything. I scooted to the edge of the seat. The flirty fabric of the dress didn't give my limbs much protection from the metal rim pressing into the back of my thighs. I hoped it didn't leave mark.

"Here's the gist of the case. Wealthy elderly ladies come onto the ship with expensive diamonds and go home with high-quality fakes. In looking at the manifests, William Hastings not only cruises a lot, but his companions of choice are wealthy women over the age of seventy-five. Last year, he sailed on over thirty-five cruises and is already on his fifth for this year."

My grandmothers flashed into my mind. They were my world, and I'd hurt anyone who harmed them. Did Ronnie know her brother preyed on elderly women? "He's taking advantage of those women."

"Or he has a lot of widowed grandmas who take him on trips." John leaned forward. "Lately, his favorite companion is Ruth

Ballard, a disabled widow. They booked this cruise at the last minute. His official job title is home health aide and he's listed as coming to care for the person he's cruising with. He has a strong interest in gems. He's taken quite a few classes on the subject."

"It's a hobby."

John raised his eyebrows.

"He said that to Ruth when she asked him to help a friend of hers pick out an anniversary gift for his wife."

Interest sparked in John's eyes. "Names?"

"Paul and Glenda. I don't know their last names."

"It'll be easy for me to find out."

"I'm curious why your suspect list is so short? I haven't been on this cruise long, and I already have more people on mine. The costume designer Quinn. Ronnie."

"Because Quinn doesn't have it in him to mastermind anything."

"He designs the costumes and accessories." I tapped the tiara on my head. "He made these."

"Quinn is a gossip. It's his true passion. There's no way he could stay quiet about it. His one deficiency in fashion is gem recognition. He can't tell a diamond from a clear crystal. It's the reason the only designing job he could find was on a cruise ship. They don't mind having someone double-check his work. Odessa orders all the gems supplies, real and fake, and Quinn's assistant sorts them out."

"Why not just hire the assistant for the job?"

"Because Ronnie can't even sew a hem."

"Why isn't she a suspect?"

"There's a reason for that," John said.

"I want to know what it is."

"The last place I want to be is on this cruise. I know how it'll look when my kids see me here, but it's the best time for me to investigate. With the wedding taking place, I can discreetly talk to Odessa's coworkers without tipping her off."

"That doesn't explain it. Why do you think your ex-wife is

involved instead of Ronnie?" He had no rationalization for tying Odessa's name to the case.

"Since Odessa was promoted to managing the stage shows, the number of decorative gems orders has increased."

"Because everyone knows buying crystals makes one a jewel thief." I didn't even attempt to stop the sarcastic tone from oozing out.

"The captain is concerned because the new crystals ordered resemble authentic gems. After an heir received his mother's jewelry, he and his wife had it appraised. The most expensive pieces were high-quality fakes. She'd been on one of the cruises before she died."

"Maybe they were never real."

John shook his head. "They had the original appraisal from when his mom bought the pieces."

"How did Odessa and William happen to hook up for this jewel heist project?"

"There's the one leak in my boat. That's my main goal of this trip, finding the piece to plug it up."

"She could be innocent."

"Or not. The captain knows his crew better than me, and if she's top on the list, I have to go with it."

How convenient for him.

The reunion crew started singing a loud and drunken rendition of "Copacabana."

"I'm taking all your questions to mean you're on the case," John said.

I nodded even as a part of my brain screamed no. Why was John focusing on Odessa? Ronnie was a performer. She'd have access to the costumes and William was her brother. Why discount her involvement so easily? Ronnie had been very insistent about retrieving the tiara. She and her brother might need the large clear crystal on it to replace the diamond in Ruth's ring.

"Good. Now I just have one more favor to ask." Nervousness flashed in John's eyes for a second.

I squirmed.

"Tell Ted I'm here."

"I thought—"

"My sons are going to find out I'm on the ship. I can't assume none of the crew members will mention seeing my name on the manifest or the diner seating chart, so the boys should be told. You can tell Ted, and he'll inform Bob."

"Why don't you?" I didn't like the idea of being the one to jump up and shout "surprise!" on this secret. If anyone should suffer the consequences for him being on this cruise, it should be John.

"I don't want you having to keep me being here from Ted. He'll find out, and I don't want to be the cause of any disharmony between you two."

"But you don't want me to tell him about the diamonds and what you suspect about Odessa."

"Correct. If he finds out, Ted might throw me overboard. Bob actually would."

And that would definitely put a damper on Bob's honeymoon.

I paced back and forth in front of the elevators on the ninth deck, waiting for Ted. I wished I could've gone to his room, but he had forgotten to give me the number. I checked the ship directory, hoping the Presidential and other suites were listed on it by name, but everything was listed as cabin number with no indication if it was a balcony or suite room.

Why the heck was I going along with John's plan? It allowed me to tell Ted part of the truth. Eventually, I'd have to fess up to all of it. Right before his brother's wedding wasn't the proper time to mention that his father was trying to prove his mother was a jewel thief.

The elevator doors opened. A man and two little girls wearing bathing suits stepped out.

"Going down?"

The man held his arm out, stopping the door from closing as the two girls waited patiently by his side.

"I'm waiting for someone. Thanks."

The man smiled and went on his way. The doors leading to the outside slid open. The little girls squealed, huddling against their father's legs as the cold air greeted them.

"I don't think it's a good time for a swim."

"Daddy, you promised," one wailed while the other nodded her head in agreement.

"We'll go check out the hot tub. Until then, I'll keep my girls warm." The man lifted them up, one in each arm, and cuddled them close. His daughters giggled.

A pang of longing mixed with jealousy washed through me. My parents died in a crash when I was an infant, so I never knew life with them. On occasion the bitterness rose up in me. When I was a child, it was something I felt and hid from my grandparents. I didn't want them to think I wasn't happy with them. I just wished I had both: parents and grandparents.

The elevator pinged. Ted stepped out, one arm around his daughter and the other resting comfortably on his ex-wife's shoulders. They were smiling and laughing, portraying very much the cute family on vacation. When Ted spotted me, his smile froze and his arm quickly slipped from his ex-wife's shoulder, causing her long blonde hair to ripple for a moment before it fell back into place. The woman was stunning.

His ex-wife's brow furrowed as she gazed up at Ted. Her bright blue eyes looked at him and then shifted to me. She peered over at Ted again, rolled her eyes, then smiled and walked over to me. "Hi, I'm Elizabeth, and this is Claire. I'm guessing you're Faith."

"Yes." Additional words fled my brain as Claire evil-eyed me. Claire had her mother's eyes, and her hair was a beautiful strawberry blond, a mix between her mother's wheat color and her father's red.

I had hoped we'd get along, but it appeared I had work to do, as the little girl seemed intent on disliking me. I usually didn't bring out that kind of emotion on a first meeting—except with homicide detectives.

Ted stood a few feet behind his ex-wife, doing a really good impression of a statue, and blocked the elevator. An older woman almost rammed into him with her walker as she tried to exit.

I hated giving Claire another reason to dislike me, but I needed Ted alone. I didn't want to say anything about her grandfather in front of her. "We need to talk. In private."

"We do." Ted finally came to life and moved away from the traffic area of the elevator.

"Daddy, we promised Uncle Bob and Uncle Garrison we'd arrive early." Claire tugged at her father's arm. "Talk to her later."

Her didn't sound very complimentary coming from Claire.

"I'll be there in a minute." Ted's voice was loving yet firm.

"You'll be late. Uncle Bob will be sad." Claire's lower lip quivered.

Ted released a pained sigh and sent a pleading look to his ex-wife. If I didn't know any better, Ted was about to cave.

"It won't take long. It's important." I had planned on working my way up to the information rather than just dumping it on him. Instead I'd have to blurt it out.

"So's Uncle Bob. This cruise is for him and Uncle Garrison. It's not for you." Claire wrinkled her nose.

My dreams of having some alone time with Ted faded away.

"Claire, there's no need for rudeness," Ted said.

"I'm not being rude, Daddy. She is. She's trying to make us late." Tears welled in Claire's eyes.

"I'm sure Faith won't make him late. She's in the wedding also." Elizabeth readjusted the little girl's tiara on her head. "She has one just like you."

"Grandma told me mine was special. It's not like hers. At all. My stones are green to match my eyes."

"It does look more sparkly than mine." I hoped I said the right thing for a truce. Though I wasn't sure what started the battle between me and an eleven-year-old.

Claire stomped out the door. Elizabeth offered me a sympathetic smile. "I'm sorry. Claire is normally a polite and friendly child. I'll go have a chat with her right now."

Ted scrubbed his fingers through his red hair, messing up the plastered-down hairdo. "I don't know what's gotten into my daughter."

"She's a girl. We have our snippy moments." I had hoped for a better introduction moment with Claire, but it was over. We had seven, okay, more like six and a half, days to get to know each other. I'd grow on her. I'd brought a travel journal for Claire, along with some coloring books and artist coloring pencils. I knew the tween loved to draw and paint, and I planned on bonding with her over crafts.

"I appreciate you being understanding," Ted said.

What was up with Ted? Why so formal? No hello hug or kiss. Cruises were romantic. I'd have thought I'd have gotten some reaction from my dress. Stop, I thought. Now wasn't the time to fret over not wowing Ted. I had a more important mission. "I need—"

"I need—"

Ted and I started the same sentence.

"You go first."

"Your dad is on the cruise." I blurted out the information, not playing the usual "No, you first" game.

Ted's eyes almost bugged out of his head. "What?"

"Your father is on the cruise. I ran into him at the muster drill."

"How?" Ted frowned. I could feel his annoyance, and I wasn't sure if it was directed at me or his wedding-crashing father.

"It's a long story."

"Give me the Cliff's notes."

I twisted the story to hint at what his father was up to. "An elderly woman lost her diamond bracelet. We miraculously found it right where a guy named William had looked. My tiara fell onto a lifeboat. Ronnie rescued it. John and I talked."

"Ronnie?"

"Garrison's best friend. Blonde. An entertainer." He still appeared confused. "Works on this ship with your mom. An aerialist."

Ted's green eyes darkened and he frowned. "Veronica. Yes, I'm aware of her."

Apparently there was no love lost between Ronnie and Ted. Why didn't he like her? Never mind, I had a good guess. Ronnie was headstrong, opinionated, and willing to risk life and limb for a thrill. Just the kind of person Ted found trying beyond reason.

"We have to keep my dad away from the wedding. I'll warn my brother and mom. You watch for my father and stall him. I don't care how. Trip him. Play damsel in distress—"

A loud, enraged screech shattered the air.

FOUR

Ted and I ran toward the scream, which was also the place designated for the wedding. We rounded the corner at the stern and stumbled to a stop before we crashed into Quinn or an awning decorated with purple and green streamers. He turned, scanned me from head to toe, and heaved out a sigh before heading over for a table set up with champagne glasses. A sommelier hovered protectively around the flutes and bottles of champagne, an open bottle in one hand.

"What is he doing here?" Ronnie pointed at Quinn. Her body practically vibrated with hostility.

"I invited him." An older woman wearing a matching fairy dress and tiara held her head regally. Odessa.

"How dare you." Ronnie stamped her foot. "He's the reason I can't perform."

"My wedding, my choice on guests," Odessa said.

"It's our—" Bob was silenced by a scalding look from his mom.

Garrison wrapped an arm around Ronnie. "Honey, take it easy. Just ignore him."

"But Odessa knew. She knows what he's said about me." Tears filled her voice. "He did it on purpose."

"Oh please, you did it to yourself." Quinn snagged a glass of champagne from the table and downed it.

"At least it's not my dad," Ted whispered to me, wrapping an arm around my shoulders and nudging me into the middle of the fray. "Let's defuse this."

"Your mother seems content to let this to play out," I said.

"That's why we have to stop it."

"You were afraid I'd get your job." Ronnie made a drinking motion. "*Glub. Glub. Glub.*"

"You wench!" Quinn tossed the glass and went for Ronnie's throat.

Ronnie squealed and scampered behind Garrison. Bob blocked Quinn from getting any closer to Garrison and Ronnie. Behind the couple was the officiant, clutching the Bible tightly in her hands. Claire huddled against her mother.

Ted positioned me near his mom and wedged himself between the grooms and Quinn. "Mom, this is Faith."

Odessa looked me over. Quick. "Nice meeting you. As you can see, Ted, we're in the middle of something."

"I'm seeing it, along with half the people on the ship. This is a wedding, not a battle of the cruise ship stars. So how about we focus on the purpose of this cruise and get on with it." A nerve in Ted's jaw twitched.

"Why in such a rush, Ted?" Bob eyed his brother suspiciously.

"It's the quickest way to stop Mom from antagonizing everyone."

"Me?" Odessa fluttered her hand near her throat, hurt flashing on her face.

"You did invite Quinn to the wedding knowing what he did to Ronnie," Garrison said.

"Ronnie's behavior made her unemployed, not me reporting it." Quinn pointed at me. "If it's anyone's fault I'm at the wedding, it's hers. Odessa had wanted me to make sure Faith's dress fit correctly, and she wouldn't cooperate when I stopped by her stateroom to complete the alterations. That's why I'm here. I also wanted to check the tiara. I heard there was a mishap." Quinn's eyes gleamed as he focused on Ronnie.

"And you blamed me, Ted." Odessa gave me another once-over. "All I want is a perfect wedding for Garrison and Bob. Is that so horrible?"

"Faith's dress is fine." Anger seeped into Garrison's voice.

"Wanting, no," Ted said. "Controlling, yes."

Odessa drew in a sharp breath. Her tight expression said to me fireworks were about to commence. Way to go on defusing the situation, Ted. It was my turn.

I slipped off the borrowed jacket. "Dress is perfect. Nothing needs done on it."

Quinn gasped. "Dirt. I see dirt."

There were smudges near my knees. Scrap it all. I brushed it.

"Stop it. Stop it." Quinn hit my hands. "You're setting it in."

"No, I'm not. It's almost gone," I said.

"It's fine, Quinn. Tell him, Bob."

Bob repeated Garrison's statement.

"If that's the way you want it." Quinn spun on his heels, grabbed a bottle of champagne, and strolled off.

Ronnie whirled around, her gaze containing a small amount of craziness. She scooped a handful of trinkets from her purse. "I'm the better jewelry designer. Look at the bracelets I made for the wedding party." She held them out. "I'm Garrison's best friend. Odessa should've let me make the tiaras. But no, Quinn said either he designed the dresses and tiaras or he'd do neither, so Odessa let him have his way. I wanted to create something special for Garrison's day."

"In your alternate world, you're better," Odessa said.

"Mother," Ted said. At least my name wasn't the only one he turned into a warning.

Bob remained uncharacteristically silent.

Garrison fixed a hard stare on his soon-to-be spouse, then switched to offering sympathy to Ronnie. "Honey, I didn't know you wanted to make the tiaras. I thought you were still perfecting your designs. You should've asked me."

Ronnie sniffed. "I wanted it to be a surprise for you. But Odessa wouldn't give me a chance."

Another hard stare floated from Garrison to Bob, who drew in a deep breath and shook his head.

"When I get married," I said, trying to soothe Ronnie's feelings, "you can make my headpiece."

Ronnie grinned. "Really? You mean that? Any way I want?"

A shiver worked its way up my spine. I ignored it, not wanting to know who was throwing invisible daggers into my back. "Absolutely."

"We should get back to this wedding," Odessa said, "not some fictional one that someone's dreaming will take place in the future."

Ouch.

Claire giggled.

"Let's not blame this on Faith and be rude to her." Ted spoke at such a rapid pace, I almost didn't understand him. "Everyone's here, so let's get to the I do's."

"You're acting real nervous." Bob narrowed his eyes on Ted. "Have you been—"

"No," Ted cut off his brother. "I'm fine."

"Now that Bob's mentioned it..." Odessa crossed her arms. "You are acting out of sorts. Why is that?"

"Her," Claire grumbled.

Everyone's gaze shifted toward me. My high hopes for a lovely time with Ted and his family plummeted.

"Dad's on the cruise," Ted blurted out.

"John? John is on this cruise?" Odessa wringed her hands. "He wants to ruin the wedding."

"We have no idea what he's doing," Ted said, his voice tight.

"Who told him?" Odessa took menacing steps in my direction. "Who tried to ruin my son's wedding?"

I backed up and stopped when the railing prevented me from going any farther. I wasn't sure if that was fortunate or not. A tumble might hurt less than the pain Odessa wanted to unleash on me. "How would I know how to contact your ex-husband?"

"Maybe Ted?" Garrison wiggled between me and his future mother-in-law. "Faith had nothing to do with John finding out."

"I just found out awhile ago," Ted said.

"Ted wouldn't do that to me," Odessa said. "But someone else would. Isn't that right, Ronnie? You wanted to make the tiaras and couldn't, so you ruined this day."

"I did no such thing." Ronnie drew herself to her full height and planted herself, readying for a battle. "I'd never hurt Garrison. There is no way I'd do anything to ruin this day for him. Maybe you contacted John to prove to your sons how much better you are than their father. That's what you've always done."

Odessa gasped, her face paling then turning fire engine red. "I want—"

Ted maneuvered his mother to stand near the decorative awning. "Everyone who should be here is. Let's start the ceremony."

"Where's your father?" Odessa's gaze swept the deck. "I'm sick and tired of that man believing he has a right to say anything. Bob and Garrison love each other and have a right to legally share their life together. John needs to butt out of what isn't his business. How dare he ruin this wedding?"

Ted sighed. "Mom, he's not here."

"He's on this ship."

"But he's not here. Dad isn't doing anything," Ted said. "He's not going to jeopardize the consulting he does for the FBI by creating a disturbance on this ship."

Sadness washed over me. I wished Ted believed his dad would behave because he didn't want to break his son's heart.

"He crashed this wedding," Odessa screeched. "I want to know who told him. Who deliberately tried to destroy this day for Bob? It's someone here. When I find out, they won't be attending this wedding. Or staying on this ship, if I have my way."

Elizabeth made a small moaning sound. I turned to her. Her face was chalk white. "Odessa, no. Please, I'm sure it was a misunderstanding."

"I don't care. Ted, if you told—" Odessa began.

Claire burst into tears and yanked the tiara from her head. "I told Grandpa. I ruined everything!" She hurled her tiara over the rail and ran.

Without making an appearance, John Roget stopped the wedding ceremony.

FIVE

"Claire!" Ted chased after his fleeing daughter.

A shaken Elizabeth sat on a deck chair, eyes focused straight ahead.

"Way to go, Mom," Bob said.

Odessa chugged down a glass of champagne and snagged the open bottle. "I'll be in my room."

"That won't end well," Garrison said.

"I'll deal with it." Bob started after his mother.

Elizabeth reached out and placed a hand on his arm. "I'll go see to her."

"I should handle it."

Using Bob as leverage, Elizabeth pulled herself up. "It's best if I speak with her. You should figure out what your father is up to."

"I can't be civil to that man," Bob said.

"Try." Elizabeth headed for the elevators.

"I'll go with you." Ronnie linked one arm through Bob's and the other with Garrison. "I'm good at being the peacekeeper."

Bob appeared ready to argue when Garrison caught his gaze over Ronnie's head and tilted his head back. Two security guards were approaching. Bob nodded, and the trio walked away.

That left me alone. I'd make myself useful, and score some points with Claire, by finding her tiara. I was sure she'd regret her hasty decision. Hopefully, I'd spot the tiara on the ground. If someone had picked it up, I'd explain that my boyfriend's daughter accidentally dropped it over the railing.

Resettling the tiara on my head, I went down the stairs to the deck where the sail away party was happening. There was a large group of people dancing and drinking. Crew members were at the railings on the upper decks throwing down beads and other goodies for the passengers. Great. Someone was going to think Claire's tiara was a gift rained down from above.

I walked on the outskirts of the dance party, alternating my gaze from the ground to my surroundings. So far, all I spotted was abandoned heels, empty glasses, and beer cans. No tiara. I reached the end of the deck and rounded the corner. I'd check out the perimeter first. I didn't think Claire's throw was hard enough to send it into the middle of the crowd.

Off in a corner, an item glittered from under a deck chair that was right against the railing. I walked over to the chair and peered under it. The item was way in the back. I had two options: crawl on the ground or move the heavy deck chair. I took hold of the back of the chair, scooting it over a few inches. The metal frame made a squealing sound. I cringed.

I looked down. Still couldn't see the object. I grabbed the deck chair again, lifting it higher to drag it away from the railing. As I leaned over to place the chair down, the strap of my dress caught on a sliver of rough metal and ripped.

Scrap it all. The strap was now hanging by a couple of threads. Wonderful. How was I going to fix it? I should've bought one of those traveling sewing kits. I heaved out a sigh. Worse. It was all for nothing. The object I saw was a pair of children's sunglasses bedazzled on the sides with crystals shaped like four-leaf clovers.

Someone sidled up into my personal space. I startled, nearly smacking them from an instinct of self-preservation kicking into high gear. William, Ronnie's brother. Possible suspect. I edged back.

"I was hoping to see you again. I wanted to apologize for knocking your tiara overboard."

"Things happen." I checked out the makeshift dance floor for Claire's tiara.

Giving me an eye-appraisal, William's smile slowly stretched. "The princess look is right for you."

A blush crept along my cheeks even as annoyance skittered around in my brain. I was more perturbed over the fact Ted hadn't noticed my outfit than over William's flirting. "Thanks. I think."

William chuckled and bowed. "Again, my apologies. I should introduce myself first. I'm William Hastings."

"Faith Hunter."

"You do look lovely. I have to say I especially love your crown. Mind if I take a look?" He reached for it.

I placed my hand over it. "Actually, I do. I almost lost it once today and rather not have it happen again."

"I won't lose it standing here beside you."

"Last time you were near me, it got knocked off my head and took a nose dive off the deck. I'd rather not repeat that performance."

"I doubt it would happen again." William tried to touch the tiara.

I blocked his hand. "Of course it won't because I'm wearing it. Why are you so interested in seeing it?"

"I have a friend who does jewelry design and I wanted to see the clasps Quinn used. I want to get her some hobby stuff for her birthday and have no idea what to buy."

Right. I wasn't naive enough to fall for the excuse. Something else was going on. Like gem stealing. Though how he'd covertly steal it in my presence taxed even my imagination. "Maybe Ronnie can help you. She designs jewelry."

The cruise director announced it was time for the conga. Passengers excused themselves around me and William.

"She's who I'm buying them for."

Why did he refer to her as a friend instead of sister? Before I asked, William threw a question at me. "Can I help you look for whatever you lost?"

"I'm about to give up. I don't think I'll find it now. Too many people on the dance floor."

The conga line stretched halfway across the deck. The leader was snaking it through the deck chairs and around the pool.

"Then the best thing to do is join the conga line. We'll be able to cover the whole deck."

The guy actually had a great suggestion. The line would weave through the deck and I'd be able to check out all the passengers as we walked by to see if anyone was wearing an almost-matching tiara. I took a risk and filled William in. "I'm looking for a tiara similar to mine."

"How about if I look to the left, and you the right?"

"Sounds good."

When the line reached us, we joined at the end. I lightly placed my hands on the waist of the woman in front of me, while William's grip was a little tighter and familiar on mine. I was starting to think this was a very bad idea.

We walked-walked-kicked our way through the area. No tiara in sight. When the line headed up the stairs to the deck above, and William's hands inched up higher, I escaped by making an excuse about needing to meet my police detective boyfriend.

SIX

The seas rocked the ship to and fro. I grabbed the handrails, stumbling my way down the hallway toward the main dining room. I should've gone with my first choice of attire: pants, long-sleeve blouse, and flats. The maroon dress I chose, while sexier, best matched the almost three-inch beige heels I brought along, but didn't help me maintain balance with the unpredictable movements of the ship. I had also opted for the more formal attire in case Odessa had kept the reservation for the private room where we were to have dinner tonight to celebrate Bob and Garrison's marriage. The actual reception was scheduled for Mardi Gras to take advantage of the costume ball. I hadn't heard from anyone since we split up, not even Ted.

Maybe tonight I could charm Ted's daughter. Or at least move her attitude away from dislike to tolerance. Odessa had linked all of our reservations so we'd share a large table at dinner. The only chance I had of spending alone time with Ted at meals was arranging some private breakfasts or lunches.

The end of the line crept toward me. As I was about to join the end of the line, I spotted William's elderly companion Ruth navigating through the sea of people. The boat listed to the left and she stumbled into the wall. Her cane slipped from her hand. I hurried over.

"Are you okay?" I picked up her cane then handed it to her.

"Thank you, honey. I'm fine. The boat is rocking a little more than usual tonight." Even with her cane, she was unsteady on her feet. She almost banged into the wall again.

I went on the other side, putting my body between her and the wall and offered her my arm for extra support. We walked toward the main dining hall. "I'm glad to see someone I know. I really didn't want to walk into the dining room all alone."

Ruth blushed. "Oh my goodness, I'm ashamed to admit that I've forgotten you."

Guilt wiggled through me. Ruth was elderly and might think her memory was going. I knew who she was because I had been keeping tabs on William at the muster drill, while she had no reason to take notice of me. "I'm Faith Hunter. I saw you at the muster drill. You were with William. He introduced himself to me at the sail away party."

The line stopped by moving. Hosts greeted each group of diners, escorting them to their tables. We'd have a little bit of a wait.

"Ruth Ballard." Her blue eyes twinkled. "So that was what William was off doing this afternoon. He was taking some time away from his duties to chat up a pretty girl who caught his eye."

I demurely looked down. Now was the perfect time to get a little information from Ruth about William, and drop a hint that the guy was a little shady. Though, I wasn't quite sure how. I might hold off on that mission for a few days. Today was day one of our seven-day cruise. I had time. "I'm sorry. I didn't know William worked on the ship. Was he at the muster drill as our leader for our lifeboat station."

Ruth let out a tinkling laugh. "William isn't a crew member. He's my health care aide. As you notice, I need help getting around. My doctor hasn't wanted me to travel alone the last two years. This is likely my last cruise." She tapped her chest. "My heart is wearing down and won't be able to keep this body going much longer. My doctor told me to take one last trip, so I booked this cruise and am planning on having the time of my life."

The poor woman. Anger surged through me. How dare William take advantage of her?

She patted my arm. "I can see you're riled up. Don't think poorly of my William. I love knowing he's spending some time with younger people rather than just with old folks. I want him to have a lovely trip also. William didn't grow up with a lot of luxuries and it makes me feel good knowing I'm able to show him places he might not ever see. It makes me happy. He's so appreciative of it."

Our turn was next. My eyes widened at the extravagance before me.

Crystals dripped from the curved ends of gold chandeliers placed twenty feet apart. The main dining room was huge and filled with a mix of round and square tables covered with purple and black tablecloths trimmed with gold sequins.

Ruth smiled at me. "It is quite a sight."

"This is a dream come true for me," I said.

"Table number, please?" The host smiled and held out his arm.

"We're at different tables." Ruth held out a small card that had her table number on it.

"Right this way." A host led her away.

I blushed. I hadn't taken time to look through any of the brochures in my room. I smiled apologetically at the host waiting on me. "I'm not sure if it's changed, but we were supposed to be in the private dining area. Odessa Roget party. I didn't think to bring down my ticket."

The host took my hand and placed it on his arm. "No worries. As Odessa works on the ship, we all know her and were made aware of her party and changes to tonight's plan." He guided me to a table.

"You'll be dining at the regular table tonight. The special dinner will be rescheduled for later this week. The wait staff will be with you in a few minutes." He led me to a round table in the middle of the room, pulling out a chair before rushing back to greet other guests.

A moment later, a waiter arrived and handed me a menu. The assistant waiter filled my water glass. "We are pleased to have you join us. Tonight is our welcome menu. We're showcasing food from the Caribbean. Would you like to order now?"

"The rest of my party should be arriving soon," I said.

"We'll be right back with you." He walked over to the table.

The assistant waiter tipped a basket toward me, displaying fragrant choices of artisan bread. "Would you care for a roll while you wait? Cheese and onion is my personal favorite. Pairs nicely with the herb butter."

"Perfect."

She placed one on a small plate and joined the waiter at a table filled with a large happy family.

I nibbled at my roll, hoping someone else showed up soon. I was smack dab in the middle of the room. Alone. Some of the diners were receiving their appetizers, and I hadn't even ordered. My stomach grumbled. Where was everyone? Or at least Ted. He should've come to tell me what was going on. I felt a gaze on me. I turned. The woman behind me dipped her head and leaned toward her companion. Great. I bet she was wondering what I had done to become the outcast in my own group on the first day of the cruise.

"Alone?" William knelt beside me, resting a hand on my leg. I shoved it off.

"Everyone is running a little a late."

"If you'd like, you can join me and my companion for dinner." William nodded toward a private table near the windows. Ruth, the elderly woman from earlier, waved at me, a bright smile on her face. "A beautiful young woman shouldn't dine alone."

"Your table is set for two." A war waged within me. I didn't want to eat with William. His presence kicked my warning-vibe into high gear, but I wanted a chance to warn the woman that William was a suspected predator.

"We can ask for another chair." William stood and held his hand out to me.

"We're ready to order." Ronnie raised her hand in the air, knocking William out of the way.

The waiter scurried over.

"I'll take the cold watermelon soup with the sea salt rim and the halibut." Ronnie pulled back a chair and tossed the ends of a pastel-hued scarf over her shoulders. "Don't worry about bringing over the bread basket. I'll skip it tonight." She patted her hips, then smoothed the sides of her beige silk pants before dropping down into the chair. "Can't have too many carbs if I'm going to be spinning in the air next month."

William returned to his table.

I tapped the block on the menu listing the chef's recommendations for the evening. "I'll go with those."

"Wonderful," he said, throwing a look of disdain at Ronnie before heading toward the kitchen. Ronnie wasn't a favorite on the ship. Were rumors circulating about her sanity over the deck incident today, or something else, like stolen gems? She had been aggrieved over not creating the tiaras.

"Odessa isn't feeling well, so she's having her family's meal delivered to the Presidential suite." Ronnie fiddled with her long scarf, adjusting it until it cascaded against her chest in soft folds rather than one lump of material.

The room dipped, and I grabbed hold of the table. "Ted could've come and told me."

"Claire was having a meltdown." Ronnie continued as if the ship wasn't moving.

"If someone had time to tell you, they could've told me." I wasn't ready to let Ted off the hook.

"I found out because Garrison made me apologize for my minor outburst. I'd rather not, but I'd do anything for him, including grovel to Odessa."

"You don't like her much."

"Let's just say our opinions clash quite frequently."

The waiter arrived with our food, trying hard to keep his balance as the boat shifted again. One of our appetizer plates slid from his hand. Nonchalantly, Ronnie held out her hand and the plate transferred over to her, and she placed it on the table. The waiter left without even a small smile of thanks. Whatever issue he had with Ronnie, he should've appreciated the fact she saved him from dumping food on a guest. Then again, maybe I didn't rate very high since I was her dining companion.

"How long have you worked on the ship?"

"Six years."

"Does the crew change over a lot or does everyone usually stay on?"

"Entertainers stay on for many contracts. There's not much of a job market for me on the outside. Besides cruise ships and theme parks, no one is hiring an aerialist."

Those skills would come in handy for a thief. The boat began doing a little cha-cha, sending our water glasses skittering across the table.

"That's the seas for you." Ronnie stopped a goblet from sliding off the table. "It's never constant. It'll be smooth as ice then the next moment a roller coaster. You have to love change to live on a cruise ship."

"It seems like it would be same old, same old," I said. "Every week is a repeat. Mealtimes. Shows. Same ports."

"But different people. It's the personalities of the cruisers that shape how your week will go. You can have rough weather all week and it can be one of your best weeks at work, or you can have the nicest weather you've ever seen and you're praying for it to end."

"True. Bob and Garrison were going to be husband and husband tonight. Now they're still unmarried."

"They'll be mister and mister soon." Ronnie scooted closer to me. "Odessa is already working on rescheduling the ceremony, and this time John won't be able to ruin it."

I refrained from mentioning that John hadn't actually done anything. "I hope my dress is cleaned by then."

"Let's finish dinner, then head to your room. If your room host hasn't sent it to the laundry service, I'll take it there myself." Ronnie batted her lashes and fluffed her hair. "There's a certain supervisor who's sweet on me. I'm sure I can talk her into making sure your dress is given priority."

"Do you know anyone who can repair it? The strap has a slight tear."

Ronnie pushed away from the table. "Quinn. But you'll have to ask him. I'll sneak you down to the crew's cabins and bring you back up."

"Won't I get in trouble?"

"Not if you're with me."

I doubted that. Ronnie seemed like a woman who found trouble and hugged it. "I don't think he'll do me any favors. We got off to a bad start."

"Admit he's right. You were terribly wrong about not needing his sewing skills. Nothing he loves more than being the only one capable of doing something. If that doesn't work, say Odessa sent you. Since she became his boss, he's all about being her simpering minion."

After we ate, we retrieved the dress and went down to the first floor. Ronnie held the dress high above her head like she was waving a war flag. Every crew member we passed averted their eyes without us saying a word about a guest invading their space.

"His room is at the end of the hall."

Of course it was. It would be way too easy if it was the first one, giving us—or at least me—a good excuse for not knowing this was the crew members' floor. Would security believe I had drank too much to read the "Crew Members Only. Guests Not Permitted" sign?

Ronnie knocked on the door, then pushed me in front of her, using the dress as if it held invisibility cloak powers.

"Well, who do we have here?" Quinn swayed back and forth, planting his hands on either side of the door frame. "Miss My Dress is Perfect with her new best friend. Beware the diva's other half."

Ronnie lowered the dress and elbowed me out of the way. "Shut up, Quinn. You won. I'm on sabbatical. No need to say any more."

He grinned wickedly. "You mean fired."

"We need a little favor." Ronnie redirected the conversation. "Her dress got ripped."

"You need the matching thread? No problem." Quinn stumbled back into the cabin, returning a few moments later to throw a spool of thread at Ronnie's head. "Have fun sewing, Miss I'm-a-Designer-Give-Me-Quinn's-Job."

This wasn't the reception Ronnie predicted. I picked up the thread. A needle was poked in the top of the spool. At least he gave us all the necessary tools.

Ronnie glared at him. "Why are you acting like—"

"I'm not the one who has another side." Quinn swayed. He braced himself against the door frame, still mimicking the movements of the boat. Watching him weave back and forth made me nauseous. "Go to hell." He spit out the garbled words.

"Drop dead!" Ronnie screeched at him.

His complexion grayed right before he keeled over at her feet.

I dropped to my knees, shaking his shoulder. "Quinn?"

A foam like substance bubbled from his mouth. His chest was still.

Ronnie banged on the door across the hall. "Francis. We need you."

The door flung open and a half-dressed man adjusted his shorts. "What are you doing down here, Ronnie?"

"Call the ship's doctor. Quinn is down for the count."

"I think he's dead." I sat back on my heels.

"What?" Francis came over. He peeled back one of Quinn's eyelids. The spirited designer's gaze was vacant. Empty. "You're right. He's dead."

Ronnie swooned, crumbling to the floor.

"She never was one to rely on in an emergency." Francis stepped over her. "I'll grab a sheet from my room and call security."

I had investigated enough murders to know this wasn't a natural death. I hurried into his room. Scattered around his room was a mix of fabric samples, ribbon, and a basket containing plastic sandwich bags filled with a mix of gems. Using my cell phone, I snapped pictures of the baskets, zooming in on a few. I had a more important task right now, but I would need the photos to study later.

There was a bottle of champagne and a prescription bottle on the floor near his bed. The champagne had the personal label Odessa created for the wedding. Garrison and Bob's name stacked on top of the other, the longer one on top and both welded together. A simple, elegant heart framed the names and underneath was today's date. The prescription bottle had numerous warning labels slapped on it. Some crisscrossed others. The cure might have been worse than whatever had ailed him.

One of the labels read, "When taking this medication do not drink alcoholic beverages." Quinn had drunk a whole bottle.

Since I found what I believed was the cause of Quinn's death, I walked over to the baskets and looked at the jewels, being careful not to touch them. The bags were sorted into color and type. Faux emeralds. Faux rubies. Swarovski crystals. I bumped the table with my hip, hoping it jostled the baggies so I could see the labels on the ones underneath. So far, nothing was a precious gem. Though, he might keep those in a room safe. If the rooms in the crew quarters had one.

"Care to explain what you are doing in here?" An angry voice demanded.

Slowly, I turned. The captain of the ship glared at me. Beside him, a security guard crossed his arms and scowled.

While the doctor attended to Quinn's body, the captain dealt with us.

"I shall ask one more time. What are you ladies doing here?" Captain Henderson made us sit against the wall outside Quinn's room and glared down at us.

"Faith's dress needed mending, so we brought it down." Holding a wet washrag to her forehead, Ronnie pointed at the garment stretched across my lap.

I was glad I took the risk of rescuing it, even though it meant a sharp look from the captain and a threat of being thrown in the brig. A lot more people had joined our meeting and it would've likely been stepped on. If that happened, there was no way I'd get out of explaining this to Ted. I rather hoped it was kept quiet. The captain's hard gaze zeroed in on me.

"What she said," I said.

"Can you not read?" His dark brown eyes looked fathomless and angry. Very angry.

"I can." I wished the wall or floor would split open and transport me into another realm.

"Then do you not understand?" He walked over to a sign and tapped it. "You are not a crew member. You are a guest. You do not belong here."

"Ronnie said it was okay."

She jabbed me in the side. I wasn't fond of snitching, but she sure wasn't helping me out. It was her idea. She should own it.

Captain Henderson now switched his ire to Francis. "Why did you not make these women leave?"

"When I saw them, Quinn was on the floor. I called the doctor and security. Wasn't it better to let them stay down here?"

I wished he had chased us off, though that might have looked worse for us. What I really should've done was stay out of Quinn's room.

The doctor and a security guard lifted Quinn's body onto a gurney.

"I warned him he was going to kill himself doing that." Francis shook his head. "Always laughed it off."

The doctor pushed the gurney down the hall and turned a sharp corner. The wheels squeaked.

"Please get dressed then escort these ladies to their rooms. They are quarantined for the night." The captain glowered at us.

"Why?" I jumped up. The wedding garment dropped to the floor. I had no other plans for the night, but I hated being locked up. Even if it was in a room with a balcony.

Ronnie draped the dress over her shoulder and stood.

"Must you ask?" The captain's patience was wearing thin with me, and it hadn't exactly been thick when the conversation began. "You also will not speak of this to anyone. Understood?"

I nodded. Ronnie sighed and inspected her nails. I elbowed her.

She shrugged. "Fine by me."

"What will happen to Quinn?" I asked.

"He'll be taken to the morgue."

"There's a morgue on the ship?" I shuddered.

"Yes." The captain smiled, a sardonic twist of his lips. "Right next to the brig. My other choice for your accommodations for the night."

I'd behave. I avoided horror films. Halloween was my least favorite holiday. Okay, I hated it. I was never fond of scary, creepy things and Halloween was devoted to them. Being locked up next to a morgue—with a dead body in it—was a nightmare of epic portions. No way, no how was I ending up there. Even for an hour. This time, I'd mind my own business.

SEVEN

Yawning, I forced myself out of bed to take on the day ahead of me. I'd had trouble falling asleep last night. Quinn's death had replayed in my mind, along with Captain Henderson's warning about remaining silent. My anger had gotten the best of me a few times, and I'd plotted out the perfect scolding to heave at Ted for standing me up at dinner. It also didn't help that I spent a few hours trying to inventory the different type of gems I had pictures of on my phone. Even zooming in, I couldn't read many of the labels on the small screen. When I saw John today, I'd get his cell phone number and send them to him. I bet he had some kind of electronic device with him that would enable him to get a better look at the photos.

Before I was escorted back to my stateroom last night, Ted had slipped an invitation under my door for breakfast with a hand-drawn map to a secluded spot, and John Roget left an activity guide with a shopping seminar highlighted. Either John thought I had no idea how to shop, the presenter Lucinda was on his list of suspects, or he wanted to up his chances of winning a two-carat diamond tennis bracelet.

I took extra care in choosing my attire. I wanted something casual yet sexy for the romantic breakfast. After twenty minutes of discarding combinations, I pulled together the perfect outfit that said everything I didn't want to have to actually say. The black leggings were sheer enough I wouldn't roast and gave me the perfect coverage to go along with the flowing red and black top I picked. The bead work around the tasteful V-neck showed off a smidgen of cleavage.

I grabbed the handle of a small tote with a blue anchor

embroidered containing my cell, travel journal, and e-reader. Depending on the buffet line, it might take Ted some time to get our breakfast. I liked keeping myself entertained while I waited.

When I reached the foyer, the universe was with me and the elevator opened. I let the man juggling three cups of coffee out first, then stepped inside and pressed the up button. Anticipation danced through me. I hurried out of the elevator, my earlier anger ebbing away. If I read the map correctly, our breakfast hideaway spot was around the corner.

The beauty of the sun gleaming off the ocean drew me toward the front railings, distracting me from my mission. The view was so different than anything I'd ever seen before. Instead of tall mountains surrounding me, it was blue waters with an occasional white cap breaking the surface. The glistening water was so smooth it looked like a mirror. The world looked so inviting and peaceful.

I leaned against the railing, wanting to soak in every moment of the serenity God had set before me. No matter what else the day held for me, I wanted to remember this moment and let it fill me with hope. I took out my cell, wishing I'd thought to grab my camera, and snapped a picture. This was definitely a scrapbook-worthy moment. I pivoted to get some shots from different angles. Ideas for a layout churned through my mind. Using an app on my phone, I jotted down notes for a page.

"Why aren't you with my son?"

My attention jerked away from my phone. Odessa glowered at me before slipping on a pair of sunglasses.

I fixed a smile on my face, telling myself to ignore the attitude. For all I knew, that was always Odessa's morning personality. Some people need a few hours, and cups of coffee, before they were pleasant. "The view is so gorgeous. I stopped for a few minutes and was caught up in it. I'm hoping I'll find Ted soon."

"Is that so?" For some reason, Odessa was a little brusque. Was it because Ted bailed on breakfast plans with the family for me, or some other reason? Whatever was the reason for her attitude, she could keep it to herself.

"Yes," I said. "What are the plans for today?"

"How would I know what you have planned?" Odessa looked around, pushing her glasses back up the bridge of her nose.

"I thought the wedding might be rescheduled for some time today."

"When it is I'll be sure to let you know."

An uncomfortable feeling wiggled through me, almost like when going up and down dips on a mountain road. Odessa was engaging in conversation to be polite, but wasn't going to actually respond in a polite way. She didn't want to talk me.

"I need to find Ted," I said, using the only good excuse to get out of the uncomfortable conversation.

"Yes, you should." Odessa walked away.

I stared after her. Had she seen me with John? That would explain her coldness to me, or she wanted Ted back with Elizabeth—just like her granddaughter.

"You're just as lovely this morning as yesterday evening." William propped himself on the rail beside me, gazing out at the horizon before shifting his attention to me. "As beautiful and refreshing as the sun shining off the smooth ocean."

I stopped myself from rolling my eyes, giving an unneeded critique of his flirting. I didn't want him to leave. Now was the perfect time to get some information from him. Odessa was just on the deck. Had she been meeting William? I reined my musings in. If she had arranged a clandestine meeting, she wouldn't have let me know that she had been here. Focus on William and what he's up to. Quickly, I plotted out a couple of questions in my head, trying to make sure they sounded like I was engaging in small talk rather than conducting an inquisition. "How's your grandmother?"

He grinned at me and gently knocked his shoulder into mine. "She's not my grandmother, and I think you already know that. This is my favorite spot to start the day. I stand here to mediate. Reflect on the day behind me and the one stretching out before me."

"How many cruises have you been on? This is my first."

"My job requires travel, so I've taken many journeys on this ship." William ran his hand lovingly over the railing. "We've become good friends."

"What do you do?" I asked. "Most people I know who travel for work go by plane or car."

"Consulting." William's gaze never left the ocean.

"What kind of consulting?"

"It's a specialty, so it's complicated. It's too lovely a day to waste on boring shoptalk."

Interesting. Why the evasiveness? Why not say he was a home health aide? "Is the woman you're traveling with a friend or a client?"

"You are very inquisitive, Miss Hunter." William smiled down at me.

I switched up the questions, hoping to throw him off guard a bit. "So, you don't come on the ship to visit your sister? Watch her performance?"

For the first time, he actually looked at me. He let out a small laugh. "Ronnie told you about me? I'm surprised. She usually keeps it a secret."

"Why?" When I first met Ronnie, she had said she was on the cruise alone. After she retrieved the tiara, she told me he was her brother. I focused on the memory, trying to pinpoint a reason for her to admit it. Nothing. What had I forgot?

"Ronnie has always danced to a song no one else can hear." William inched closer to me, our arms touching. "Since Ronnie told you about our relationship, how about you tell me what the two of you were up to last night? Ronnie seems out of sorts this morning."

I swallowed hard. "Fixing my dress."

"Is that so?" William's expression said "liar."

I straightened and crossed my arms, putting some inches between us.

"There you are, Faith." Ted called out. "I couldn't reach you on your cell. I was starting to worry."

"I forgot to switch it from airplane mode when our flight

landed." I pulled out my phone and changed the settings. It pinged. Ted had texted me last night to explain about dinner, wanting to know if I wanted to join him for a moonlight walk after things settled down in his room. Oops.

"Until later." William saluted and strolled down the deck, his canvas shoes making a shuffling sound on the wooden deck.

"You must've thought I was ignoring you." I tucked the cell back into my purse.

"It had entered my mind. Who's your friend?" Ted aimed a narrowed eye glance at William's retreating form.

"Someone I met during the muster drill." I kept my tone light and mysterious. I liked the hint of jealousy in Ted's expression. For some reason, I omitted the fact about him being Ronnie's brother. I wasn't sure if my motivation was because Ted hadn't seemed fond of Ronnie or if I didn't want him asking me any more questions.

Ted placed a hand on the small of my back, directing me toward a stairwell leading to the tenth deck. "Does the someone have a name?"

Big fail on my part. He was still asking questions. "William. Ronnie's brother."

"I'd stay away from the guy."

"Why?"

Ted paused in front of a small alcove created by the stairwell. "Ever meet someone and just instantly dislike them? It's nothing they said or did to make you feel that way, but something deep inside you says there's something off about the person." Without waiting for an answer, Ted ducked his head to get into the small enclosure.

I followed. There was a table and two chairs set up in the private area. The table had a lace tablecloth covering it, and the metal chairs had small cushions on them. It looked like Ted had been hard at work this morning.

There was orange and apple juice and a carafe of coffee on the table, along with a pile of eggs, bacon, toast, pastries, and fruit. Enough food to feed a small army—or a small family. My stomach plummeted. Had our private breakfast turned into a family affair?

"How many people are on this date?" I asked Ted.

"Two. You and me."

I kissed him on the cheek. "This is so romantic. Thank you so much."

Ted grinned. "That's kind of the reaction I was hoping for."

"Kind of?" I wound my arms around his neck. "Were you hoping for something more like this?"

I stood on my toes, and roamed my mouth lightly over his. His hands drifted to my waist, wandering down to rest on my hips. I pressed myself more firmly to him, feeling his heart race against me. Ted cupped the back of my head, increasing the pressure of the kiss. What I started as a light teasing kiss Ted turned into an intense one. I responded by exploring his chest and back with my hands.

Ted moved us farther into the darkness. My back touched the cool metal of the ship and I shivered. Ted held me tighter, one hand lingering near the decorative beads of my shirt.

We were in public. My grandmothers wouldn't approve. Even as I sent my brain reminders of proper behavior, I arched up, heating up the kiss. I didn't want it to end. I wanted more. Needed more from Ted. My head swam and my legs seemed almost unable to hold me up. Ted clasped me firmly to him, and everything in his touch told me he had me. I was safe. I was loved. I was his. My heart and head tripped over themselves, trying to assert control over the situation in which I so wanted temptation to win.

Children's laughter drifted toward us, bringing us back under control quicker than a bucket of ice water.

"Breakfast. Food," Ted said, his voice unsteady.

I nodded, knowing I couldn't trust my voice to say anything more than an agreement spoken in breathless regret.

I plopped onto a chair, pressing my hands onto my still shaking legs. My grandmothers had insisted I make sure Ted and I had separate rooms so nothing improper went on. They had raised me from almost day one, and I hated to disappoint them. They held to traditional ideals about relationships and wanted their granddaughter to follow suit. I loved and respected them so much, I had followed their rules for how I should conduct myself—at least when it came to romantic relationships. Now, I wished I'd been able to stand up to my grandmothers a little more. I was almost thirty years old. A grown-up. A woman should make choices based on her emotions and desires rather than rules laid out when she was a child. Right now, on this cruise, with the man I knew I was in love with, I so wanted improper goings-on happening between us. I wanted our relationship to go to the next level. With or without a ring.

I smiled seductively at Ted. "Breakfast tomorrow in my room?"

"Can't." Ted dumped a spoon of scrambled eggs onto my plate. "I promised Claire tomorrow was daddy-daughter day."

That was understandable. "How about Tuesday before we dock at the first port? We can spend the evening dancing until dawn, go back to my room, and mark our choices on the breakfast menu door hanger and hang it along with a 'do not disturb' sign." No one would be worrying about where I was, as the people who would do that—my grandmothers—were back in Eden.

Ted stroked my hand. "I want to say the hell with breakfast and go back to your cabin. I do."

"Your nos aren't giving me that impression."

My come-hither expression was morphing into one of annoyance. Maybe I shouldn't be so hasty about adding a sexual component to our relationship.

"All of your invitations are making some tempting images spring into my brain. I want to prove that the reality is so much better."

My cheeks felt warm. Very warm. "Do you? Really?"

Ted caressed my cheeks. "Yes. But I don't want to rush you."

"How can you be when I'm the one asking?" Almost begging.

"Daddy!" Claire's tearful voice reached us.

Over his shoulder, I saw Claire running down the deck right

toward our secluded spot. Elizabeth was trailing after their daughter and smiled apologetically.

"Why did you leave me? Are you mad at me? Is it because I invited Grandpa?"

"I'm so sorry, Faith." Regret filled Ted's eyes. Claire threw herself into her father's arms.

"I don't hate you, Daddy. I don't. Please don't leave me again." Claire broke out into full-fledged sobs.

Ted winced. "Jelly bean, I'm not leaving you. I just came to have breakfast with Faith."

"I woke up and you were just gone. Like before."

Ted rocked his daughter back and forth, exchanging a pained look with his ex-wife. "I'm sorry about that. Daddy handled that all wrong."

"So did Mom." Elizabeth squeezed Ted's shoulder, then rubbed her daughter's back.

Ted hadn't talked much about his marriage or divorce from Elizabeth, just giving me a few key details here and there since we met.

After an investigation involving the brutal murder of a teenage girl, Ted had turned to alcohol to stop the images haunting him. Ted didn't blame Elizabeth for throwing him out, nor did he blame her for going through with the promised divorce and ending his visitation. It wasn't until a few months after the divorce, and not being permitted to see his daughter, that Ted fought his demons. Bob had encouraged Ted to move out of Morgantown for a fresh start. Elizabeth had agreed, even offering to drive Claire to him for weekend visitation. She wanted her ex-husband to have the opportunity to heal without dealing with gossiping coworkers.

It never bothered me that Ted was friends with his ex-wife. I actually thought it was admirable. Of course, it was easier to feel that way when I wasn't witnessing the camaraderie between them, and it was obvious to me that Claire wanted her parents back together.

Quietly, I slipped out of the alcove. There was a section of the deck where the sun was shining so I made my way to a chair and sat down. The movie playing on the huge screen at the pool didn't interest me, so I pulled out my e-reader and my phone. I settled myself into a deck chair and browsed through the books.

I skipped over the romance books, not feeling it at the moment, and also bypassed the mysteries. I didn't need anyone else planting whodunit thoughts into my head. I had John for that. There was a reason Ronnie had originally not mentioned her brother being on the cruise. Why did she change her mind? Or had it slipped out? What was it about William walking off with Ruth that concerned her so much she lowered her guard?

My mind tumbled all the questions around and around. The words on the screen made no sense. I turned off the reader and exchanged it for my travel planner, hoping the act of writing would focus my brain on something else. Instead of journaling about the pleasant events of the trip, I scribbled down my theories and tried connecting them with wavy arrows.

"What are you writing?" Ronnie lowered a large cream-colored beach tote onto the floor and flopped onto a seat beside me. She arranged the flowing fabric of her caftan around her, exposing her mint-green bikini. She slipped off dainty silver sandals and placed them underneath the chair.

I slapped the book shut, slipping it into my tote. "About the trip. How are you this morning? William's concerned about you."

"I'm fine. No reason for any concern." Ronnie slathered sunscreen on her long legs and rubbed it in, catching the eye of men walking by. The silver bracelets with tiny crystals adorning her wrists clanked together.

"He's family. Of course he'd be worried. Someone you know died."

Ronnie collapsed back and draped her arm over her eyes. "My tiara went missing. That's my biggest problem right now. Quinn made his own choices and there's nothing I can do about it."

"Went missing?" That bothered her? Not a man dropping dead at her feet?

"I swear I placed it on the vanity in the bathroom, but this morning it's gone." Ronnie tapped her lip. "If I can't find it, I can always remake it. I have some jewelry-making supplies with me. If you let me borrow yours, I can copy it."

Whatever William was involved with, so was his sister. Quinn's death had no effect on her, and she knew my tiara was the last one and had an excuse for why she needed it. She had watched Claire pitch hers over the rail in the midst of a tantrum.

John was wrong about Odessa. There was no way she'd have matching, or almost matching, tiaras made if she knew it'd get her granddaughter caught up in a jewelry scam. John needed to focus on Ronnie and her brother.

"It's kind of intricate," I said. No way was I letting her switch any stones.

"If Quinn made it while half-drunk, I can do it sober." Her voice grew deeper, a coldness creeping into her gaze for a brief moment before disappearing after a rapid series of blinks. She fidgeted, covering her legs with the caftan.

"Why did you originally tell me you were cruising alone?"

"What?" Her blue eyes widened.

"When we first met, you said you were traveling alone, then later you said William was your brother. I'm confused about that."

Ronnie whipped a pair of sunglasses from her beach tote and perched them on her nose. "I'd rather not talk about it."

"That question sure does annoy you. You weren't too happy I asked it yesterday."

"And yet you're still asking it." Ronnie rubbed the bridge of her nose. "I'm on a medication that leaves me confused at times and I forget things on occasion. And, I hadn't known William was on the ship until I saw him at the muster drill."

A shadow fell over us. A security guard nodded briefly at me before turning his attention to Ronnie. "Captain Henderson requests your presence."

She shooed him away. "I'm a guest. He can't order me around."

"Even a guest can be questioned about a death." The guard locked a hand around her wrist.

"I'll come. Let me get my stuff." Slowly, she folded her towel and whispered. "Don't tell anyone they're questioning me, Faith."

By anyone, I assumed she meant Garrison. "You need help."

"I'll handle this on my own. It's better that way."

"I can help you."

"No, you can't."

Four people who weren't sitting in jail would testify otherwise. "Trust me. I can."

She whispered in my ear, "A month ago, I threatened to kill him. And the month before that, you can say I kind of tried. Or at least that's what a witness to the incident said. I don't quite remember it. Four people know about that. Me. The captain. You. Odessa. Let's keep it that way."

EIGHT

Ronnie's confession shook me. I felt off-kilter. A scrapbooking class was being held on deck six, so I headed there, needing to clear my mind while I figured out what to do. Scrapbooking calmed me and centered my spirit. I knew this trip would rev up some anxiety, so I bought a travel planner. It was more portable than a scrapbook, yet the same techniques were used for decorating it. Instead of pictures, words were the main focal point. I had brought colored pencils and an array of travel stickers for decorating the pages.

I spotted a crew member pushing a cart loaded down with cruise-themed scrapbooking supplies and followed. Other women and a few men joined our parade to the lounge area in the back of the ship.

"Find a spot while I set up." The young woman began sorting through the packages of products and stacking them by theme onto a table.

I spotted Garrison sitting at a table in the back, flipping through a book. When I sat down, he closed the leather book about the size of an 8x8 album. The cover was embossed. I tried reading the script font, but he covered the writing with his forearm.

"Here to scrapbook or just looking for some peace and quiet to read?" I asked.

"I've wanted to learn some new techniques and now was the perfect time."

"You and Bob didn't have anything special planned for this morning?"

"Odessa stopped by this morning to tell Bob the captain wanted to meet with him."

"About what?"

"I'd rather not know, so I kissed Bob goodbye and told him I'd be here. I'm sure it has something to do with John. I wonder where Ronnie is. She had said she'd meet me here."

"When did you talk to her?" I doodled in my travel journal.

"At breakfast. Why?"

"Curious," I said. "No other reason. She might have lost track of time or something unexpected came up." The captain had issued a gag order. Ronnie said to stay quiet. And here I was blabbing—or almost blabbing, which was just as bad. "This probably isn't the wedding you dreamed of."

"The event meant more to Odessa than us, so we caved on pretty much everything. Our only sticking point was no alcohol at the event out of respect and love for Ted, and yet she had the champagne flowing freely, and now we also have John Roget to contend with. I'm not looking forward to him and Odessa coming face to face."

"He's stayed away so far."

"That's true. Maybe he only came to spend time with Claire and not to stop the wedding. John is a hard one to figure out."

"He isn't the only one."

Garrison's eyebrows rose. "Do tell."

"Ronnie was the only one who showed up at dinner last night, so we had time to chat."

Garrison scooted his chair back from the table, taking his book with him. "What about Ronnie?" There was an edge to his voice.

He thought I was judging her. About what? "I like her. She made me feel welcome from the first moment we met at the muster drill. She even went out of her way to get my tiara when it was knocked onto a lifeboat."

Garrison groaned, lowering his head into his hands. "Please don't tell me she climbed down to get it."

"Twirled down. I told her not to. She insisted. It was kind of amazing, though security wasn't thrilled with the impromptu show."

"I'm sure they weren't. Looks like scrapbooking items are being sold. We should get up there before they run out."

"You don't seem too surprised about Ronnie doing an aerial performance from a deck rail."

"Because she's done it before." Garrison weaved his way between two women deciding between getting a family fun cruise layout or a relaxing day at sea packet.

We paid for our items and returned to our table where we perused our goodies a little more thoroughly. I was excited over all the chipboard pieces that had the logo for the cruise line. I had scoured the internet for items and lost hours of sleep with nothing to buy. Maybe I should pick up a few extra packs. Claire might be interested in making an album of the trip, or I could make a gift album for her. Even better, the next time she visited her dad, I could bring over a scrapbook and the embellishments for the three of us to work on a memory book together.

"I'm going to be showing everyone how to use two sheets of pattern paper to make a background for a layout." The instructor chose two sheets from the kit and held them up. "These are the ones I'll be using. Feel free to use any two you'd like."

Garrison opened up on the packs and took out two coordinating sheets.

Suddenly, we could hear a small argument at the entrance to the lounge area. William was in a heated exchange with a crew member. Had William created another ruckus with a passenger or was he having it out because the guard hauled Ronnie to the captain's office?

William's companion hobbled over to him and rested a dainty hand on his arm. "Dear one, have you seen my bracelet? I thought for sure I placed it by my side of the bed. I can't find it anywhere. I'm not able to look underneath the bed. Can you help me find it?"

William caught me staring. The look he centered on me sent a chill down my spine.

"I don't believe it."

Garrison stood, clutching onto the table. His knuckles turned white and I felt a crackle in the air. William and Garrison stared at each other and both men had the classic old west showdown look on their faces.

Ruth practically dragged William out of there. The elderly lady wasn't as fragile as she appeared.

"I'm taking it you don't like him." I tugged Garrison back down to the seat. "Want to talk about it?"

"It's a long story."

"We have time. Everyone is working on their scrapbook pages." I pointed at the sample board the instructor placed on the table. "I'd rather use my own design, especially since I'm not sure what size I want to make my cruise album."

"I wasn't planning on making a cruise album. I just wanted to get some ideas for our adoption book."

I grinned. "Your what?"

"Adoption album." Garrison turned over the book he had been hiding from me, running his hand longingly over the leather cover. "Bob and I want a child and had agreed to start the process once we were married."

"You'll be married soon." I squeezed his hand. "From what I've come to know about Odessa, nothing will stop her from achieving her goals."

"We consulted with an attorney and an adoption agency in Morgantown for advice. The agency recommended putting together a family book about Bob and me. There are many couples looking to adopt and a book will help the mothers get to know us. Bob and I will have an uphill battle already, considering we're a same-sex couple."

"You two will be awesome parents. You're both caring, smart, resourceful, and have great jobs."

"Jobs that could hurt us in the long run." Garrison gripped my hand. "I have a question to ask you, though Bob wanted to hold off on us talking to anyone until we formally sign with the agency.

Being a planner, I prefer to know all the viable options we have before we get our hearts in too deep."

Tears welled in my eyes. I couldn't even imagine the hope and despair that were intertwined in their dream. "Ask away."

"Once we adopt, I'm planning on taking a year off to bond with our child. It's a little easier for me to do that because my specialty in the medical field makes me extremely employable. I'm ninety-nine percent certain the hospital will hire me back as the hospital director has always said I'm their best ER doctor. But Bob owns his own business and if he takes a large amount of time off, he won't have anything to go back to, and one of us has to bring in an income."

"How can I help?"

"Right now, Bob works alone and spends a lot of time on his cases. If he had a research assistant, it would cut down the time he was in the office for each case. He'd need someone to help him out on occasion. It wouldn't be much over minimum wage as Bob will be the only wage earner, though we are saving a chunk of my salary right now. Would you be interested? You wouldn't be in danger. It'll consist mainly of tracking down records and other information on a computer."

The idea intrigued me. Our finances had taken a hit trying to repair the damage done to Scrap This by a fire, so an extra income would benefit my family, but I couldn't abandon my grandmothers.

"It's a bad idea. I shouldn't have said anything." Garrison said.

"I like the idea. I'm just worried about the logistics. I'm not sure I'm up for a three-hour commute for a side job." Not to mention gas would eat up most of my pay.

Garrison's blue eyes sparkled. "You wouldn't have to commute from Eden. The majority of your work would be computer research. Bob might need you to come in and man the office on occasion, but you could stay over at our house and we'll pay you mileage."

"It sounds great..." I allowed myself to trail off. I wasn't a split-second-decision type of gal. Heck, I had enough trouble committing on where to place an embellishment on a layout. I sure couldn't make a life-altering decision on the spur of the moment that also affected my grandmothers.

"I don't expect an answer now. I know you need some time to think it over and come up with a plan. It's just something to muse over for a bit. You have plenty of time."

"Time for what?" Ted dropped into a seat beside me, drifting a kiss across my cheek.

"Catching up on sleep, working on some crafts, watching some movies, whatever I want, since I seem to be on my own during this cruise," I said, immediately regretting it. I sounded shrew-like instead of playful.

Garrison's eyebrows lifted and he pressed his lips together, taking great interest in the layout kits on our table. I hadn't meant to be so snippy, but I allowed instinct rather than careful thought to rule. It was the reason I didn't want to give Garrison an answer. My impetuous choices always came back to drop around my neck like a noose. Things worked out better when I angsted through all the potential outcomes.

"I'm trying, Faith. It's not my fault our breakfast was interrupted."

"I know. I was just looking forward to it. I don't expect to have all your attention on the cruise. You should spend time with your daughter. I just hoped we'd have a little time for each other."

"There are plenty of us here to keep Claire entertained," Garrison said. "Bob and I would love to spend some quality time with her. There's an excursion we'd love to take her on."

"Which one?" I tried not to sound too excited.

Ted rubbed his forehead. "I have no problem with it, but I'm afraid Claire would."

Garrison let out a grunt of a laugh. "Oh please, that little girl loves her Uncle Bob and Garrison. She knows she has Bob wrapped around her finger."

"But Claire isn't happy if I'm away from her," Ted said.

"Then have a talk with her before it gets worse." Garrison discreetly placed his cruise kits on top of the adoption album. "I understand you want to spend as much time as you can with her, but I think this has less to do with you and more to do with Claire wanting you and Elizabeth back together."

"That's not true. Elizabeth has been dating Neal for a year. Claire is acting up because she feels bad about telling her grandpa about the wedding, and her grandma is upset because he showed up," Ted said.

"Maybe," Garrison said. "But I think I'm right. Bob would agree with me..."

"That the wedding should take place off the ship?" Odessa joined us, with Claire in tow. "It should be on here like originally planned. I assured him that John would not interfere with the new ceremony. I had the captain promise him also."

"How can the captain do that?" Ted asked.

Odessa smiled sweetly at her son. "He'll explain it to you during our discussion."

"Discussion?" Ted frowned.

I shrank back into my chair, hoping everyone continued to forget I was there in case my expression gave away the nervousness creeping inside me.

"Daddy!" Claire wiggled herself between me and Ted. "I've been looking for you. Mom isn't feeling well, and said me and you will hang out together."

"That's not fair," Garrison said in a playful tone. "Uncle Bob and I were hoping to have some time with our favorite niece. Bob and I wanted to race you up the climbing wall then get some ice cream." He leaned closer to her. "Not the free ice cream that's in the buffet, but the extra special one you have to buy at the ice cream parlor. I also want to browse around the shops with a shopping buddy. Bob is no fun to take shopping."

Claire nibbled at her lip, indecision in her eyes.

Please choose the afternoon with your amazing uncles, I thought.

"Can Daddy come with us?"

"No." Garrison acted put-out. "He's even a worse shopper than your Uncle Bob. I bet your dad won't let you eat the triple scoop sundae with cookie crumbs, gummy worms, hot fudge, and caramel sauce."

"That's true," Ted said. "As a dad, I can't let you eat that much sugar in a day."

"But an uncle can." Garrison grinned at her.

Placing my hands under the table, I crossed my fingers.

"As lovely as all that sounds," Odessa said, "today is not good for it. I need you and Ted to come with me and talk with the captain and the security detail. Apparently there was an incident last night," her gaze slid in my direction, "and the captain is a little concerned something was overlooked. He'd like your advice."

"About what?" Ted asked.

"I'm not at liberty to say." Again, her cool gaze skittered in my direction.

"Then I'm not inclined to go," Ted said.

"Since when do you talk to your mother like that?" Another look in my direction.

"I'm done with your games, Mom."

Garrison stood. "Claire and I are going to explore the ship. She doesn't want to hear the two of you argue."

"I'm not upset." The little girl clung to her dad's arm.

My cue to leave. The person I really wanted to talk to right now was Garrison. He had found a great way to distract me from getting the truth I wanted—why he disliked William—and now he had a perfect excuse to leave. What was it that no one wanted to say about William?

"I need you and Garrison to come with me," Odessa said. "It's for professional advice."

"What about Claire?" Garrison placed his hands on the girl's shoulder. "It's not fair to make her sit through a boring meeting."

"It definitely isn't a conversation my sweet granddaughter should hear."

"How about I come with you and Garrison stays with Claire?" Ted asked. "I don't want her wandering around the ship by herself."

Garrison looked relieved.

"No." Odessa stared at me. "What about you?"

"I have plans to attend the gem shopping seminar."

"Sounds like a perfect activity for the girls," Odessa said.

"I'm not sure that's a good idea," Ted said.

Claire evil-eyed me.

"Surely Faith can look after an eleven-year-old girl for a couple of hours," Odessa said, the challenge quite clear.

Here was my chance to change her opinion of me, and prove Ted wrong. "Of course I can."

NINE

No. No, I couldn't. I had thought looking after my friend's three elementary-school-aged boys nicknamed the Hooligans was a challenge. Claire was testing parts of my patience those boys had never stretched a smidgen. The girl was letting me know she did not like me. At all. She had argued with all my suggestions, even tossing aside every gift I had bought for her.

"Are we going to stay in your room all day?" Claire stomped her foot and scowled. "I'm bored. I thought you were taking me to the jewelry thing."

Not when I knew John wanted me there. "What would you like to do?" I asked, plastering a smile on my face. Patience. Patience. Patience. Even with Patience being my middle name, it wasn't one of my strong suits and I hoped begging for it helped.

"I just told you." She stomped her foot again. "Take me now."

If I didn't take her, I'd face the wrath of Odessa and Ted. Once John saw me there with his granddaughter, he'd nix his brilliant idea on uncovering the jewelry stealing ring. Right?

"And I want to find my tiara."

"We'll do both," I relented, praying nothing went wrong. "The seminar will have a jewelry appraiser there. Maybe whoever found your tiara will bring it."

"No, they won't." Tears welled in her eyes. "Grandma is picking a new date for the wedding. I won't have my tiara to wear. Can I have yours?"

Indecision rippled through me. How could I say yes? How

could I say no? I opened up the room safe and took out my tiara. Cradling it in the palms of my hands, I presented it. "You're more of a princess than me."

Claire's green eyes, so like her dad's, lit up. She reached for it, her hand stopping a few inches from the gift. A frown twisted her face, and she slapped it out of my hands. The tiara landed on the bed. "It's broken. That's why you don't want it."

Was that why William wanted to see the tiara up close and personal? To check and see which stone was missing? I retrieved my tiara. Yep. The stone in the middle was gone. How would I get that fixed on the ship? It would have to wait until later. "Let's go to the seminar and see if anyone brings your tiara."

"I'll never get it back. I ruined the wedding." Her lip trembled.

My heart went out to the girl. Odessa had inadvertently blamed her granddaughter for the delayed ceremony. No wonder Claire was in such a foul mood. She thought her grandmother was mad at her and found herself pawned off on the woman she really didn't want to know. I needed to have more empathy for her. "The cruise director said some of the items being thrown down to the passengers were valuable. I'm sure people will show up to see how much their prize was worth."

"Okay."

"There sure are a lot of people here." Claire drew closer, placing a hand on my sleeve.

My heart did a little happy dance. Many of the attendees were carrying jewelry pouches and bags. Let one of the items be Claire's tiara, I thought. I stayed right next to Claire, but allowed her to control the contact between us. I didn't want to set off one of her tantrums. One, not good for her to do so in public. Two, I didn't want any interest drawn toward us. Blending in was my motto for today.

I spotted John at the far end of the room. The look he shot across the theater told me his view on bringing Claire. Not happy at all. Matter of fact, it said if he could strangle me in that moment he would. Two things held him back: I was his sting operation, and Claire. At least I knew he was protective of her. Hopefully, his love for his granddaughter would keep his behavior in check when the wedding happened.

A swarm of excited cruisers staked out their spots. Claire dragged me forward, quickening her pace. It was nice to see her excited about something besides giving me a hard time.

"I want to sit in the front." Claire tugged me in the opposite direction. "We'll be closer to the shopping lady."

"Sounds good. We can see what everyone brought for appraisal."

William stood near the front of the theater, chatting with a lovely woman dressed in a little black dress and the cruise director. In the center of the floor, in front of the stage, was a long table filled with gift bags and brochures. Microphones and bar stools were at opposite ends of the table. William must have felt my stare because he turned, darkness flashing across his face for a brief moment before our gazes met. Claire and I started to sit. William shook his head slightly, then tilted his head to the side twice as if he was stretching out a kink in his neck.

At the opposite end of the row, William's companion was maneuvering through the tight quarters, one hand on a seat back and the other clutching her cane. A huge tote weighed down her arm. She struggled to make her way to the center of the aisle. A large diamond bracelet glittered as the light hit it. It was an impressive piece. My knowledge was lacking when it came to fine jewels, any type of gem actually, but I'd have to say each stone making up the bracelet was at least one carat. It snagged on the fabric cushion of the seat.

"Oh dear." Ruth tried to untangle it while keeping hold of her cane.

"Let's sit here." I dropped my tote onto the seat William had directed me to then went to help Ruth. "We'll get a better view here."

Claire plopped into the seat beside me. "This better not be boring."

The seminar hadn't even started and Claire was complaining. I hoped the elderly woman sitting beside me was in the mood for small talk.

"Let me see if I can get you unstuck," I said.

Ruth smiled at me. "Thank you so much honey. This bracelet is always getting in the way. I don't know why I let William talk me into buying it."

I wrestled a sharp edge of the clasp from the fabric. "I think it's very pretty. I love the setting. It looks like there's some square stones mixed in with the round ones."

"There are. William said it reminded him of the letters used for hugs and kisses. We were browsing in my favorite jewelry store in St. John when William spotted this piece. Once he said that, I had to buy it. I had told him how my husband and I had ended all our correspondence with those symbols. It's also why I wear it even though it keeps getting caught as it makes me feel like my husband is always with me."

My heart ached for her and was filled with fury at William. He was probably one of the worst people I knew—and I've run into quite a few horrible people.

Ruth dropped into the seat next to me and fanned herself with her hands. "Goodness me. Either aisles are shrinking or my hips are expanding at an alarming rate. I swear it wasn't that hard to make it to a seat last month."

"You cruise often?" I asked, giving her a friendly, but not overly friendly, smile as I took my seat.

"Once a month. I love people and going out, but this eighty-year-old body of mine has issues getting around. It's so much easier on the ship where everything I love is in one place. Movies. Fancy dinner." She fluffed her curls. "My hair done. When I'm home, it seems the only time I go out is for doctor's appointments."

"This is my first cruise."

She smiled at me. Warmth and laughter sparkled in her eyes.

She reminded me of my grandmother Hope, who never met a stranger she didn't like. It made me even angrier that William was likely taking advantage of her.

"Be sure to experience as much on the ship as you can," she said. "Some people like to spend the whole time by the pools, but I find it's better to explore the ship and take in all the classes you can. One never knows when a new activity will become a love and passion."

"That's why I decided to come to this seminar. A girl should know what she can about diamonds."

Claire rolled her eyes. "Keep dreaming."

The woman raised her eyebrows and her lips quirked up. "Charming child."

I leaned toward the woman and whispered, "I'm dating her father. She's not happy."

"You don't say." She grinned.

The cruise director cleared his throat. The cruisers grew quiet. He introduced the lady in black.

"Welcome to our diamond shopping seminar. This is the lovely Lucinda Wells."

Lucinda beamed at all of us and clapped her hands. "I'm excited to see so many here today. For those that don't know, the Caribbean has the best shopping for fine jewelry, especially diamonds. You'll find the best prices, value, and there's no tax."

Some of the attendees were impressed; others, like Claire, had their eyes on the gift bags or on the bowl a crew member was carrying down the aisle. Silver bracelets gleamed under the lights. Even from a distance, I noticed the jewelry wasn't sterling silver. Granted, I wasn't an expert, but I never saw sterling silver packaged in plastic sandwich bags.

"I'll have a friend of mine pass out the free gifts." Lucinda rested a hand on William's knee and gave a little squeeze. His cheeks turned pink; he'd almost perfected the look of humble embarrassment. "We placed the gifts in bags to keep them from getting scratched. I'll be sharing my expertise on the best places to buy your diamonds and other fine gems. The best quality purple tanzanite can also be bought on St. Thomas."

William handed everyone a bag, lingering near me and Claire. William's fingers drifted across my skin from my wrist to my fingertips. His smoldering gaze caused me to narrow mine. He winked and moved on to the cruisers sitting on the opposite side of the aisle. I was starting to believe William was one of those people who was a natural flirt, for a lack of a better term, since there wasn't a phrase for a male who was a shameless hussy.

Ruth wiggled her fingers at him. "Going to give me one of those, dear one?"

"I was saving the best one for you." He winked at her and handed her a bag before moving to the row behind us.

Claire elbowed me, a true smile on her face for the first time during my babysitting duty. "He likes you. You should go out with him."

I stopped myself from reminding her I was dating her father. No way did I want to send Claire into meltdown mode.

"Why don't you take out the bracelet and see if it fits?" I tapped the gift bag on Claire's lap. "If not, we can go to check the shops onboard and find you one that does."

"Because I don't want to." Claire crossed her arms and glared at the stage.

There was a loud rustle as many people stood and made their way for the exit. I guess they were interested in the gift and not the shopping information.

"Coming around the room are maps showing the best shops to purchase your jewelry," Lucinda said. "For those interested in having a more personal shopping experience, I have some slots available for a guided tour through the shopping district. If you have an item you'd like appraised, please raise your hand." Lucinda counted out the number of people needing appraisals. "Six. Perfect. We'll have enough time to get to everyone after the short film that explains everything to look for when buying a diamond."

Ruth fiddled with her bracelet.

The lights dimmed and the movie rolled. A bored disembodied voice educated us about diamonds. Chairs creaked as more attendees headed out of the theater for something new to occupy their time. I was on the verge of going with them.

"This is stupid." Claire slumped down and kicked the back of the chair in front of her. Since no one was sitting in front of her, I let it go. I fumbled through my memory, trying to recall the other activities taking place.

"It'll end soon, sweetie," Ruth said. "Then they'll do a couple of appraisals before the big giveaway." She rummaged around in her purse and drew out a bottle of a soda and a package of frosted cookies. "I have some snacks if you're hungry."

"She'll be fine," I said. "We'll stay put. We don't want to ruin the film for those interested in it."

Ruth dropped the goodies back into her large purse while Claire switched positions and accidentally-on-purpose kicked me in the shins. The lights came back on. Cruisers yawned and stretched. A couple of people glanced at their watches.

Lucinda stood and beamed at everyone, a long velvet box held reverently in her hand. "I hope that answers all your questions, and if not, please feel free to pop into Dazzles, the best diamond store on any cruise ship, and ask to see me. The cruise director wanted me to remind everyone that there's a dance party happening on the ninth deck. I'll announce the name of the winner of this two-carat diamond bracelet so you call all be on your way. There are tons of other activities happening today including some great sales on the fifth deck. Those with items needing to be appraised, please come down to the front of the theater. The winner is..."

Everyone froze. A couple of women leaned forward, eyes gleaming. Claire scooted to the end of the chair, fingers on both hands crossed tightly. Ted would have a heck of a time getting the diamond bracelet away from his daughter if she won. There was no way he'd want his daughter walking around with two carats of diamonds adorning her wrist.

We waited. And waited some more. A few people grumbled.

Lucinda giggled. "Actually, the person who will announce the winning name is you. Look under the chair you're sitting in. If there's a ticket taped underneath, the bracelet is yours."

"What if no one is sitting there?" someone asked.

"The first one to find the ticket gets it."

There was a mad scramble. Claire flipped up her chair then worked her way to the end of the aisle.

Dread washed over me. I had a feeling I knew who the winner was. I peered at the underside of my seat. Yep. I had the diamond ticket. As I reached for it, William blurted out, "We have a winner. The lovely brunette in the fourth row."

A smattering of polite claps replaced the sounds of squeaking chair cushions.

Claire glared at me. "You cheated."

Fortunately, no one overheard her. "No, I didn't."

"Congratulations, darling. I bet it'll look lovely with whatever you're wearing for formal night." Ruth used her cane to help push herself up and hobbled out of the row.

"Here you go." Lucinda walked over and handed me the velvet box.

"Be sure to wear it to dinner tonight and let everyone know you won by coming to the shopping seminar. There will be more prizes at the next one."

"Thank you." I placed the box into my tote. "I was wondering-"

"I'm hungry. Take me to Surf's Up." Claire stamped her foot.

"I just want to ask one quick question. And didn't you want to see if anyone brought your tiara for appraisal?"

Claire's face turned a light shade of pink. She had forgotten.

"You lost your tiara?" Lucinda asked, bestowing a sympathetic smile onto Claire.

She looked down at the floor.

I placed my hand on Claire's shoulder and it was quickly shrugged off. "She was near the railing during the sail away party and it slipped off. I thought maybe someone would bring it to your appraisal."

"I'd be happy to keep a look out for it." Even though Lucinda was answering me, her gaze was on Claire. "Can you describe it to me?"

Claire shrugged.

I wouldn't have thought the child had a shy bone in her body. "It has multicolored crystals on it. The setting is silver."

"Anything distinguishing about it?" Lucinda asked.

I remembered my selfie and pulled it up on my phone, zooming in on the tiara. "It's very similar to this one."

Lucinda took my phone to get a better look at it. She frowned slightly and squinted. "This is very similar to one I've seen before."

"You saw my tiara?" Hope lit Claire's eyes. "Mine is prettier and has one big heart-shaped stone in the middle."

There was grumbling behind us. The cruisers wanting appraisals were getting restless.

"I haven't but I'll be on the lookout for it. The tiara in the picture reminds me of one that William's friend has. I saw her wear it on formal night not too long ago."

I tucked the information away. How had Quinn come up with the same design? Did he get it from William or his helper Ronnie? "Quinn must've really loved the design. I hope Ruth doesn't get upset that he copied it."

Lucinda handed the phone back, the corners of her mouth dipping down. "Quinn doesn't mingle or pay much attention to the passengers. It must've just been one of those weird coincidences that sometimes happen."

I seriously doubted it. If it wasn't William and Quinn masterminding a switch of real jewels or fake ones, then it had to be William and Ronnie.

"Can we go eat now?" Claire tugged on my arm.

"Sure."

"I thought you had a question," Lucinda said.

Question. Yes. I patted my tote bag. "I was wondering if there's any paperwork showing how much the bracelet is worth in case I should insure it."

Lucinda blushed. "Usually, I also bring down the diamond certificate with me to hand to the winner, but I left it at Dazzles. I can meet you there in an hour and give it to you. It'll have everything you need to have it insured."

"Thanks."

Beaming, Lucinda walked to the rather impatient cruisers with their items. Fortunately, she had one of those bubbly, but not overly perky, personalities that made people smile. The grumpy expressions soon changed into playful ones.

"Can we go eat? I'm starving."

"As you wish." I hated the tone she used, but I was hungry so I ignored the behavior. There was a long line for the elevators so we opted for the stairs.

"I was going to say something to that lady but didn't."

"What were you going to say?" I was annoyed at the hesitation in my voice. I couldn't believe I was scared about what a little girl almost said.

"About what that guy did. It wasn't fair," she said as we walked up the stairs. "You were led to the prize. You shouldn't keep it."

"You're right, Claire. I'll tell the captain and give it to him."

"Why not just give it back and let them do another drawing? Or give it to someone else." Hope shone in her eyes.

There was no way I was giving a diamond bracelet to a little girl. Ted wouldn't be happy, and I didn't trust William. There was a reason he wanted me to have it. I doubted it was because he had fallen madly in love with me. "Because the captain should know what's going on."

"I guess," Claire said. "And since the guy already cheated, he might just keep it for himself."

There was that.

TEN

Claire and I had a delightful lunch at the buffet. It seemed our agreement over William cheating offered us a bonding moment. As we stepped out of Surf's Up, laughter drifted from past the doors that separated the small alcove between the restaurant and the deck.

"Sounds like a party out there. How about we check it out?" I asked.

"Sure."

The warm air held a hint of salt with a mix of chlorine from the pool. Around us, adults and a few children were dancing and singing. The outside movie screen had been turned into a huge karaoke screen. Four crew members stood on the raised concrete edge of the pool and demonstrated a line dance to go along with a Top 40 classic.

"This is stupid." Claire crossed her arms.

Her favorite word reappeared, stealing away the hope in my heart. Our getting-along moment was short-lived.

"There's a kid's club on the ship. Want to check it out? I bet you can find a few friends."

"You want to get rid of me so you can have my dad all to yourself."

"That's not true. I'd never interfere in the time your dad wants to spend with you. I care about your dad. And you."

"How can you? You don't know me," she snapped.

"I'd like to." I rested a hand on her thin shoulder.

She pulled away. "I don't. My dad is getting back with my mom, and you're too stupid to figure that out."

I took in a few calming breaths, reining in my temper. Part of me wanted to have a "come to Jesus" talk with Claire, but another part of me screamed it wasn't my place. Let Ted handle it. The last thing I wanted was to make things worse, though I wasn't sure how I could possibly do that.

"I want to go back to my room." Claire held out a keycard in a folder, the room number visible to anyone walking by.

"You shouldn't let people see the number."

"I guess that's not safe." There was a sly smile on her face. "Can we go? Our room is big. Maybe we can even do one of those stupid craft kits you brought."

I hated not to trust Ted's child, but I didn't. The girl had something devious in mind. It was one ill-conceived scheme I refused to take part in. "No. We can stay at this dance party or go back to my room."

The crew members jumped down. "It's conga time. Come and join the fun. Even you loungers around the pool. You're on vacation, so let's get the party energy flowing."

Adults and children scrambled to join the conga line. A few women good-naturedly fought over who got to put their hands on the waist of the hotter of the two male crew members.

"Want to join?" I asked. "I'll stand here and watch you."

"This is better than your room." Claire made her way to the end of the line. After a few step-step-kicks, a smile blossomed on her face and she got into the conga, swinging her hips in time with the music and laughing. I tugged out my phone and captured a few shots. Ted would love them.

From the corner of my eye, I spotted a little girl wearing a sparkling crown running to the end of the conga line. A familiar-looking crown. Claire's tiara. My mind flickered to all the discarded craft kits I had bought for Claire. Maybe the little girl, who looked about four, would like them in exchange for the tiara. I wished there was a way I could get them from my cabin without Claire noticing I was gone. I knew the kid would take off the second I left and tattle to her dad and grandmother. I'd make the offer now and schedule to meet at the ice cream parlor, adding in a sundae to make the barter even sweeter.

"Now we're going to see how low we can go," the cruise director announced. "Let's bring this conga under the limbo stick."

A few of the older members of the line scattered back to their deck chairs, while others in the line stretched and did some quick calisthenics. Claire glanced over her shoulder, her gaze settling on me for a second. Her face reddened. Unfortunately for her, I was right where she left me.

Claire left the line and zoomed over to the tiara-wearing little girl, who was returning to her mother's side. "That's mine." Claire snatched the tiara off the preschooler's head.

The little girl wailed.

I froze. I usually reacted in some manner during a crisis, but never before had I been responsible for the bad behavior of another. I ordered myself to move and hurried over.

"How dare you!" Shaking with anger, the mom cuddled the little girl to her with one arm and snatched the tiara back. "That belongs to my daughter."

"It's mine," Claire screeched, going again for the tiara. I inserted myself between the girls, bumping Claire with my hip.

"That girl almost hurt my daughter." Fisting a hand, the mother glared at me.

"I'm so sorry." I didn't blame her one bit for wanting to throttle someone. I squatted down to smile at the little girl. "Thank you so much for finding Claire's crown, sweetie. We've been looking for that tiara everywhere."

"It's mine," the little girl said, hiding the tiara between her and her mom's bodies.

"It was made special for Claire. Her—"

"Stop talking to her." Claire smacked me in the back. "Take it back."

I glared at Ted's badly behaving daughter. "You made her cry. She deserves an apology and a reward for finding your bridesmaid's crown." I added in the last bit hoping it swayed the mom.

"It belongs to me. She stole it. Don't give her anything."

"My daughter is not a thief." The mother picked up her toddler, cuddling the crying child to her bosom.

One. Two. Three. Four. Five. Six. I wasn't sure there were enough numbers to count for my temper to cool. "I know she didn't steal it. Claire is a little high-strung this morning because she dropped the tiara over the railing and didn't think we'd ever find it." I fudged the truth a little bit.

The cruise director walked over to us. "Is there a problem over here?"

"Yes. Her." The mother jabbed a finger in Claire's direction.

I sure was doing a bang-up job of watching Claire. Odessa and Ted would be furious if the girl was carted off to the brig—or wherever they put unruly kids. I took a page from Ronnie's playbook. "Claire lost her tiara yesterday when Bob and Garrison's wedding was postponed. Odessa's been looking for it."

The cruise director edged backwards. It worked.

I continued on with my overdrawn explanation to diffuse the situation. "The tiara is very special to Claire. She's a bridesmaid in her uncles' wedding and the tiara was made for her to wear to it. Since you found it, I'd like to give you a reward. I have a Disney Princess coloring book, a fancy one, and special coloring pencils. There are seventy-two in the box."

The little girl lifted her head from her mother's shoulder, wide eyes fixed on me. At her age, I'd have also been enthralled with that many different colors to use.

"I'd also like to treat you to a sundae at the ice cream shop on the sixth deck."

"Take me to my dad." Claire shoved me, nearly knocking me into the mother and child.

I whirled around. "You almost hurt this little girl. Her mom is being very patient with you, considering you ripped the tiara off her daughter's head. You need to apologize."

"It's—"

"Don't say it again." I made a cutting motion in the air with my hand. "It's yours. We got it. But that doesn't give you the right to just rip it off her head. You ask nicely."

"They aren't giving it back."

"You haven't given them the chance," I snapped at her.

"I hate you!" Claire screeched. "My dad will never, ever marry you. I won't let him."

I was done with her poor behavior. I took a gentle, yet firm, hold of her arm. "We're going back to my cabin."

"Stop hurting me!" Claire stiff-armed me, sending me tumbling to the deck. She ran.

I scrambled to my feet.

Sympathy flashed on the mother's face.

"She's a brat," the little girl muttered.

Silently, I agreed.

"I got this," Bob called out, taking off after his niece.

Bob, Ted, Odessa, and Garrison stood a few yards away. They had witnessed the end of the exchange. Worry crept into my brain. Odessa's narrowed eyes told me her view. I refused to meet Ted's gaze, fearing I'd see the same thing on his face. I couldn't deal with that right now. I wanted to curl into a ball and cry. I couldn't remember the last time someone had treated me so hatefully.

"Here you go, honey." The mom handed over the tiara. "Stepmoms have to stick together."

I nodded a thanks, words getting stuck in my throat. Stepmom. That was where a romance with Ted led, unless I was content with dating forever. And I wasn't. I also wasn't willing to become the object of scorn and hate for the rest of my life.

I looked over at Ted. He was gone. No coming to check on me. No asking what happened. Just going to comfort his daughter.

My gut screamed that I was watching my future play out before me. Was it what I really wanted?

"Sorry about Claire's behavior."

I whirled around. John was standing against the railing, a pair of binoculars trained toward the ocean. "How long have you been there?" I asked.

"For pretty much the whole thing." John settled the binoculars against his chest and readjusted the strap around his neck.

"Thanks for helping." I made sure my tone conveyed just how little I appreciated him watching.

"If I said anything to Claire, I'd create a worse incident. In case you haven't caught on, Odessa doesn't want me here." He pointed to the faux-glass structure that separated the family pool area from the adult area. "Let's go into the atrium. I'll get you a drink. We need to chat."

"I have some information for you."

John placed a hand on my back and encouraged me to walk in the direction he requested. The Rogets sure were bossy people.

We sat down at a table in the far corner, away from the pool, bar, and sunlight. John ordered two frozen non-alcoholic drinks from an approaching waiter.

I rested my elbows on the table, cupping my chin in my hands. "You're wrong about Odessa."

"I'm certain she doesn't want me here," John said.

"I agree with you about that. I mean she's not involved in the bling thing," I said, being as vague as possible and still making sense.

"You're allowed to have your own opinion on the matter."

"It isn't an opinion, it's a fact. Quinn had different types of gems in his room. Yesterday, William really wanted to get his hands on my tiara, and today I found out that Ruth, the woman William is the health aide for, has a tiara similar to mine. I bet William was trying to swap them out."

"Did you see the tiara for a comparison?"

"No. Claire lost hers and I showed a picture to Lucinda. She told me it looked like one Ruth had worn."

John stared at me, rubbing his chin. "We need to find a way to get a look at Ruth's tiara, and figure out how Odessa fits into it."

I heaved out a sigh. "She's not involved. That's why you have nothing on her. You realize, trying to prove she's a criminal isn't going to endear either of your sons to you."

He stretched out his legs. "If I was trying to prove a situation was true, I'd agree with you. I'm not out to create a truth, I'm showing the truth for what it is. Can't blame me for that."

"Sometimes the truth isn't what people want."

"True. But that doesn't mean you turn away and allow someone else to take the fall, especially now with murder involved."

"Quinn," I squeaked out his name. The waiter placed our drinks on the table. Before I pulled out my keycard, John paid with his own.

"That's how it appears."

"He didn't drink himself to death? I saw the bottle of champagne and the empty prescription bottle in his room."

"I heard all about that. The captain wanted to bring you in for questioning, but I told him you worked for me." John handed me a beverage. "The drinking did him in, but there was an added ingredient in the bottle."

Poisoned. I stared at mine suspiciously.

"I'm sure your drink is fine. Someone isn't randomly poisoning cruisers. Besides it wasn't the champagne that was tampered with, it was his medication. And that's why I'm certain it was my ex. William wouldn't have access to his medication, and Ronnie has been on sabbatical for a few months."

I hoped not. I took a sip of my drink. It was a banana and coconut daiquiri. Watery and warm. There were a few of the specials pre-made and sitting on the counter for the waiters to grab. "But you think Odessa was able to get her hands on his meds?"

"She's been working with him on the wedding outfits. I've confirmed with multiple crew members that Odessa had been spending a lot of time in his room. Sometimes in there alone when he had to deal with a show's costume emergency."

"Couldn't William or Ronnie have sneaked into his room and tampered with his medication?"

"William could've snuck down onto the crew's deck, but not into Quinn's room. Ronnie wouldn't have gone near Quinn with Garrison being on board."

"One, she did. I know it because I was with her. Two, why would Garrison being on the cruise stop her from getting into it with Quinn? They had a heck of an argument before the wedding that didn't take place."

"You sure do ask a lot of questions." John scowled.

"And you aren't asking enough," I fired back.

He leaned back. The shock on his face was soon replaced by a large grin. "I like you."

I guessed that was a good thing and meant he wouldn't try and frame me for something. Now, if I could just convince him to take the bull's-eye off Odessa long enough to consider another suspect. "So, how does Garrison's mere presence keep Ronnie in check?"

"He's always been a calming influence on her. They've been best friends since grade school and he just knows the right things to say to calm her down."

"She's been a little reckless, rappelling down to get my tiara, otherwise seems pretty relaxed about everything to me."

"Seems is your key word, Faith. Ronnie is good at keeping her temper in check, but there have been times when she hasn't."

Her earlier confession popped into my mind. "Do you think Quinn was killed because of the diamonds."

"Yes. I know for a fact Quinn was about to roll on someone."

"He came to you?"

John nodded. "No name, but with enough details that I knew he was telling the truth, and also involved in the matter."

"Why wouldn't he give you the name?"

"Leverage. First he wanted complete forgiveness for his sins."

"Naturally, you'd think the name he was planning on giving you was Odessa."

"She was responsible for buying the jewels."

"Maybe Quinn just told her what he needed, and that information he got from William. It is William's hobby and..." I pulled out the velvet box containing the diamond bracelet from my tote bag and opened it. "I have William to thank for me winning this at the seminar."

John lifted it from the box. "It's an unusual setting that makes it look like some stones are round and others square."

An image flashed in my brain: a similar bracelet around Ruth's wrist. I took it out of the box, lifting the bracelet right up to my eyes. The setting around the stones were larger, making the diamonds appear bigger. "This looks like a bracelet Ruth was wearing."

"Are you sure?"

"Yes. I got a close look at it when it snagged on a chair."

John draped it over my wrist and fastened it. "Let's see if Ruth has a reaction to your bracelet. We already know William won't as he doesn't want to give himself away. He probably doesn't realize you saw Ruth's lookalike bracelet. Also, drop a hint to Ruth that she should get her bracelet fixed when the *Serenade* stops in St. Johns. I'll follow them and see if he suggests any other purchases to her."

The diamonds sparkled on my wrist. "I can find a way to walk by their table during dinner."

"Good plan. It should come across as a natural and not planned meeting."

I stood. "I'm heading to Dazzle to pick up the certificate."

"I'll hang around in the area and get it from you for safe keeping."

I didn't know how it would be less safe with me, but it might be better to split up the items in case someone else found a way to sweet-talk their way into my stateroom.

ELEVEN

What had I walked into? A mass of bodies filled the shopping district, a.k.a. the hallway that stretched from mid-point on Deck Five to the bow. Cruisers occupied every inch of the area near a kiosk in the middle of the area. Pieces of gray fabric covered the items on the shopping tables. The tall tables of the kiosk protected four clerks from the shoppers desperate to get to the goods underneath. Four other tables were lined up against the walls with crew members stopping shoppers from taking off the covers too early.

Two women with heads bent toward each other marked out a battle plan on a hastily drawn map. Another woman gave her husband a list of items: leather bags, wallets, and makeup cases. She was going for the memory charm bracelets, necklaces, and watches. I had never seen so many overeager shoppers, even on Black Friday. Frantically, I scanned the growing crowd. Where was John? He'd excused himself for a moment and was now swallowed up in the masses.

"Two more minutes, folks, before the unveiling."

I tried excusing my way through the crowd but was thwarted at every attempt to get closer to the jewelry shop Dazzles. "I have an appointment to pick something up at the jewelry store."

The group in front of me closed ranks. Not even a breath could squeeze between their bodies. Why had Lucinda picked this time? This was a pickpocket's dream. I covered the bracelet on my left wrist with my right hand, holding it pressed to my stomach.

Had John come to the same conclusions and decided to use

me as the mark? I hated to think he'd put me in danger, but I didn't know the man very well. Stop with the drama, I thought. I was in the midst of hundreds of people, and besides some squished toes and an elbow or two to my body, I was safe from harm. If I could only get across the sea of shoppers and to Dazzles, I'd be able to get this task done and head to my next one: giving Claire her tiara. Of the two, I was certain this one sent me into less of a minefield. But I was willing to risk life and limb to wiggle partway into Claire's good graces.

"I want to get to the store." I pointed over their heads.

"We're not falling for that," one of them snapped at me. "You just want to cut in front of us."

Cruisers pressed around me. The strap of my tote fell into the crook of my arm, gaping open. Claire's tiara twinkled. Would someone try and snatch it? I lifted my arm up, cradling the tote to my chest, and placed my unadorned arm on top of the other.

"The sale is on!"

People rushed forward. I started toward Dazzles and my foot hooked around something. I pitched forward and into a woman in front of me. She veered away so quickly, I lost my balance. Another shopper jabbed their elbow into me and I fell backwards. I used my hands to brace myself from the fall. The items in my tote scattered to and fro. About an inch out of reach, in opposite directions, were the tiara and my e-reader. Which one did I save first? I snagged the tiara. It was easier to replace the reader than recreate Claire's fairy crown.

A heavy boot stomped on my hand, nearly crushing the tiara. I bit back a scream and quickly shoved the rescued tiara into my tote. At least it didn't sustain any harm.

"Are you okay?" Ruth used her cane to move my e-reader closer to me. "I am so sorry. It's so hard for me to maneuver around in these crowds. I seemed to have accidentally tripped you with my cane."

Tears glittered in Ruth's eyes and her woebegone expression told me she was sincere. It had been an accident. I plastered a smile on my face, not wanting her to see my pain as I shoved the e-reader into my bag. "I'm fine." My hand hurt when I moved my fingers, but I was able to flex them. I tried pushing myself up, but my hand was too sore. Instead, I rolled to my knees before standing.

"Oh my goodness, you're hurt. Let me get someone over here to help."

"Please, don't do that. It's just a little sprain. It's a little sore from being stepped on." I was sure it would feel better in a moment. If not, I'd have Garrison take a look at it.

"You should at least put some ice on it so it doesn't swell up."

I looked at my hand. It was a little puffy. I poked a spot and hissed in a breath. That wasn't a smart idea.

"I'm taking you to my room right now." Ruth hooked her arm through mine. "No arguments from you, young lady. William always carries medical supplies, and I know he has some gel ice packs in the room. He gets them from the medical facility after we board."

"I'll go since it'll save me a trip to the medical facility." It also got me into Ruth and William's room so I could snoop around, and it provided the opportunity for Ruth to take a look at the bracelet I'd won.

We took the elevator to the eighth floor. "We're in a suite at the end of the hall," Ruth said, leading the way. She kept a tight hold on my arm. I wasn't sure if it was to keep herself steady or she was afraid I'd run off.

Stewards in the hallway smiled at us as we passed by. Mid-afternoon must be the time for sprucing up the rooms. I made a mental note to pass on the information to John, in case we needed to do searching later on.

"Here we are." Ruth hooked her cane onto her arm before removing her room key from her purse. She waved it in front of the lock then pushed the door open. "William has the second room."

I stepped inside. The suite was huge. I wondered if the room Ted shared with his mom and daughter matched it. This was the way to travel. There was a large couch and plenty of space to spread out. The curtains were pulled back and showed off a large deck that wrapped around the corner of the boat.

"William keeps the ice pack in the refrigerator." Ruth headed for a medium sized fridge near the TV console. It wasn't a full-size fridge but larger than the mini one in my room.

"Would it be all right if I peeked into the rooms?" I felt a blush heating my cheeks. "This room is a lot fancier than mine."

Grinning, Ruth handed me an ice pack. "Feel free to start in my room. I have the better view. I'm going to pop into the restroom to freshen up then order some room service. Would you like anything?"

"I ate lunch earlier."

"Not even a dessert?" Her blue eyes twinkled. "Calories don't count on a cruise. I always have a post lunch dessert."

"In that case, I'd love to have dessert with you."

Ruth clapped her hands. "Wonderful. Maybe William will get back in time from his meeting with Lucinda to join us. I'll order an extra slice of cheesecake just in case."

"Okay," I said, not quite sure if I was good with it. I pressed the ice bag onto my hand. Was being here when William arrived a good thing? Should I find a way to leave before then? My thousand questions and I entered Ruth's room and looked around.

There was nothing out in plain sight. Of course not. Ruth was a woman who routinely traveled with expensive items, she'd know to keep them tucked away in a safe. Now what? It wasn't like I could ask to see her tiara. Maybe she'd wear it on formal night. That was it. I've never been on a cruise ship before so it wouldn't be out of the ordinary for me to have questions regarding what to wear.

I reeled in my excitement so I didn't skip out of the room. "It's amazing. Maybe one day I can cruise in this kind of style."

"That might be possible to arrange." Ruth winked at me.

My face heated. I hoped she didn't think I was trying to wrangle an invitation to cruise with her.

"Is something wrong?"

"I'm an over thinker, what some would call a worrier, and for some reason formal night popped into my head. I have a tiara I was thinking about wearing and wonder if it would be too much."

"Most certainly not. Not everyone gets dressed up but most women do and they are jeweled up. I have a tiara that I wear on occasions."

"Are you planning on wearing yours?"

"I still haven't made up my mind, but I did bring it along."

I bet William was planning a switcheroo. I had a feeling knocking my tiara onto the lifeboat wasn't an accident.

There was a pounding on the door.

"Room service is here and a little anxious. They must have a lot of orders." Ruth started to push herself from the couch.

"I'll get it."

I opened the door. Ronnie stepped back, a shocked look on her face. Ronnie was dripping in scarves. The entire skirt of her dress seemed to be made from different lengths and hues of silk pastel scarves. The bodice was a form-fitting silver sequined tank top. A white cape floated behind her, a brooch in the shape of an anchor keeping it secured around her neck.

"What are you doing here?" She asked.

"Visiting Ruth. And you?"

She heaved out an impatient sigh. "Looking for my brother."

"He's not here, dear." Ruth joined us at the door. "Lucinda, the diamond shopping woman, said she had something important to chat with him about in private. I figure he should be back soon if you'd like to wait. I've ordered room service."

"I'll catch up with him later. There's a class I want to join but I need a partner. I'll just have Faith come with me." She smiled at me. It shook.

There wasn't a class. Ronnie needed a listening ear, and I wanted to know what happened at the meeting with the captain. "As long as I can do it one handed." I held up my injured hand which still had an ice bag draped on it.

"Faith, are you okay?" Ronnie took hold of my hand.

"That's a lovely bracelet." A tight smile played at Ruth's lips.

"Looks similar to mine."

Good. I had her attention. "It's the one I won at the seminar."

"The swelling is going down," Ruth said. "I can get you a new ice pack."

"I'm fine." I waved goodbye to Ruth, gently pushing Ronnie away from the door and getting us away from the suite.

"What happened?" Ronnie's gaze filled with concern.

"Someone stepped on it," I said.

"You should get it checked out."

"I'd rather stay out of the infirmary."

"I don't blame you. If the doctor thinks it's broken, they might have you taken off the ship at the next port for medical reasons. The ice pack will help take the swelling down, and I have some medication in my room that'll take the edge off the pain."

Right. Like I'd accept pills from someone I didn't know very well. "I came stocked with pain medication, ginger pills, band-aids, and cough syrup. I'm prepared for anything. I just really want to get the certificate for my bracelet. Once we get to our class."

"There's no class."

We stepped into the elevator.

"I didn't think so."

Ronnie pushed the button for the fifth floor.

"What happened in your meeting with the captain?" I asked as the elevator doors shut.

"Let's go get some ice cream and I'll tell you all about it."

"Sounds good."

Ronnie linked her arm through mine, dragging me out of the elevator. "It's been a long time since I've had a girlfriend to hang out with."

I felt a little bad knowing I had ulterior motives for befriending her—getting to the bottom of the jewelry theft ring so I could eliminate Odessa as a suspect.

We headed for the parlor. I placed the warm ice pack into my tote and spotted Claire's tiara. After I finished my ice cream, I'd take it to her.

"The captain and I squared everything away," Ronnie said. "He wasn't happy I took you down there, but he knows there's no way I was involved. I'm alibied up."

I cringed. The last person I knew with a solid alibi had a partner in lying. "Who do they think killed Quinn?"

"Quinn."

Not what I heard.

"He's lucky drinking that much while taking his medications hadn't killed him before now."

"And what about what you said earlier? Captain Henderson just agreed to forget about your prior arguments with Quinn?"

Ronnie waved off my words. "I'm prone to drama. I did threaten him and lock him in a trunk. There were plenty of people around, so unless half the stage crew ignored his cries for help, Quinn wasn't in any real danger. Let's dish about your day. I heard you've had a rough or interesting one, depending whose opinion I want to take."

The whirlwind conversation left me dizzy. "Let me guess, Garrison said rough, Odessa offered up interesting."

She smiled and gave my arm a quick, friendly squeeze. "You got it. Claire is acting like quite the handful on this cruise."

That was one way to describe her behavior. "She's very, very vocal about her dislike of her dad inviting me."

"From what I know, Garrison and Bob invited you. Claire and Ted didn't have much of a say."

Ouch. Did Ted really not want me to come, and it was Bob and Garrison who went against his wishes? Was that why Ted hadn't been trying very hard to make alone time for us? Or was Ronnie making a simple statement about her feelings on the matter? Why would she and Garrison be talking about Ted and me before the cruise? Ronnie didn't know either of us.

I was being too sensitive. It was possible I heard Ronnie's comment wrong. That was all. Understandable, considering the horrendous day I was having so far. Nothing that a nice big sundae with a lot of sugary goodness on top wouldn't turn around.

We arrived at the ice cream parlor. "You get us a seat and I'll buy. I get an employee discount, and since I have someone to share with and don't have to watch my weight right now, I was planning on getting the marshmallow mammoth. It's meant for a couple to share." Ronnie whipped out her room key from a small purse disguised as a scarf.

The woman sure loved her scarves. I read the menu board. The marshmallow mammoth was three scoops of chocolate and two scoops of vanilla ice cream, with fresh pineapple, strawberry, and blueberries, topped with hot fudge, cookie crumble pieces, sprinkles, and whipped cream...all surrounded by a mix of mini and gigantic marshmallows. I could feel my mood lifting already. "I'll be your other half."

The parlor was tucked in a corner before the gateway to the shopping area. There was a small section in the back with three small round tables. I chose the one in the corner, since we'd be there for a while eating our snack.

I dropped into a chair and propped my elbows on the table, resting my chin in my right hand. I splayed my left one out. The area between my index and middle finger was turning purple and the swelling had gotten worse. The ice pack didn't do the trick. I really didn't want to make a trip to the infirmary. A shiver worked its way down my back. Someone was checking me out, and not in a good way. I leaned slightly, scoping out the reading area on the other side.

There were clusters of passengers in the seating area near the windows. Some played cards, others chatted and enjoyed their cocktails. Ruth was playing Scrabble with Glenda. Someone rushed around the corner. All I made out was a flash of white trousers and the sole of a dress shoe.

Ronnie carried over the ice cream. "Here we go. Hope you have a sweet tooth."

It was a sight to behold. Mounds of ice cream were piled six inches above the bowl. Fruit toppled off the edges onto the tray while hot fudge dripped down the sides. We dug in.

"I heard you got the tiara back for Claire. Did it get damaged?" Ronnie asked.

Ugh. I hadn't even checked. I'd been so annoyed I had shoved it into my tote without checking it over. "No, but mine is. One of the crystals must've fallen out when it hit the deck."

"How about we go get it once we're done eating? I'll fix it for you. I have all my tools out because I was making the basic shape for Claire's replacement tiara. It won't take me long at all to pop another one in there. I'm sure I have something that will match. We can change your bracelet to match."

I placed my spoon down, needing a break before I went to town on my share of the two scoops of chocolate. "I like the bracelet, and I don't think changing it would be good. I won it at the seminar."

Ronnie's eyes widened. "Wow. They sure are being generous."

"They are. I'm going to give Elizabeth the tiara after we're done with the ice cream. I think it's better if I speak to her and give her the tiara rather than Ted. I don't want to come across as the girlfriend jealous of the daughter."

"Are you sure that's a good idea?" Ronnie asked. "How is talking to Elizabeth going to help with that impression?"

"Because Claire is usually with Ted."

"Maybe you should just let it go. I don't think explaining your side is going to make a difference. You have no idea what you're stepping into."

No, I had a pretty good idea on what I was stepping into—a minefield—but it needed to be done. Pain gripped my stomach. I wasn't sure if it was from all the ice cream I'd eaten or thinking about talking to Elizabeth. Either way, my snack binging was over. "I'm going to get it over with."

"If you want, we could go to your room first. I'll get your tiara and repair it. Garrison said the redo of the ceremony is tomorrow at sunrise." Ronnie sighed. "Isn't that so romantic?"

It was. And early. I'd add an afternoon nap into tomorrow's schedule. "I don't know what room Elizabeth is in, so I'll need to find Odessa and ask her." Since Claire flashed her keycard, I knew the Rogets' suite number.

"Good luck with that. If you end up with time on your hands and would like to fix your tiara, I'm in room 5106. One of my friends in the costume department stopped by my room and I asked her to mend your dress. It's good as new."

"Thanks. I'm two cabins over from you. 5110. When can I pick it up?"

"Stop by any time. I'm usually there or sunbathing on the eighth deck." Ronnie picked up our almost-empty dish and headed for the trash can.

I walked up the remaining two flights to the eighth deck and checked the directory on the wall, stifling a groan. Room 9001, the Presidential suite, was the last room on the opposite side of the ship from where I was standing. After a long walk, I found the stateroom, pausing for a few moments to rehearse my speech. I'd start with asking if Claire was all right, and then tell Odessa I had the tiara and wanted to return it.

I knocked on the door. And waited. And waited some more. What if she was napping? Or not even in the room? I'd knock once more, and if no one came, I'd give it to Claire before we took portraits tonight.

The door opened. Odessa stepped out of the room, easing the door into the frame to make sure it didn't close all the way. "What do you want?"

It was nice to know I'd made such a good impression on her. "I'd like to know Elizabeth's room number. I have Claire's tiara and would like to return it."

Odessa tilted her head to the side, confusion blooming in her blue eyes. "Elizabeth's room?"

"Her cabin number." Come on, like Odessa couldn't really figure out what I meant.

Odessa pushed the door open a bit and pointed to a door at the far end of the large suite. "I'd invite you in, but Elizabeth is napping in her room."

Ted was staying in the Presidential suite with his mother, daughter, and ex-wife. That was why Claire saw me as an interloper.

Why had Ted brought me along? Ronnie's words rushed through my brain. Or had he? Tears burned in my eyes.

"Don't think I don't know you've been secretly meeting with John." Odessa raised her index finger in the air and made a circle. "I have eyes everywhere on this ship."

Odessa was pleased about the situation. The hurt in my heart was immediately replaced with anger. "I'll make sure to pass that along."

Odessa grabbed my arm. "What does that mean?"

"You should know. You know everything that happens on this ship. Right?"

She drew back, eyes wide. "John's on this cruise because of the stolen jewelry. He's befriending you because he thinks I have something to do with it and Ted's helping me."

I should've kept quiet. I knew it was never wise to hand over control of my mouth to my fury.

"What better way for John to learn my secrets than to weasel the information out of Ted's girlfriend. Unfortunately for John, I don't have any dark secrets, and even if I did and shared them with my sons, they'd never betray me." Odessa leaned toward me, a smile flittering on her lips. "Not for anyone."

I yanked open the closet door in my cabin, regretting it immediately when my hand throbbed. She had eyes everywhere. Knew everything. And she'd thrown down the gauntlet—she was the number one woman in Ted's life. Anger churned in my gut.

Unfortunately for her, she'd just talked herself right into being a good suspect for the gem-swapping shenanigans happening on the ship. If she knew everything that was going on, that meant she was keeping quiet about the criminal activity because she was involved or was protecting the guilty party. At least it eliminated

Ronnie from the suspect list, because if she was involved, Odessa would've invited the authorities to the wedding and handed Ronnie over after the I dos were exchanged.

I flipped through the hangers. As much as I wanted to avoid certain members of the Roget clan tonight, it was formal night, and Odessa had arranged special backdrops for wedding photos for Bob and Garrison. I didn't want to ruin the evening for them, so I'd suck it up and deal with it. I'd unleash my outrage at Ted tomorrow. After the wedding. But where was my dress?

Ronnie's cabin. My anger was soaking up all my brainpower. I took a deep breath. Settle down. Good thing we were on the same floor. Odessa had enough reason to dislike me; no need to show up late and add another one. Ronnie was a fashionista, so I knew she'd be in her cabin getting ready.

I knocked on the door. "Ronnie, I need my dress."

Some harsh whispers floated from the room. There was a bang followed by a moan.

I pounded on the door. "Are you all right?"

"A moment, please," Ronnie moaned.

"Let me in right now, or I'm going to get Garrison." If William was in there, I hoped dropping Garrison's name got him away from Ronnie.

"Hold on." Ronnie's voice was stronger and annoyed. She yanked the door open. "Why are you so impatient?"

I drew back. Now I knew what death warmed over looked like. Ronnie's face was ashen with bright red splotches on her mascara-streaked cheeks. She had changed into a baggy pair of gray sweatpants and an equally baggy white t-shirt.

"Sorry. I don't want to be late for pictures and dinner."

She looked at me like I had lost my mind.

"My dress. You picked it up from Quinn's room."

"That's right." She allowed me in.

I scanned the area, allowing my gaze to drift to the balcony. The curtains were drawn back. Nobody was out there. On the coffee table was a collection of crystals in various colors, wire, and a diagram. Ronnie had started remaking her missing—likely stolen—tiara. "I thought I heard you arguing with someone."

"I was. Myself. I was debating about ditching tonight's pictures. I either caught a stomach bug or my medication is reacting to something I ate."

I edged back toward the door. Whatever plague attacked Ronnie hit hard and fast. She'd been happy and stunning a few hours ago, and now she looked like an extra on *The Walking Dead*. If what she had was contagious, I didn't want to get it and end up quarantined to my room for the remainder of the cruise. Though it'd certainly make Claire and Odessa happy.

"I don't know if I can pull myself together in time. I'm still feeling groggy, though my stomach is feeling better." She offered a weak smile. "My tiara isn't coming along. I've drawn out a couple but none look right. Worse than not having it is making it wrong and standing out. Odessa doesn't like anything or anyone directing the spotlight in a direction she didn't choose."

"Claire's tiara is in my room and mine is still missing a stone, so you wouldn't be the only one without one."

"If Odessa knows you have Claire's tiara, I'd bring it. You don't want to be accused of sabotaging her perfectly planned evening."

No, I didn't. "As long as Claire has hers, Odessa should be thrilled. Claire will be overjoyed if she's the only one with a tiara. She wasn't happy when she saw I had one."

"It'll be better if you wear yours." Ronnie walked over to the table and collected up some items, placing them into a plastic bag. She handed me the bag. "You're a crafter. You should be able to replace the gem pretty easily. I put some wire, pliers, cutters, and a few gem options in the bag. I'll let you borrow my hot glue gun."

"You were able to get one of those on the ship?"

Ronnie opened her closet and withdrew my dress. "Since I helped Quinn with making some the accessories for the performers, I was given permission to bring them on board. I had left some of my crafting supplies with a friend and picked them up the other day."

"Won't you need it?" I pointed at the remainder of the jewelry supplies on the table. "At least my tiara is fully formed, minus one crystal."

"I have another one. That's my fine-tip glue gun. It'll work for you. I'll see you at dinner." Color had returned to Ronnie's cheeks. The talk of crafting perked her up.

TWELVE

I returned to my stateroom and changed into my dress. The straps were a little loose, but at least firmly attached. I decided for once not to overthink a situation. I hot glued in the only crystal that fit into the space on the tiara and tossed the bag with the remaining gems and tools into the safe. I'd give them back to Ronnie tomorrow.

I twisted my hair into a knot and secured it at the nape of my neck, allowing a few tendrils to escape. I smiled. For once, my hair cooperated. I touched up my makeup, watching the diamond bracelet I won sparkle under the lights in the bathroom. So far, it didn't seem like anyone was taking any interest in my prize. Of course, I hadn't spent too much time out and about today. I'd flaunt it tonight and attend as many activities as possible tomorrow to show it off.

I grabbed a beaded clutch and Claire's tiara and headed for the lobby where we were meeting. Fortunately, my preoccupation with retrieving my dress and getting ready had occupied my mind. With that problem gone, my anger and hurt over Ted's omission of his other roommate revved back up. Did he really think I wouldn't find out? Not now. Remain pleasant. For Bob and Garrison. Deal with Ted later, I thought.

The ship showcased luxury and elegance in every nook and cranny. The crew members had redecorated the place in a hurry. The mammoth crystal chandelier in the atrium sparkled and all the coffee tables were draped in elegant white linens. The captain and crew members were in black tuxedos. Waiters walked around with crystal trays, carrying flutes filled with champagne or apple juice. There were formal portrait stations set up around the area, including one at the circular staircase with a sign stating it was for portraits with the captain.

"Champagne?" A waiter held out a tray.

"Thank you." The chilled liquid tickled my throat and calmness settled around me. I felt better. I stared into the bubbly liquid, uneasiness skittering through me. Knowing Ted's history with alcohol, I was unsettled about my reaction to the sip. I wanted to drink the beverage because I enjoyed the taste, not because it changed my emotions. I wanted to feel happy and calm because it was true, not mask the truth with alcohol. I walked over to a table filled with empty plastic flutes and put mine down.

I stood in the prearranged meeting place and looked around. Where were the Rogets? Was I being stood up again? At least this time I didn't care. It was better for Ted if I had more time for my temper to cool off. I had a feeling Ronnie's earlier comments were her trying to clue me in on the situation without being the one to tattle. Was I the only who didn't know about the room arrangements? Probably. No wonder Ted wanted to sleep the whole entire flight. I bet he faked it. I flexed my hand. The swelling made it feel tight. The extravagant diamond bracelet twinkled.

At the far end of the large foyer, I heard a heated conversation that grew louder every second. Odessa. Surprise, surprise, there was something Odessa wasn't happy about. I went over, wishing for a brief second I still had the drink. There was no amount of drinking—where I'd remain standing—that would turn this evening around anyway.

"You have to do something." Odessa glared at the photographer.

"I don't control the weather. There is fog. No moon." He gestured toward the glass doors leading out to the deck. "If you want to take your party outside for pictures, go right ahead."

"I had it all arranged," Odessa said.

"I guess God didn't get your request in time to change His plans for the weather," the photographer said.

Elizabeth's mouth gaped open. Bob coughed a laugh while Garrison leaned into Bob's shoulder to smother his own. Claire blinked up at her grandmother in wide-eyed wonder. Ted remained silent. I bet John would wish he'd been around to see this. Or was he around? I stood at the end of the huddled mass of Rogets and looked around. Either John was getting better at melding into the crowd or he wasn't here. Matter of fact, neither was Ronnie. I thought for sure she'd make an appearance.

"I have Claire's tiara." I held it out, hoping it stopped the explosion brewing in Odessa's blue eyes.

She snatched it from me. Her attitude swiveled one-eighty when she faced Claire. "Here you go, sweetie. Grandma has your tiara for you." She settled it on Claire's head.

"Thank you, Grandma." Claire adjusted the tiara, beaming at her grandmother.

Bob looked at his niece. "Thank you, Faith."

"Thanks," Claire said to the floor.

Ted remained quiet. I never knew the man to have so little to say.

"We have to get our portraits taken before dinner," Odessa said. "If you can't take them outside, then why didn't you set up in another area for us? I will not make my family stand in one of those lines for generic pictures everyone else will have."

"Because you didn't make arrangements for an alternative location. I can't push another photographer out of their spot to please you."

"Why not?" Odessa stepped closer to the photographer.

We must've been getting the side-eye from others on the cruise because a swarm of waiters headed over with drinks and appetizers.

"How about a cocktail while you wait for your pictures?" A bartender rushed over with a tray of a specialty drink, holding it out toward us.

"I want cranberry juice," Claire said.

Captain Henderson joined us and placed his hand on Odessa's wrist. "What is troubling you this evening, my dear lady?"

His smooth, lilting voice had a calming effect on Odessa. "Nothing is going right for me," she simpered. "My ex-husband ruined the wedding yesterday, and now I'm told we can't have our pictures taken out on the deck with the moon as our backdrop."

"That's because there is no moon," the photographer defended himself.

"I'll make sure a photographer is available to take your portraits outside later on tonight. The weather will be clearing in a few hours." The captain took Odessa's hand and looped it into the crook of his arm. "Let us go on the stairwell. It be will perfect for your lovely family. You shall have the wedding portraits of your dream, Odessa."

We followed after the sweet-talking captain and the now-appeased Odessa. Garrison appeared perturbed by the whole thing, while Bob and Ted were relieved. I just wanted it over and done.

A waiter returned with a tray of beverages. "I have some sparkling cider and a cranberry juice."

"No drinks in the pictures," Odessa said.

"We have to wait for Ronnie." Garrison accepted a glass.

For the first time since I joined the group, Ted acknowledged me by handing me a flute. "Talk later? Please?"

"Maybe." I wanted to talk to him, but I also wanted him worried for a bit. Let him think I planned on the silent treatment. Of course, he might find that a better alternative to the airing of my grievances.

"Dinner will be soon," Odessa said. "We can't wait any longer."

"We can do it later, Mom." Bob patted her shoulder. "I'm sure the captain will be agreeable to appearing in the portrait any time you ask."

"Someone might get dirty."

Ted let out a deep sigh. "Mother, we are mainly adults. We can get through a dinner without destroying our attire."

"Things happen." Odessa crossed her arms and glared at Ted.

I fiddled with the waist of my dress, twisting it so the skirt settled better over my hips. No way was I going to venture into this argument.

"Then we'll tie our napkins around our necks or wear bibs. I'm sure the ship has some available."

"I know the gift shop does," Garrison said. "I'll go buy some right now."

"There's no need for that. We'll take our portraits now. Ronnie knew the time. She's sabotaging this." Odessa squared her shoulders back. "I will not tolerate that."

"She wouldn't do that." A small flicker of concern crossed Garrison's face.

"Ronnie wasn't feeling well earlier." I didn't want Garrison to think his best friend bailed on him.

"She wasn't?" he asked.

"No. A reaction to something she ate for lunch. I saw her right before I got here. She was starting to feel better and hoped to make it."

"She isn't coming," Odessa said. "Let's get the pictures done. If she does make it, we can take extra photographs after dinner."

"Fine," Garrison relented, fixing an unhappy look on Bob. Bob drew Garrison to his side and said something. Garrison's face relaxed.

Odessa sure was a force to be reckoned with. John was toast if she found out what he was up to.

"Places, everyone." Odessa stood on the left-hand side of the Captain. "Claire, Ted, and Elizabeth beside me. Bob, Garrison, and Faith on the other side of the captain."

Garrison cringed and elbowed Bob.

Bob sent a do-something look at Ted.

I quietly smoldered.

"I think it's better for Faith to stand with Ted." Elizabeth crossed in front of the group and nudged me to head over to Ted's side.

"I'll stay here," I said.

"I insist." Elizabeth prodded me out of my spot and claimed it.

"Will everyone please stop wasting time," Odessa said.

I excused myself around the photographer.

"Let me take your purse," he said. "We have a spot for it. The photograph will look nicer without you holding it."

I held it out to him; the bracelet caught the light and twinkled.

"I don't want that gaudy bracelet showing up in the pictures," Odessa said.

She had us wearing overly bejeweled tiaras and was worried about a diamond bracelet being seen in the pictures? "This is a diamond bracelet in a traditional setting."

"Please, Faith, just take it off," Ted said.

I aimed a drop-into-a-fiery-pit glare at Ted.

"For me, Faith?" Garrison asked, adding a beseeching look for additional pleading effect.

"Fine. For Garrison and Bob." I took off the bracelet and placed it in my evening bag. I placed the clutch in front of the photographer. No way was I going to lose it. I stepped back into the group, taking my spot by Ted.

"It's not my fault Ronnie isn't here," Odessa said. "The group needs to be a little balanced. No need for so much drama about the arrangement. If Faith had been on this side also—"

"I want to stand by my mom," Claire said.

"Then come over here with us." Bob grinned at his niece and waved her over. "We're the fun side."

"Fine." As Claire started over, she tripped and her arm jerked out. Cranberry juice drenched the bodice of my dress.

I froze, staring at the red liquid staining the beautiful garment, trying my best not to yell at her or start crying.

"Claire!" Ted tugged off his suit jacket and tried blotting my dress. I swatted him away.

"I'm sorry. It was an accident." Claire worked up some tears. She stood near the photographer, swishing her body back and forth, hands clasped behind her back.

I wasn't falling for the Miss Innocent routine. She did it on purpose. I think everyone knew it, but no one wanted to confront the girl. Ted and his family were creating a monster.

The captain raised his hand in the air. A waitress rushed over with club soda and napkins. The photographer, captain, and two waitresses flocked around me.

"We can get some of this out." The waitress with the club soda blotted away.

The photographer opened a box of props and threw out scarves. "I know I have one that will blend in with your dress. We can cover the stain."

"Grandma, I'm getting hungry. Can't we just take a couple of pictures today without Faith?" Claire asked.

I knew just the way to put a damper on Claire's plans. "Since Ronnie still isn't feeling well, I'll borrow her dress for tonight's pictures. I'm sure Odessa can arrange to have my dress dry-cleaned by tomorrow morning. I'll be back in fifteen minutes."

The photographer handed me my purse and winked.

Take that, Claire. There's no way you can ruin two dresses and have it come off as accidental.

"Wait, Faith." Ted came after me.

"I don't want to talk."

Ted hustled me off into a corner, away from some of the prying gazes. He wrapped his arms around me. I pushed away. "Please, I need to talk to you. I heard about your visit to the Presidential suite."

"Your mother won't be happy if I delay the portrait session any longer."

Ted reeled me toward him. "My mom didn't know I hadn't told you I was sharing a cabin with her, Claire, and Elizabeth."

The hurt I worked so hard to ignore crept up on me. Closing my eyes, I drew in a shaky breath. My purse slipped down, the chain landing on both our arms. "I know now."

Ted tilted my head up, his finger lightly grazing my chin. "I didn't know until I got on the ship. I had thought my mom booked me in my own cabin. You have to believe me."

I saw fear and despair in Ted's green eyes. He was terrified of losing me. My heart thawed a little. And I did believe him. Ted had never lied to me. He always told me the truth, even when he knew it wasn't something I wanted to hear. "I wish you hadn't hidden it from me. I don't like games."

"I tried to tell you. Every time I was about to explain my room situation, Claire interrupted us. I've tried to find another accommodation. For some reason, Garrison and Bob don't want me rooming with them." With great exaggeration, he rolled his eyes.

"Gee, I wonder why." Ted wouldn't ask me. He knew my grandmothers' feelings about cohabiting before marriage, even on a vacation, and he respected them too much to breach their trust, even if they'd never find out.

"Just so you know, my mom has one of the rooms in the suite, Elizabeth and Claire the other. I'm sleeping on a pull-out couch for the next seven days."

"Six," I said. "Don't be such a big baby about it."

He smiled. "So you're not mad."

"Oh, I'm mad. Just not about that."

The smile vanished. "About what? I want things right between us. These first two days of vacation haven't matched the picture I had in my brain. Me, you, and Claire having lunch together, doing some of the family activities as a unit."

"It might've worked better if Claire and I met beforehand."

"I'm seeing that now. Elizabeth had told her a few weeks ago that she and Neal were dating, not just friends, and Claire wasn't happy. I felt it was best to wait."

"That's working for us."

Ted drew me into his arms, cradling me against his chest. I relented and wrapped my arms around him. It felt good. "I know I'm not making enough time for you. Claire is so sensitive lately, and I don't want her thinking I'm choosing you over her. And my mom is acting more controlling than usual. She's jumpy about something. That's not her. My mom is usually cool and can settle any drama with a single look, not create more. I think she might be drinking again. Knowing my father is somewhere on this ship is affecting her."

Or she didn't want Garrison to find out she was the one who told the captain about Ronnie shoving Quinn into a trunk. An ugly thought crept in. If John was right about Odessa's involvement in the jewelry theft ring, Odessa might have used that knowledge to get rid of Quinn, knowing the blame would fall onto Ronnie's shoulders.

Ted tipped my chin up. "What is it?"

"Nothing. Worried about the time." I shoved the horrible thought out of my head. John's assumption was taking root in my head. "Your mom and daughter are probably flipping out right now. You've been gone awhile." Placing my hands on his waist, I spun him toward the atrium. "Go."

His shoulders hunched forward as he obeyed my command.

I needed a brief break from Ted and his family to sort out all the thoughts in my head. I was driving myself crazy. I should tell John I was out. Done. Claire's behavior toward me was making this trip stressful enough; playing master spy with John quadrupled it.

I pressed the button for the elevator and in no time made it to our deck level. I walked down the hall. A figure hurried toward the end of the hallway and turned the corner.

The ship lurched. The waves were tossing me to and fro. I pressed my hand to the wall. Ronnie's cabin door wasn't closed all the way. I tapped on the door then opened it. It was empty and the lights were dimmed. A scream came from outside. Jazz music floated into the room. The sliding glass door was open, and a cool breeze blew into the room, fluttering the curtains that hadn't been drawn back. "Are you out there, Ronnie?"

More screams. Terrified, not gleeful. The music stopped.

"Oscar! Oscar! Oscar!" The announcement came over the loudspeaker.

Man overboard. I ran to the balcony and leaned over. The boat dipped again. I clamped down tight to the rail, my purse slipping from my hand as I righted myself, fearing I'd get pitched over. The cabin door banged shut. A white scarf fluttered down to the deck. Another scarf was tied to the railing. People were pointing out to the water while others looked up. Toward me. Ronnie's balcony.

"She jumped. A woman jumped!" The cries reached my ears. "From there."

Ronnie! I spun and ran into the room. "Ronnie, where are you?" No answer.

I yanked open the bathroom. I doubled over, a deep pain twisted my insides.

On the mirror, written in bright pink lipstick were the words: "I caused too much pain. I'm sorry."

THIRTEEN

The ship continued its slow circle in the vicinity where Ronnie had fallen. Crew members stood around the railing, shining lights down onto the water. Other passengers, like me, strained their eyes, hoping for a glimpse of Ronnie in the dark waters below. Please let her surface. Please let us see her, I thought. With every passing second, the chances of Ronnie being alive diminished. She'd already been in the water for about four hours. It was past midnight. Ronnie and I should be complaining about Odessa's controlling ways together, not me standing in the dark, praying for her life.

How did it happen? I remembered the boat lurching. Had Ronnie been looking down at the party and tipped over? Or had the boat made the movement because Ronnie had fallen from the balcony and the boat was slowing down and turning? I grasped what everyone was saying—she jumped—but my mind refused to believe it. Garrison was getting married. Her best friend. She wouldn't ruin that for him. My mind swirled with images. She had looked horrible earlier. Not herself at all. She practically chased me out of her room. No. No. No. I pressed my hands to my ears, not wanting to hear the voice in my head or those outside of it.

In the inky blackness, I made out the lights of another cruise ship joining the search for our missing cruiser. It was easier on my heart to think of the person overboard as a cruiser rather than Ronnie. I'd deal with the whole truth later. Right now, I wanted to do what little I could, and that was staring out at the dark water, hoping to see a person waving for help.

It was a slim hope, but I clung to it tightly. With every white cap that rose, I held my breath, willing to see our missing person being brought up out of the ocean to us. Each cap disappearing back into the water made the reality of the situation so much more real. She wasn't going to come back. Ronnie was gone. Lost in the ocean.

Garrison had followed me to Ronnie's room. The moment he saw the note, he screamed her name and ran for the balcony. I shivered, recalling the mix of horror and heartbreak that crossed his face. Not long after, a security guard showed up. She gently escorted us out of the room. The captain wanted it sealed until they investigated what had happened.

What had happened in that hour's time that made Ronnie do such a horrific thing? I shivered. Ted draped a trench coat around my shoulders, then pulled me into his side. "You should go inside, sweetheart. You've been standing out here for three hours. There's nothing—"

"Don't say it." Rationally, I knew there was nothing I could do for her, but I hated the word *nothing* with every fiber of my being. It was hopeless. Dark. It took away all control.

"All that can be done is being done," Ted said instead. "The Coast Guard should be here in a few hours to help."

"How's Garrison?"

"He's at the stern of the ship with Bob. He doesn't want to leave in case Ronnie is found and needs more medical attention than the ship's doctor can provide."

"We aren't going to find her, are we?" I shivered again, knowing it was more from the situation than any cold in the air. Going inside wouldn't take it away. I'd still feel it in my bones.

"I want to say yes so much. I hate seeing you hurting."

"Why are people saying she jumped? It makes no sense."

"I think Ronnie said she was sorry because of Quinn," Ted said.

I stared at him. "She murdered him? No. I don't believe that."

"Sweetheart, you didn't know her that well. What else could she have meant?"

Stealing diamonds and selling them. "Garrison does. He wouldn't be best friends with a killer."

"You married one," Ted said softly. "Unfortunately, the people we love turn into someone we don't know sometimes. It's hard to know what will push someone to commit a horrific crime."

I understood what he said. Agreed with him even. But I still believed Ronnie was innocent.

"I've heard snatches of conversation and some cruisers said they saw a woman on the balcony. She stood on a deck chair and placed one leg over the railing," Ted said.

The scarf fluttered into my mind. I grabbed his arm. Soreness crept across my hand. I had to remember that hand was still bruised from the stomping it took. "A show. Ronnie was going to do an aerial performance from the balcony. The boat made a sudden movement and she slipped before she secured her scarf. I saw one floating down from the balcony below hers right after it happened."

"That sounds dangerous and unlikely."

"It's something she'd do."

"How do you know that? I know you and Ronnie were becoming friends, but you didn't know her that well."

I fisted my hands around the lapels of the jacket. How dare he make me explain my friendship with Ronnie? "I knew her enough to know she loved to perform and had to take a sabbatical because she was caught doing her routine off the railing before. And she loves Garrison. She wouldn't take her own life the day before his wedding."

A crew member tapped Ted on the shoulder. "Excuse me, sir. I hate to interrupt, but the captain would like to speak with you. It's urgent."

"Will you be okay?" The expression on Ted's face told me he was torn between staying with me and accompanying the crew member to the captain's office.

"You should go. It's probably related to Ronnie going overboard."

"I'll walk you back to your room first."

"No. I'm going to see how Garrison is holding up." I wanted to commiserate with someone else who liked Ronnie and wouldn't believe she was a killer.

"I'll come by your room later and check on you."

"I don't need you to take care of me."

"You might not need it, but I do," Ted said.

I shrugged on Ted's coat all the way and went in search of Bob and Garrison. I weaved my way through people returning to their cabins and crew members who were shifting positions. The spotlights swept over the ocean, revealing only water. I found Garrison and Bob at the stern. Bob had an arm around Garrison's waist.

I stood behind them for a few moments. What should I say? How should I announce myself? I didn't want to intrude on their grief, but I needed to talk to someone and have them agree that Ronnie hadn't killed herself. It made no sense. "Garrison." I choked out his name.

He turned and held out his arms to me. "I can't believe she's gone."

I accepted his embrace. "I don't believe what everyone is saying. She didn't jump. Or kill Quinn."

"Who's saying that?" Garrison's grip tightened. The anger flowed from him into my body.

"Talk," I said.

"From who? Quinn's death being a possible murder isn't common knowledge," Bob said.

I sent him a look, begging for no more questions.

"It's Ted." Garrison spun. He jabbed a finger into Bob's shoulder. "Your brother is calling Ronnie a murderer. Do something."

"Love, I'm sure Ted's not proclaiming that from the rafters. It's what Ronnie's note hinted at. I'm sure that's all he meant." Bob moved forward to gather Garrison into his arms.

Garrison stepped back, shaking his head. "Ronnie wasn't capable of that. Make Ted stop saying it."

"He's not," Bob said.

"First your mom, now Ted. You're never going to stand up to your family."

Bob's jaw tightened. "I disowned my father. My mom and Ted are nothing like him. My mom is bossy and a little controlling, not cruel or demeaning. Ted has always supported us."

"But Ronnie..."

Bob drew in a deep breath and pressed his lips together. He had a comeback, but knew it was better unsaid.

"I'm sorry. I didn't come over here to start a fight." I retreated a few paces.

"Faith, wait." Bob motioned for me. "This isn't your fault. This week has gone downhill since we first boarded. We've all reached our limit. I'll talk with Ted. Tell him if he's thinking what Ronnie wrote was a confession of murder, he's wrong. Okay?"

Lights in the distance were nearing us. Another boat was arriving to join the search.

Garrison pulled in a shaky breath and leaned into the railing, his attention once again on the dark water.

"Something happened to Ronnie. She didn't jump," I said.

"Faith, please stop," Bob said. "You're making this harder for Garrison."

Tears filled my eyes. "Ronnie's stateroom door wasn't closed all the way. I figured room service left it open. When I went inside, I heard screaming and went to the balcony. A scarf fluttered down from the balcony below. I think it got caught there."

"You think Ronnie was doing a performance?" Bob asked.

Another image popped into my mind. Someone rushing down the hallway. "Or trying to escape. I saw a person in the hallway."

"It was nothing," Bob said. He was lying to me. He had the same distant look Ted got when he knew something but didn't want me to know. "But I'll mention it to the captain. He can have someone check her shipboard account. Ronnie might have ordered room service and the waiter noticed what she was up to and left to sound an alarm."

That was plausible.

"If you guys will be okay, I'll go talk with Ted and John. I want him to stay away from us. This week is bad enough," Bob said.

I took hold of Garrison's hand and squeezed. "We'll be fine together."

He squeezed back. "Absolutely. We'll go have a drink and find a deck chair out of the way to watch."

"Love—" Bob started.

Garrison held up a hand. "I know. Believe me, I know. Ronnie won't come back to us alive. I need to be here for her. If it'll make you feel better, I'll get some blankets from our cabin so Faith and I don't get cold while we wait."

"It could be a long wait."

"We'll be waiting no matter where we are," I said. "This way, we'll know when it happens and won't have to keep asking people for information."

"All right." Bob headed for the sliding door, casting a look back over his shoulder. He was too far away for me to read his expression, though I was sure I knew what was on his mind. Worry with a hint of suspicion. And rightly so. We were up to something.

"I have a key to Ronnie's room," Garrison said. "Let's go see if we can figure out who was in there with her."

"We have to make it quick. Bob will be checking up on us. He doesn't believe us."

"We'll be fine. Bob is up to something on his own," Garrison said. "He's sworn for the last five years the only time he'd willingly go see his father is at the man's funeral. Unless he's murdering John, there's something else he's up to."

FOURTEEN

Garrison leaned his head against Ronnie's door. "I need a moment."

I patted his back and stepped away, giving him a little privacy. Garrison's shoulders shook and I heard his muffled sobs. "I'm going to take a quick look out here in the hallway." I wanted to test Bob's theory and see if there was an alarm at the end of the hallway or around the corner. If the waiter had seen something—like Ronnie preparing to go over the side of the balcony rail—he'd find the closest alarm to pull.

Carefully, I shuffled down the hallway, alternating my gaze from the carpet to where I was going. There weren't any clues to lead me to the identity of the mystery person I glimpsed. All I spotted was discarded straw wrappers, wet footprints, and glitter...or something that was sparkling under the hallway safety lights.

I knelt. The objects were minuscule crystals. I tried picking one up with my fingernails, but couldn't grip it. I licked my finger and touched one of the crystals, lifting it from the carpet. It was pale pink, almost white. There were a few more on the carpet, like Hansel and Gretel's trail. I followed it around the corner where it vanished, and I saw an emergency phone on the wall. The small crystals were probably from a beaded dress and a few escaped the vacuum when a crew member cleaned the hallway.

There was an alarm at the end of the hall. Bob's theory had some weight to it. I was a little ashamed at the disappointment flooding through me. I rubbed my forehead, weariness settling into my being. This happy occasion was now a nightmare, leaving my emotions off-balance. I had no idea why someone killing Ronnie was a better alternative than her ending her life on her own terms.

I went back to Ronnie's room. The door was cracked open. I entered quietly, securing the door. I didn't want anyone spotting us. The main lights were off. The TV was on and muted. Flickering lights from the television washed over Garrison as he stood in front of the sliding glass door. Mists of rain were being blown into the carpet, and the sounds of the crew members continuing their search reached us. My shoes squished on the wet carpet. The slow movements of the boat felt more threatening than the shifting we experienced earlier. Ronnie still hadn't been found.

"I can't believe she'd do this."

"I don't either." I flipped on the main light. "Something in this room will tell us the truth."

Garrison and I searched, neither of us knowing what we were looking for. I wanted to check out the balcony for more wayward scarves, but there'd be a lot of unhappy people if we were spotted out there. I was sure the captain and the security detail preferred to get the first look at the room.

"We need to be careful about moving items," I said. "Just make a note of what we find. We don't want to find ourselves thrown in the brig."

"Or locked in our rooms by Bob or Ted." Garrison flattened himself on the floor and looked under the bed. "There's something here. There has to be."

I pivoted, taking in every inch of the room. Or more importantly, what wasn't there. Ronnie's jewelry items. I hurried to the closet and opened it. "Check the drawers near the bed. See if her jewelry-making supplies are in there."

Garrison opened one up.

The top two drawers in the closet bureau were empty, the bottom holding Ronnie's undergarments. Why were those drawers empty? My stomach tightened. Where were her scarves? "Ronnie had her jewelry makings out earlier. She gave me a few crystals to fix my tiara so Odessa didn't flip out over it being broken. The rest of her jewelry items aren't here."

"She might have stored them in the safe. Some of her crystals are pricey." Garrison opened the cabinet where the safe was located. He pulled out his wallet and took out a credit card. "Ronnie gave me her extra card in case she lost hers. She has a habit of forgetting where she places things and didn't want to be locked out of her safe."

"Are her scarves in there?" I flipped through all the hung-up clothes. It was a silly question, but there weren't any in the closet. Slowing down, I went through all the dresses, skirts, and blouses again. There wasn't one scarf. I didn't know much about Ronnie, but I knew she loved her scarves.

"No, she'd have kept them in the closet." Garrison looked into the safe.

"There aren't any here."

"Are you sure?" Garrison headed over. "There's nothing in the safe. I don't like this."

Ronnie didn't jump. I felt it deep in my soul. She was pushed. I bet the person I saw in the hallway was responsible or knew something about her fall. "Neither am I. Not only am I not seeing any of her favorite accessories, but her dress for the wedding is gone. Earlier she told me her tiara was missing. I bet she figured out who stole it and confronted them." My guess was her brother.

"Missing?" Garrison turned me. "I saw her with it earlier."

"Maybe she finished her new one." No. Garrison hadn't known she was sick so he hadn't seen her since earlier this morning. Ronnie had been working on the tiara when I stopped at her room for my dress.

"She would've told me. There's no way she'd have passed on the opportunity to prove she was a better designer, and that Odessa had made a mistake not letting her design them."

Was Ronnie wearing the dress and the tiara when she fell? Or had someone taken them? Why?

The door handle inched down. There was singing coming from

the hallway and the handle sprang back up. As soon as the voices faded, the handle moved again.

Trouble was walking in. "Light," I whispered, mimicking the motion with my hand.

Quietly, he hurried to the light and turned it off. He slipped onto the veranda, grabbing the dark blue comforter from the bed and wrapping himself in it, allowing him to blend into the night.

The door creaked open. I hid in the closet, maneuvering myself so I faced out. With my uninjured hand, I picked up one of Ronnie's pumps, holding it with the heel facing out. Thankfully, she liked her heels high and spiked. My heart thudded. Someone shuffled around the room. A thin light swept through the crack of the closet door. I shuffled deeper into Ronnie's clothes. The space wasn't big enough to hide all of me from view, and if whoever was searching the room moved the garments, I was caught. Drawing in small breaths, I calmed myself. I needed my wits about me. Besides, I had backup standing on the balcony.

What if the intruder also brought someone along? My hand trembled. The doors opened. I tightened my hold on my weapon of choice, or rather desperation. A hand reached in, moving the hangers and flashing the light inside. I inched back. My back found the end of the closet. The light headed in my direction. Not wanting to be blinded, I ducked down and charged, knocking the person flat on his back. The element of surprise worked for me. I grabbed the flashlight and threw it. The man rolled me off of him. I sprung to my feet as he clambered to his, readying the shoe for attack.

Garrison flew from the patio, wrapping the man in a bear hug and lifting him from his feet.

The guy twisted, throwing the pair off balance. They crashed to the ground. I flipped on the light.

"What the hell?" John Roget blinked at me, rising to his feet.

"What are you doing here?" I asked. "How did you get in here?"

"I have a key." John showed it to us. "I could ask you two the same question."

"She was my best friend." Garrison fisted his hands. "How did you get a key? Ronnie would've never given you one."

"I have one." John walked over to the sliding glass door, inspecting every inch of the frame. "Doesn't matter to me if you believe me or not."

I placed my hand over the phone receiver. "It should. One call and I'll have security here."

"Honey, that won't work on me." John pulled out a small camera and took pictures of the frame, then the carpet. "If you call security, they'll want to know why you and Garrison are in here. It'll get back to Ted and Bob, which I know neither of you want to happen."

"But then they'll know you're here in Ronnie's room." I crossed my arms and glared at him. I so disliked when my ace hand was trumped. "You don't want them to find out."

"I don't care." John walked back to the closet and examined it. "My sons aren't overly fond of me anyway. Finding out I'm searching Ronnie's room won't ruin our relationship."

True. While I didn't think being in Ronnie's room would ruin mine and Ted's relationships, it sure wouldn't help.

Garrison, on the other hand, wasn't backing down. "I have every right to be in here. Ronnie gave me a key to her room. She's my best friend. It wouldn't be strange for me to be in here."

"You got me there," John said. "But you don't want anyone knowing I'm in here."

"And why wouldn't I?" Garrison crossed his arms and sent a death stare at John.

"You'll end up in the brig and thrown off at the next port. Make this trip better for Bob."

"Because there's a jewel theft ring on this boat and his mother is involved in this mess. It's likely the reason Ronnie went overboard was to protect her brother who I'm positive was Odessa's partner."

I stared at him. Except to me, the guy had kept mute about the case for the last two days. Telling Garrison his future mother-in-law might be involved in a matter that caused his best friend's death was heartless.

"You're a liar." Garrison fisted his hands.

I had to get John out of there before Garrison knocked him out. The man had it coming, but there was no way I wanted Garrison in trouble. Sometime this week, he was supposed to marry Bob, not get bailed out of jail by his future husband, if you could even get bailed out of a brig. For all I knew, Garrison would be stuck in a cell until we returned to the United States.

"There's nothing, besides what you think John, that links Odessa to the jewelry thefts," I said. "You need to leave. Garrison and I can explain why we're here you can't."

"Let's get out of here," John said. "The captain will be coming in here to collect Ronnie's items to send to her family. You don't want to be here."

"I do." Garrison sat on the bed. "I'll let them know I'll pack up Ronnie's belongings. I'm the only family she really has. Nothing should be given to William."

"Trust me, you don't want to be here," John said.

"We don't trust you," I said. "That's the issue."

John eyed me sideways. For some reason, my comment wiggled itself under his skin. Good.

A buzz filled the room. John glanced down at his cell phone. "We have to go. Now." He grabbed my arm, and pushed open the door. His hasty movements almost slammed me into the doorway.

"Knock it off." I tried shaking off his grasp. The man was strong.

"Get in front of me." He maneuvered me around to the front of him. "Head for the elevator. If anyone yells my name, keep walking until we get to the end of the hall. You duck around the corner, then I'll head back."

"Why?"

"Regardless of the fact that you don't trust me, you'll have to."

"What about Garrison?"

"He's on his own, darling. I'm only making myself responsible for you," he said. "I dragged you into this godforsaken mess."

We reached the end of the hall without anyone calling out to him. Keeping me in front, John pressed the button, making sure his movements didn't stop him from shielding me.

"How many of those dang things are there?" He lifted his chin to indicate the tiara I still wore.

"Four," I said. "Mine, Ronnie's, Odessa's, and Claire's."

His eyes nearly bugged out of his head. "Claire? My granddaughter was given one of those?"

"Your ex-wife had them made for the wedding," I said.

"I know that. I didn't think she'd be so stupid as to give one to our granddaughter." The elevator opened, and John placed a hand in the small of my back, pushing me inside. "I'll meet you at your room. Even if they're in Ronnie's room, I have to check one more thing."

"Who?" I tried escaping the elevator, but John blocked my exit.

"The captain, a security team, and my sons." The doors closed.

I guess meeting with the captain was what Bob had planned on doing. He had some doubts about Ronnie's accident and was checking on it. I had a feeling Bob downplayed it because he didn't want Garrison getting involved in case something criminal was going on.

My stomach tumbled to my feet. I didn't have my purse. I must've dropped it when I discovered the message. It wasn't in Ronnie's room. Who had it—and the bracelet?

FIFTEEN

I walked onto the fifth floor and went to the guest relations desk. A few passengers sat on the chairs around the atrium, gazes fixed on the windows. Even from inside, I saw the spotlights from other ships sweeping across the ocean. How long would they look? The fog made a nearly impossible search even more of a pipe dream.

I swiped at the tears pooling in my eyes. I wanted my room. I needed to decompress. Think through everything that happened today. Claire hating me. Ted. John. Ronnie's death. Garrison. A good cry was what I needed most. I hated crying in public. It left me feeling weak and out of control. Everything was so out of my control right now, I didn't want to add my emotions on top of that. I needed to have something bend to my will.

"Can I help you?" the guest relations manager asked.

"I lost my stateroom key. I'd like to get another one." I told her my room number.

"I just need to verify your identity," she said.

"That might be a problem. My driver's license is in the safe in my stateroom. I can't get it because my purse is gone, along with my room card."

She smiled at me. "We have your photo stored, so all I need to do is take a look at it, and if you are you, I'll have another one printed out for you in a jiffy."

This was pretty painless.

"Describe your purse for me? I'll check lost and found for it."

I described my purse even though I doubted it was there. Everything in me said to keep the last place I saw it—Ronnie's room—a secret.

Something tapped my shoulder. "Looking for this?"

I pivoted, and my left hand swung out and swatted the counter. I hissed out the pain.

Garrison was holding my clutch.

"My friend found it," I called out to the woman who was searching the back. "I don't need a duplicate room key."

Or at least I hoped I didn't. I should've checked before I made the bold announcement. I opened the purse. My room key was inside along with my cell. Coldness tingled across the top of my head. "My bracelet is gone. Where did you find my purse?"

Garrison took hold of my arm. "What happened to your hand? Did John hurt you?"

It was a lovely shade of purple and puffy. "It was stepped on. Not by John."

"Let's get you into better light." He led me to a set of chairs near the windows. The backdrop was the cruise ships' continual search for Ronnie. Around us gossip flowed. *Jumped. Pushed.* One woman wildly described to her friends Ronnie's descent to the water.

"My hand isn't important," I said. Garrison shouldn't have to hear anymore.

Somehow, he blocked out the voices. "Of course it is. It could be broken." He gently examined my hand.

"I can still move my fingers." I squirmed as his fingertips drifted over the injury. "I'll be fine. There are more pressing issues going on."

"At least this is one I can do something about."

I grew still and allowed Garrison to finish the examination.

"It's not broken."

I held in my "I told you so."

"I have some over-the-counter muscle relaxers in my room. It should help with the swelling and pain. I'll drop some off to you."

I had to refocus Garrison's attention. "Where did you find my purse? I have to find my bracelet."

"I advise against that. I found it on the balcony in Ronnie's room. You must've dropped it when you went outside." Garrison scooted a chair over close enough to drape an arm around my shoulders. He tugged me toward him. I dropped my head onto his shoulder and he rested his head on mine. "Someone pushed Ronnie into making that decision. I'm going to find out who."

"We will." William had kicked my tiara on purpose, sending it over the railing onto the lifeboat. Ronnie went to get it. Had it not been an accident, but planned? Quinn designed the tiaras. Were Ronnie and William using them as a way to get the diamonds off the boat?   Did the stones accidentally—or on purpose—get swapped? Had Quinn given me the wrong tiara?

"What are you thinking, Faith?"

"Craziness," I said, not wanting to share my rambling thoughts with him. I couldn't let him know I suspected Ronnie was involved in a jewel theft. To mask my thoughts, I took off my tiara and studied it, giving my brain another focus. Some of the other crystals weren't secured all the way. Quinn had brought the dress and the tiara to me. Had Quinn decided to keep the real stones for himself? Was that why he'd been killed? Because he had tried double-crossing his partner?

A bright light shined into the atrium. I squinted and turned my head. The Coast Guard had arrived and a helicopter was in the air, bright lights shining down onto the water.

Garrison walked over to the windows, gaze fixed on the copters. "Why didn't she come to me instead of jumping?"

"She didn't." I followed after him. "Ronnie was trying to get away from someone. Why else would she have used a scarf?"

"No. That's not why."

Two cruise ships, our ship, and a Coast Guard cutter continued to circle the area where Ronnie had fallen. As the sun rose, the spotlights were put away and the crew members trained binoculars on the water. Cruisers were returning to their rooms or going about their regular day. A few grumbled about the delay the search was causing and worried we wouldn't make it to port on time.

"Ronnie jumped overboard to save William." Garrison's

shoulders slumped with each word. He aged right before my eyes. "She took her tiara, the evidence, with her."

I leaned into Garrison, not wanting anyone to hear us. "You think Ronnie was involved?"

"I want to believe she wasn't. But she'd do anything to save her brother, including killing herself."

"Why not just throw the evidence overboard?"

Garrison heaved out a sigh. "Ronnie wasn't in a stable frame of mind. You mentioned she appeared ill earlier. I went to check on her and see if it was a physical illness, or her mental illness affecting her."

"Why wouldn't William help his sister?"

"William was the type of man to use Ronnie's illness to his benefit. She'd get confused and forget things, and William would make her believe she did horrible things when it was actually him."

I shuddered as fear raced through me. I'd been up against some bad people before, but never someone truly evil. If William allowed his sister to kill herself for him, there was no other word for it. He was evil to the core. What were John and I up against?

"William's working with someone on the ship and wanted Ronnie to know he was here," I said. "It wasn't a coincidence they were assigned to the same boat."

"I know one person who'd have enough clout to make it happen." Garrison stared into my eyes. He pressed his lips together and continued to keep his gaze riveted to mine.

No. No. No. I shoved, pushed, and kicked at the thought forming in my head. I couldn't go there. Heck, we shouldn't go there. Yet, not only was the name in my head, but it was embossed in large letters. Odessa, the woman who had all aspects of the wedding under her control, who clashed with Ronnie, and who the captain apparently doted on. As Odessa told me, nothing happened on the ship that she didn't know about.

"This isn't going to go over very well," I said.

"It won't. But if we take into account all the facts we have, Odessa's the answer. She bought all the supplies for the tiaras, insisted you take off the bracelet, and John Roget has been keeping a polite distance from all of us, even though he's always done his best to make my and Bob's lives miserable. Why did he decide not to crash the wedding? I'll tell you why, because he didn't want Odessa knowing he was on the boat."

I was the one who let that surprise out of the box. There was one issue with the theory: Claire. "She gave a tiara to Claire. I can't believe she'd drag her granddaughter into this."

"I agree with you on that." Garrison rubbed his temples. "I don't know what to think. It's not a coincidence William was assigned to that station. He wanted Ronnie to know he was here."

Now I was rubbing at my forehead. I didn't know if the brewing headache was from the twisting and turning of my thoughts, a lack of sleep, adrenaline wearing off, or a combination of all three. Or a fourth reason: we had to keep the truth from Ted and Bob. The only one who'd want to arrange a meeting between William, a ne'er-do-well, Ronnie, the protective sister, and John, the man on the hunt for a jewel smuggler, was Odessa. The best way to get away with a crime was hand over a suspect better than yourself.

"If we go down this route, it's going to break Ted and Bob's hearts whether we're right or wrong."

Garrison draped an arm around my shoulders and squeezed me into his side. "I have to do this, Faith. Ronnie died because she was trying to protect William. I have to know if he was guilty, and if not, who was. If you don't want to be a part of this, I understand."

The sun was rising and more cruisers ventured out to the deck to look down into the water.

"I'm in. If Odessa is innocent, we have to stop John from setting her up," I whispered. "I'll compare the tiaras. That'll let us know how involved Odessa is. There's no way she'd allow a matching tiara be made for her granddaughter for one she's involved in the jewel swapping." One problem with my brilliant plan was I gave Claire's back to her. There was no way the girl would let me borrow it, and asking Ted for it was out of the question. Or was it? I rubbed my temples. It felt like a vise was trying to squeeze my brain out of my ears.

"What's wrong?" Garrison's brows drew down.

"Claire has the tiara. How will I get it back?"

"We'll work it out later," Garrison said. "You go get some rest. I'm going to talk to the captain about conducting a memorial for Ronnie. I'm sure he'll let me. We can listen to what her coworkers are saying."

"Ted and Bob are going to know we're up to something."

"Any weirdness Bob sees from me he'll attribute to Ronnie's death. I can't give you any advice on handling Ted."

Unfortunately, I couldn't come up with an idea either.

SIXTEEN

I flipped through the channels, settling on the ship's information channel. My eyes were blurry from a lack of sleep, yet the anxiety churning through me made it impossible for my brain to settle down, not to mention the throbbing in my hand. The bruise on my hand was darker and the swelling increased. Whenever I closed my eyes, the image of the scarf blowing in the wind, Ronnie's last words written on the mirror, and her disheveled appearance rotated through my mind. At least I had the foresight to put the room service door holder on last night, and fresh brewed coffee and a basket of pastries would be delivered soon. I wasn't quite ready to join the rest of the cruisers. I felt the ship moving and wasn't ready to accept the fact we were continuing on the journey—without Ronnie.

I picked up my travel journal and wrote down the painful memories. I hoped putting them on paper would make it all fall into place. It wasn't working.

The cruise director and captain popped onto the screen. I sat up and turned up the volume.

"Good morning, cruisers." The director waved to everyone as the captain gave a small nod. "Going on right now is our Walk Around the Deck, perfect for working off any additional calories and enjoying the lovely ocean breeze. Please note we are going at a pretty good clip to make up for some lost time due to an emergency, so you might find your balance is a little off this morning."

Once again, the captain nodded.

"Plenty of activities are scheduled for today and we plan on docking on time tomorrow. Don't worry about missing any of your planned excursions." The director smiled, nothing in his demeanor suggesting something horrible happened to a passenger last night. Maybe that was for the best, to not cause a panic. Though I was sure it would be around the ship by noon. It would be hard to keep someone going overboard a secret.

There was a knock on the door. "Room service."

I pushed myself up, causing my wrist to throb. Fortunately, I was dressed appropriately and didn't need to make a hasty dash for something to wear.

"Stay tuned for some videos that our guests have taken and shared with us."

Videos. Videotaping events and posting them on YouTube was a hobby for many people. Maybe there was one that showed exactly what happened last night. I hated using some of my vacation fund to buy an internet package, but sometimes your priorities changed.

I yanked the door open.

The waiter drew back, a hint of surprise in her eyes.

"Thanks, just put it on the desk." If my hand had felt better, I'd have taken the tray from her. I really wanted to check out my theory before I lost my train of thought.

She placed the tray down, giving me a curious glance as she scurried out of the room. She left so fast, there wasn't enough time for me to hand her a tip. I must have looked a little crazed.

I poured some coffee and nibbled on a croissant before picking up my cell from the bedside table. I logged on and bought the cheapest plan available and checked a popular cruise message board. In the background, the cruise director, using an overly cheerful voice, read through the daily activity schedule. There was another diamond shopping seminar; a giveaway of a pair of diamond earrings was the incentive to show up. I'd show up and see who William directed to the winning chair this time.

I clicked on the link for the board dedicated to the *Serenade*. The first post was about the man—woman—overboard situation. With my hand shaking, I scrolled through the comments and checked the time stamps. People sure were quick to report rumors about the situation. Within two minutes of the incident, it appeared on the board.

I blew on the coffee, then took a sip. Blech. I hated bitter coffee. I dumped in two packs of sugar and added a large splash of cream, hoping it cut down on the strong flavor. I continued reading. Most of the comments on the thread were gossipy-type posts. People at home asking what happened. There were speculations ranging from a drunken brawl to a rogue wave sweeping a passenger off the ship.

I'm on the ship. It was a performer. Tragic circumstances, someone with the screen handle of LoveTheWater posted. *Suicide.*

Condolences for the family followed the announcement along with horror stories of how cruise ship staff members are overworked and underpaid. How did the poster know Ronnie was a performer? Was it because she saw Ronnie's performance when my tiara was knocked onto the lifeboat or did this mysterious cruiser know her personally?

The next message had my breath stuck in my throat.

I have a video. The blue link tempted me to click. Would it be a blessing or a curse? Either way, I had to find know. I clicked on it.

The mist and darkness made it hard to make out anything. Jazz played in the background.

"Up there."

"A woman."

Screams overpowered the music.

The lens jerked up. A person in a white dress tumbled through the air, melding into the mist. The camera was redirected at the water. The music stopped. A vague shape hit the water.

"Oscar! Oscar! Oscar!" blared from the loudspeaker.

"Right there," a young woman's voice said, the cell trained on a balcony two decks above. "That's where the woman fell from, almost hit the lifeboat," the camera shifted, "and splashed in the water."

A chill ran through me. No scream from the woman falling. I copied the link to the video, hoping it wasn't deleted before I was able to show it to John. Who wouldn't scream if they were plummeting toward the ocean? The only answer my foggy brain came up with was if they were already dead. After downing the remainder of the cooled coffee in one gulp, I gathered up needed items (cell for music, headphones, travel planner, and a book) for my new mission: waiting.

I changed into a swimsuit and cover-up. I wasn't sure how to find John, but he always knew how to find me. I'd camp out on the eighth deck and wait for him.

I stumbled my way over to a vacant chair. The increased speed of the ship made it hard for me to keep my balance. Using other empty chairs as railing, I completed my journey. I already had one minor injury and didn't want to add a broken leg to the list. My stomach roiled. Great. Seasick. I hoped the cool breeze would settle my stomach.

I sank into a chair, keeping my ears open to the conversations going on around me. There were a couple questions about the *Serenade* arriving in port on time, otherwise nothing about Ronnie going overboard. Either word wasn't spreading or vacationers preferred to keep their thoughts happy and not focus on the reason for the delay.

The sun beat down on me. I shifted the position of the deck chair and took off my cover-up. I hoped John found me soon, because I couldn't camp out here for long since I had forgotten sunscreen. I'd hang out for a while, then try and get some sleep. On this deck, the motion was having a lulling effect on my body.

Would Ronnie ever be found?

I closed my eyes, tears spilling down my cheeks, and sent out silent prayers for her. I hoped she was found, giving closure for Garrison. It was bad enough to lose your loved one in such a horrible way, but to not place them to rest was beyond anything I wanted to comprehend.

Squeezing my eyes even tighter, I drew in small breaths,

hoping to stop the panic welling up in me. I tried conjuring up more pleasant images. Nothing came into my head. All my thoughts were about Ronnie and the pain that drove her—or her killer—to that decision.

The wedding. Think about the wedding. Unfortunately, even that brought me back to Ronnie.

"Would you like a drink of the day?"

I peeked up at a worried-looking waiter. He held a tray with frozen drinks.

"You all right, miss? Can I get you anything?" He glanced over his shoulder, weaving his head back and forth like he was trying to catch someone's attention.

My throat felt parched. "I'd love one."

"Over here!" A man stood and waved. "Who do I have to kill to get some service?"

I cringed and rooted around in my bag for my keycard, which doubled as currency on the ship.

The waiter handed me a drink.

"Thanks." I took a long draw of the lemon-and-raspberry-flavored drink. The coolness coated my throat. My gaze shifted to the railing behind me. There was Plexiglas from the bottom of the floor to the top of the railing to prevent young children from climbing through and falling overboard. There was a large enough space between the railing and the top of the panel for a large knot to fit. Was the spacing the same on the stateroom balconies?

I set the drink down, realizing I'd guzzled half of it, dug out my planner, and flipped to the last page that held all my other notes about Ronnie's death. Tears welled in my eyes. I quickly scribbled down my ponderings and questions then dropped the book back into my tote.

My tote tipped over, knocking over my drink. Even though it was waterproof, I still snagged up my bag and placed it on the chair. Darn it all. Waste of a good drink. I pulled the towel from underneath me and dabbed at the spilled liquid.

A waiter rushed over, bringing me another drink. "Now, don't you worry about that, miss. We're here to take care of all of that for you. You just relax and enjoy your vacation."

"I hate leaving a mess for others to clean." I held out my card.

"Put that away." The young waiter smiled at me, dimples deepening in his unlined cheeks and his deep brown, almost black, eyes sparkled. "One free spill replacement each morning."

"Thanks."

Another crew member arrived with a mop and bucket, and in a few moments the deck around me was swabbed back to pristine condition.

I resettled back onto the deck chair. The movement of the boat and the sun in my eyes got to me. I closed my eyes and pulled the image of the balcony into my mind, trying to picture the spacing between the railing and the safety glass. Maybe if I concentrated enough, I'd remember.

Something brushed against my left arm. I jerked up. William was draping a towel over me.

He took a step back. "I was hoping not to wake you."

"What are you doing?"

"I was afraid you'd get burned," he said. "You've been sleeping for thirty minutes and your skin was getting red. I didn't think it would be appropriate to put suntan lotion on you, so I covered you up."

I pressed against the back of the seat, tucking my feet under me. Every ounce of my being was in protective mode, wanting far away from William. Even though he was doing a nice deed, it creeped me out that he had watched me while I slept. Give the guy a break, I thought. His sister just died. "Thanks for looking out for me. I had trouble sleeping last night."

William sat beside me. "I haven't gotten much either."

Shame rushed through me. Of course he hadn't. Ronnie's death affected him more than anyone, besides Garrison. "I'm so sorry for your loss. Were they able to..." I trailed off.

"No sign of her. I don't think anyone will find her." William stared off into the horizon.

"I'm so sorry."

He took hold of my left hand. "What happened?"

"It got stepped on." I drew my hand away without acting like his touch burned my skin.

"You might want to get it check out. It's really swollen."

"A doctor took a look at it. It's not broken."

"Such a shame you can't wear your bracelet."

I shaded my eyes with my hand. "I'm not really comfortable with being the winner. I feel like you cheated."

Quickly, William transferred over to my deck chair, his body crowding into my personal space.

I shrank back.

"I did no such thing." His gaze bore into mine. "Do you understand that?"

"You told me—"

The anger in his eyes silenced me. "I nodded hello at you. Why wouldn't I? You were a friend of my sister. Lucinda taped the ticket to the chair. I had no idea where it was. The place you sat at was Ruth's usual spot."

"So you wanted her to win."

"I already told you I didn't know where the ticket was placed. It was a coincidence. If you'll excuse me." He headed for the atrium.

I glanced at my phone. Today's diamond seminar was starting in half an hour. I knew I'd see John there.

I slipped on my cover-up and went back into the ship. The room was buzzing with excitement. I tuned out the voices and decided to skip the elevator and use the stairs to go down to the theater. I didn't want to get stuck listening to people chatting about Ronnie's death. I hated the fact that what happened to her was giving some people a "cruise to remember."

There must have been a demonstration in the atrium as cruisers filled the area. I weaved my way through the crowd. There was a long line at the excursions desk. A quick peek at a board told me that some of the excursions for tomorrow's first port day were sold out, including the marine park outing Odessa wanted everyone to go on. I was looking forward to it.

Off in the corner, I saw Ruth hunched over a pile of papers. Her gray curls drooped over her eyes. She bit her lip and ran a shaking finger over the paper. She looked so distraught. Alone. My heart broke at the thought of either of my grandmothers being in need and everyone being so caught up in themselves they never even noticed.

"How are you doing?" I sat across from her.

"I just don't know what to do." She looked up from the tour brochure, tears glittering in her eyes.

I switched chairs, taking the one beside her, and placed my hand on hers. "Can I help you?"

"I promised William I'd go on the ATV island tour with him. He's always wanted to go and has never been able to on the other cruises he's gone on. When he described it to me, it sounded fun. It's for couples. Snacks provided. We'd be able to see all the best spots in St. Maarten. But now I'm not sure I should go."

"Why not? It sounds lovely."

"I kind of like the idea of being considered a couple with William." A girlish giggle floated from her. "I'd love to be the subject of some juicy gossip. I sure wish my children and grandchildren, or at least one of them, would've come with me. They would've been in an uproar. Little old slow me traipsing around an island with a hot guy."

"You're missing your family?" I understood that.

"Not really. I asked them to come, but they only like the bigger ships with more adventurous activities like rock-climbing walls, ice skating, and a surf pool. This ship is boring to them."

"I'm finding plenty to do." Of course, most of my chosen activities were related to finding a criminal.

"That's because you're the type of person who's willing to make the best of a situation," she said. "Unfortunately, I spoiled my children when they were younger, turning them into adults who only find enjoyment in what they love to do. Finding pleasure in knowing your family and friends are having a wonderful time isn't in them, which is how I got myself into this mess." Ruth looked even more miserable than when I first stopped to chat with her. "I don't want to hurt William's feelings, especially considering what happened to..."

"Maybe William will change his mind about going."

"No, it makes him want to go even more. One never knows when it's their last day." Ruth tapped the paper. "I saw a bit of an informational video and it looks more intense than I can handle. Sharp curves. I don't know if I can hang on for so many hours." She rubbed her hand over the knob of her cane.

"I bet there's another excursion, even one with ATVs, that will work better for your and William's needs."

"There isn't." She sniffed. "I just don't want him to cancel because of me. It was so important to him. He's been talking about it for the last two days. It's a must-do. He's already distraught about the news I told him last night. He disappeared on me for an hour, and that's not like him."

"What news? If you don't mind me asking."

"It's fine. I wouldn't have brought it up if I didn't want to speak about it." She let out a heavy sigh. "I finally told William that this will be my last cruise. My heart is getting worse. My doctor advised me that cruise travel wasn't safe for me anymore. At times, I'll be too far away from a hospital if I have an incident."

That explained William's interest in Ruth's friends, Paul and Glenda.

"I hate knowing William won't be able to go on this excursion he's always dreamed of."

I had a solution. I smiled at her. "William won't have to go alone. I'll go with him. When is it?"

Ruth beamed and clapped. "In two days. Let's keep it a surprise."

Absolutely.

SEVENTEEN

My conversation with Ruth sidetracked me. I hoped I wasn't too late to the seminar, or have a chance to find John. This class was just the place for him. There was another prize offered for today: two-carat diamond earrings. How did the cruise line afford such expensive prizes every week?

Either I was getting better at detecting or John was predictable. He was holed up behind a tree in a corner near the theater. I headed for him and stopped short, switching direction and finding my own hidey-hole near a soda machine. Who he was with was a big surprise—Odessa. An even bigger surprise was neither of them was trying to rip the other's heart out. This was an interesting turn of events. Maybe they decided to be cordial since the cruise was tense enough. Or they both believed in the saying "keep your friends close and your enemies closer."

Odessa scanned the area, forcing me farther behind the machine. I barely saw anything now and the hum of the dispenser made it impossible to hear. What were those two up to? Odessa waved her arms around, jabbing John in the chest a time or two. He glanced down, either checking his phone or trying to avoid getting poked in the eye.

I was tempted to go over and say hi. The only thing stopping me was the possibility of saying something I shouldn't. Lack of sleep was never a good way to operate, and I knew I was near exhaustion. I was sure I was close to being placed on Odessa's enemy list and sure didn't want to firmly entrench myself on the list as number two behind John.

"You haven't seen her?" The cruise director's voice carried up the stairs.

"She's not feeling well," William said. "I stopped by her room and her stomach is bothering her. In case it's a virus, she doesn't want to get near the passengers and pass it around to them."

"I should stop by and see her."

"If she isn't feeling better soon she said she'd call the doctor. The last thing this cruise needs is for you to catch whatever she has. Passengers are already upset because of...you know."

The man patted William's shoulder. "I do know. I'm sorry about your sister. She was a good girl. Different, but good. Tell Lucinda if she needs anything to call my room. She should make sure she limits the number of people visiting her."

"It's just me. I told her I'd bring her food from the buffet when she's hungry so she doesn't infect any other crew members by calling room service."

"I'll see if I can find a replacement for Lucinda. I'll meet you inside in the theater," the cruise director said.

Had William been spending time with Lucinda during the missing hour or had he been in Ronnie's room? I wanted to find a spot in the seminar without William noticing me. If he knew I was there, I was certain he'd change whatever plan he'd devised for gifting the new prize.

I slipped into the theater and sat in a dark corner in the back. There were less people at this seminar than at the first one. I couldn't help but wonder why. Did word get around there was a lack of real information at the previous one, or with the sun shining so brightly and a nice breeze in the air everyone would rather spend all available daylight hours near the pool?

Not long after I settled into the seat, William entered. I ducked my head, pretending there was something of interest in my tote. Peering through my lashes, I watched him lean over and talk to someone sitting in a seat in front of a panel board. Dozens of knobs and switches had the crew member's rapt attention. All I understood from the brief conversation was the person didn't have an answer for William because they shrugged their shoulders.

William huffed out a breath and headed for the front of the theater. He took a seat on the edge of the stage. The attendees quieted down and waited. And waited some more. William glanced at his watch, then the door. I checked the time on my cell. The seminar was set to start soon, and there was no replacement speaker.

People fidgeted in the chairs. Creaks filled the air along with deep sighs. The group was growing restless. Ten minutes ticked by and still nothing. William looked at his watch again and dabbed a handkerchief across his brow.

"Sorry for the delay." The cruise director walked down the center of the aisle, throwing apologetic smiles to the left and right as he passed each row. "Unfortunately, our shopping diva Lucinda Wells is under the weather today and won't be able to make it."

"Best news I've heard. I'm going to play bingo." A man excused himself from his row.

"I'll be at the bar." The woman with him also left. A few other cruisers followed along behind them.

"We are very sorry for this unexpected change," the director said. "Unfortunately, even crew members get sick, and all we can do is make do how we can. Instead of the shopping seminar, we'll be doing free appraisals in Dazzles. And tomorrow we'll have extra shopping guides at the ready to take you to the best places and help you with negotiating. I'll be one of them. I have quite the knack for bargaining."

William plastered a smile on his face, but the narrowing of his eyes said he wasn't pleased about the change of plans.

"Please stop by Dazzles and enter your name to win the lovely pair of two-carat diamond earrings we had planned on giving away." The director dangled the prize bag over his head. "Don't want anyone to think this is a ruse to keep this for ourselves."

"There you are." Ted sat, weaving his fingers through mine. "I've been searching the ship for you. Garrison asked me to give you this."

I placed the small bottle he gave me into my tote. I rested my head on his shoulder. "Trying to keep busy this morning."

Grumbles echoed throughout the theater. People excused themselves around us and headed for the door. Ruth leaned heavily on her cane as she made her way up the carpeted aisle.

Ted kissed my forehead, lips lingering against my skin. I closed my eyes and enjoyed the moment, leaving crime solving behind and fantasizing for a moment that we were in a location where the simple kiss had the possibility to lead to more.

"Why aren't you wearing your new bracelet? If you love it, wear it. Don't let my mom make you feel differently about it."

"She's not. I really don't care what your mom thinks."

Ted snorted. "I would advise you not to tell her that."

"I wasn't planning on it. The bracelet was stolen sometime yesterday."

Ted swiveled to look at me, his brows drawing down. What did he hear in my tone that concerned him? "When did that happen?"

William didn't seem so eager to leave the theater. The cruise director had already left, creating a conga line to lead everyone to the change of venue. I bet he was the first person invited to a party. The man had a gift of turning a negative into a fun time.

"Either when everyone was attempting to remove juice from my dress or if I dropped it."

"Where would you have dropped it? Did you report it?"

"Aren't you the man of a thousand questions?"

"You're too nonchalant about it, which means you're up to something."

"Or maybe it's not that important, considering what else happened last night."

"I can see that." Ted squeezed my hand and leaned his head against the back of the chair. "So when does this seminar start, or did I miss it?"

"The personal shopper is sick today, so free appraisals will be given at Dazzles. I'm enjoying this alone time we're having."

Ted smiled. "This is nice, but how about we go to the

appraising event? I'd like to get my woman her bracelet back and catch a thief."

I kissed him. Good. "It's nice to know I rate above catching a criminal."

"Just barely." Keeping hold of my hand, Ted stood. "Though I do have a bit of fondness for them. Without criminals, I'd never have met you."

Dazzles was a small store situated in the middle of the shopping zone. It was bigger than the other three stores on the ship, but the crowd in it shrunk it down in size. The other places were a duty-free shop crammed full of cigars and liquor, a perfume store next door to it, and a shop dedicated to items emblazoned with *Serenade*. From a brief peek inside, I spotted everything from dresses to teddy bears branded with the ship's name and logo. There was a cute salt and pepper shaker set Grandma Hope would fancy, and Grandma Cheryl had started obsessing about anchors, so the matching pillow set was the perfect gift for her.

"What's the battle plan?" I asked. A female employee held a ring up toward the light, twisting it back and forth. I was surprised at her technique. Wouldn't a professional appraiser have some type of tool to use, like those small binocular things people use on television? Her way of figuring out the clarity and quality of the stone seemed amateurish.

"This isn't a battle." Ted wrapped an arm around my waist and pulled me into his side. I think it was more to keep me in line than to stake a claim on me. "If anything, it's a reconnaissance mission. Observe and note."

"So if someone has my bracelet, I just take a mental picture of it. Sounds productive."

"No. You tell me. I'll handle it."

"The little woman can't take care of herself? You should know I'm quite capable of it."

"I'm aware of that." The left side of his lip quirked up. "I'm also very aware of your capability of stirring up a heap of trouble. It's not you I'm looking out for, but all the innocent people in the vicinity. No reason they should get dragged into any quests of righteousness you set off on."

"This was your idea, remember?"

"I certainly do. I'm a public servant, so I do what I can to save the world."

"It doesn't need to be saved from me." I stomped over to a display case and looked at all of the rings. Diamonds of different shapes, colors, and sizes blinked at me. Calling me to try them on. Give them a chance. My gaze flickered over to my unadorned hand. Even when I was married, I never had a ring. The louse had convinced me a ring was a waste of money. He had better things to spend money on. Of course, that was the least of our issues...the whole murdering a poor man and blaming me for it outranked all of his other faults.

"Someone needs protecting." Ted faced away from the case. Using his elbows, he propped himself on it. "Okay, not so much the guilty individual, but anyone unlucky enough to be in the vicinity."

"You act like I'm a holy terror."

Ted studied each and every person who walked in. The only way I knew was the subtle muscle movement in his neck. I had never watched him detect before. He kept a half-smile on his face, body posture relaxed, yet his gaze moved constantly, muscles rippling ever-so-slightly. My cheeks heated up. It was kind of sexy.

His lips twitched. The green in his eyes darkened.

Scrap it all. The man knew.

Ted straightened. "I'll be right back. Don't react to me leaving. Keep browsing."

Did Ted want someone to think we were looking at rings? It made a good cover. He walked away. Even though my eyes were on the rings, my attention was on the goings on behind me I couldn't see. Ugh. I wanted to know what he was doing. Selfie time. I took out my cell and held it up. I tapped the button to flip the camera and instead of my face in the screen, I saw Ted watching William give an appraisal of a bracelet. I zoomed in on the jewelry. Not mine. If it had been, I'd have expected a reaction from William. There was a reason he wanted me to have it.

"Anything you'd like to try on?" A clerk smiled at me. Her blond hair was smoothed back and twisted into a knot at the nape of her neck. "Miss?" Her volume increased.

I tucked my phone back into my purse. "Just browsing. I never knew diamonds came in so many colors."

"We have pink, chocolate, white, and even a canary one." She tapped the case with her manicured nail. "Lovely, isn't it?"

"Yes. I'm more drawn to the white and pink ones."

"Let's see how one looks on you." She opened the case and pulled out a simple solitaire with a one-carat diamond. It was a soft pale pink. The white-gold setting brought out the color. "It's for fun. You're not committed to buying it because I place it on your finger."

What was the harm? I held out my hand.

She started slipping it on my finger. "This one is on sale today. It's one of our featured pieces, only six thousand dollars."

Only? I yanked my hand back. "Way out of my price range."

"It won't hurt anything to try it on."

"You never know."

"What's going on over here?" Ted stood behind me, wrapping his arms around me. "What do you know? You happened to find a pink ring." He smiled at the saleswoman. "She loves pink."

She beamed at him. "And she'd look quite lovely with this little bauble."

"No, she wouldn't," I said.

"She looks lovely even without it," Ted said. "Try it on, sweetheart."

"I don't think so." I hid my hand under my shirt. "There's no way I'm putting on a six-thousand-dollar ring."

"Ring prices sure have gone up," Ted said.

"Pink diamonds are quite rare, sir," the clerk said. "Just like your lovely lady."

"I'm not that rare."

Ted laughed. "You better be. I don't think our town can handle another one of you."

"How about this?" The clerk took out a ring in a similar style except the diamond was white instead of pink. "This one is only two thousand."

"I don't think they understand the use of 'only,'" I muttered to Ted.

He gently drew out my hand and held it out to the clerk. "Let's see how it looks."

My hand trembled. What did this mean? I slammed the door in my mind shut. Keep all thoughts about it out. No overanalyzing. No second guessing. Just enjoy the silly moment.

She slipped it onto my finger.

Ted raised my hand. The ring was a little big. The diamond sparkled. I had to admit it looked lovely. Perfect. Especially with Ted cradling my hand.

"It's a good look for you, Miss Hunter." Ted's voice was rough and trembled.

A loud shriek made Ted jump in front of me. I grabbed onto him. The clerk's eyes widened.

"I'm sorry." Elizabeth covered Claire's mouth. The girl scratched at her mother's hand.

"You're going to hurt your mother." Ted frowned. For once, his face showed displeasure in his daughter's behavior.

Some people in the shop averted their eyes, while others took undue interest in the scene before them. Claire's green eyes brimmed with tears, some streaking down her pale face. The hatred she felt for me was clear.

Elizabeth's features were drawn, her complexion matching her daughter's. I guess Claire wasn't the only one unhappy about catching Ted and me window shopping. I wanted to tell them we were just being silly, reassure them. Instead, I kept my mouth shut.

"I'm fine." Elizabeth tucked Claire against her, rubbing her sobbing daughter's back. "We hoped you could join us for a game of shuffleboard. This," she waved a thin hand around in a circle, "was a little bit of a surprise."

"Faith and I are having an enjoyable afternoon." There was a strain in his voice. "No need for hysterics from anyone."

Elizabeth death-stared Ted. "Hysterics? Your daughter is hurting and confused. It would have been nice for you to have hinted at the seriousness of the relationship."

I yanked the ring off and shoved it at the clerk. "For crying out loud. We were just goofing off. No one is getting married. At least not us. Claire doesn't need to cry. You don't need to yell at Ted. Go be a happy family. I'm leaving."

"Faith..."

Ugh. It was that stupid warning tone. I shooed at him. "Go. I have plans."

"That's what I'm worried about," I heard Ted mutter as I walked away.

I shoved the poor card into the slot, almost breaking it, and pushed the door open. It smacked against the wall. Some vacation. Instead of exploring our new romantic relationship, Ted and I were pulling apart. I'd have never thought that meeting over my amateur sleuthing and the resulting bickering would be the highlight of our relationship.

I unlatched the lock of the sliding door and stepped onto the balcony. A cool breeze drifted over me. The scent of the salt air and the warmth of the sun kissing my skin calmed me. Just a bit. I leaned against the railing and stared off into the horizon. I gripped the railing and took a deep breath, my fingers curling around the bar. I moved my hand back and forth, careful not to loosen my hold or scratch my finger. The space wasn't that big. Could Ronnie have tied a strong enough knot? Would the type of scarves she wore fit? There was less space between the Plexiglas and railing on the veranda than the ones on the main deck.

I leaned farther over the railing, looking to the right. Ronnie's stateroom was two balconies away and over the rafts where we had our muster drill. Had she decided the mist-filled night was the perfect one to try and find a missing diamond? One that her brother's life might depend on?

A security camera placed between the rooms dangled from a cord. It was broken. I scooted closer to it.

"What the hell are you doing?" Arms wrapped around my waist and yanked me back into a standing position.

"How do you keep getting in here?" I smacked at him. It felt good to relieve some anger on a Roget. They were becoming the bane of my existence. Even more disturbing than John Roget being in my room—again—was the fact I didn't hear him enter.

John tugged me back into cabin. "Someone let me in."

"Great. Crew members are conspiring with guests for breaking and entering. Just what this cruise needs." Sure complicated Ronnie's death.

"Anything interesting happen at the seminar?"

I had a feeling John was deliberately trying to draw me out of my thoughts. Maybe he feared I was plotting his demise. I broke from his grasp and dropped onto the bed. From now on, the chain was going on the door. No more uninvited visitors. "Besides Lucinda calling in sick, no. Who let you in my room?"

"Can't share that with you," he said.

"Then maybe I can't share with you." Take that. I fixed my most smug smile on my face.

"Then how are we going to find out the truth about Ronnie? I sure hope you weren't out there to pitch yourself into the ocean."

"Of course not. I was investigating." I crossed my arms and hit John with my fiercest glare. "I don't plan on letting someone get away with killing Ronnie."

"I'm not sure if she was killed or just led to do it herself."

"I think she was dead before she ever hit the water." I filled him in on what I saw online. "She didn't scream, and the security camera facing her room is broken."

He went out onto the veranda and come back in. Worry

deepened the lines on John's face. "Hundreds of cameras and that's the one not working. I don't like it. Enjoy your vacation. Find some time to spend with Ted. I'll handle it from here on out."

"You realize you're not my boss."

"Garrison just lost someone dear to him. He needs his friends around him." John handed me a postcard.

The background was black and a simple gold line trimmed the outside edges. In a white script font was the announcement for Ronnie's memorial service. This must've been what Odessa gave him earlier.

"I'm surprised Odessa invited you." I tucked the card into my tote.

"You saw us talking together?"

"Yes. I'm sure your sons would like to see a pleasant exchange between their parents."

"As long as the meetings are brief, Odessa and I can be as pleasant as an afternoon rain shower." John tucked the magazine under his arm and stood. "Any more than that, and we become a thunderstorm that brings a tornado or two with it."

"What were you guys chatting about?"

"Not that you need to know, but she was wondering if I knew anything about some damage done to a few costumes."

"Why would she ask you?"

"It's her way of accusing me of causing trouble."

EIGHTEEN

The moon shone down on us. The clear night sky showcased the glittering stars. The water lapped at the ship. It was a beautiful, breathtaking night, the backdrop for our breaking hearts. I swiped away the tears trickling down my cheeks. Ronnie deserved justice. For the first time, I didn't know how to find it for her. The captain, and everyone else it seemed, believed her death was a suicide. There was nothing in her room to prove otherwise.

I wandered the deck crowded with crew members. A few guests lingered on the outskirts, and an officer went over to quietly explain to them about the memorial. The wait staff and room stewards all wore their regular uniforms, while the performers wore dark-colored formal wear with some outfits a little more blingy than others. I wore the only black dress I'd brought with me and added a cardigan, making it more demure.

Garrison stood at the helm, gazing into the horizon. Bob was by his side, an arm draped around his love's waist. Odessa hovered protectively nearby, gaze searching the crowd for anyone who'd dare make it harder for him. The set of her shoulders told me she was itching for someone to challenge her. Ted stood on the other side of his brother. He must've felt my gaze on him, because he turned slightly and our eyes met.

I pivoted, walking away. Drawing my cardigan tighter against my body, I slipped through a crowd of room hosts and ventured my way toward the performers. Fear wiggled through me. How could I get the information needed without offending or upsetting someone? Part of me said this wasn't the time or place for sleuthing, but the other side of my brain informed me there wouldn't be another time. This was a night for memories and talking about Ronnie. It was a natural time for a person who had just become friends with Ronnie to learn about the woman she met and now misses.

On the port side was a large buffet area set up with cheese, crackers, juices, and champagne. A woman dabbed at her cheeks with a lacy handkerchief. Near her was Francis, Quinn's neighbor across the hall. I went over to him.

"I'm sorry for your loss," I said.

He tipped his head back, sucking down a goblet of champagne. He tossed the plastic stemware to the side. "I don't know how Ronnie stood drinking that stuff. It was her favorite."

"Champagne." Light. Bubbly. Sparkling. Sounded just like Ronnie.

"Not just any kind...pink." He leaned forward and grabbed another one.

That also sounded like Ronnie.

He poured the liquid over the side of the railing. "And one for you, darling girl. God. I can't believe she's gone."

"I didn't know her very long, but I'm having a hard time wrapping my head around it also."

"She was just so much larger than life," he said. "At least Quinn and Ronnie are together."

"It didn't seem like they got along," I said cautiously.

"Quinn and Ronnie were either bosom buddies or at each other's throats. There was no in between for those two. They loved to fight, so they were the perfect pair." He picked up two glasses of champagne and handed one to me.

I accepted the flute, twirling the stem between my fingers. I had taken one of the pain meds, but I had a part to play tonight. One small sip wouldn't hurt. "Love or hate?"

"More like love and hate. They held both in their hearts toward each other, one of those emotions always stronger than the other. It all depended on Ronnie."

"Depended on her?"

He nodded, slugged back the drink. "That's the way you had to be with Ronnie. Love her when she was herself. Hate her when she wasn't."

"What do you mean by when she wasn't herself?"

"Ronnie had a medical condition that made her difficult to be around at times."

"Was there anyone on the ship who was close to her? Maybe a roommate?"

"Ronnie had her own room. Why are you interested in who Ronnie hung out with?"

"I thought maybe her roommate had Ronnie's jewelry items. They weren't in her room."

A waiter walked over to us. Francis picked up two flutes and handed one to me. I placed my half-empty drink onto the tray. I hadn't realized I drank more.

"Jewelry making was a hobby she shared with Quinn. The only time I knew of her working on pieces was in his room." He held up the flute out toward me. "To Ronnie."

We clinked our glasses to glasses. I sipped mine. Francis gulped his down.

"I hope the costumes were fixed."

He hesitated for a moment before plucking another glass from another waiter making the rounds around the deck. "There wasn't an issue with the costumes."

"Are you sure?"

He snorted. "Of course I'm sure. I'm the lead costume designer since Quinn died."

"I'm sorry. I shouldn't be sharing gossip with you, or anyone for that matter. I guess I'm just not sure what to talk about."

Francis smiled softly at me and patted my shoulder. "No worries, honey. I'm a little stressed about taking over for Quinn, trying to answer passengers' questions about Ronnie's death without turning her into a sideshow or ruining the cruisers' vacation, and now a coworker of mine is spreading rumors about the costumes." He ticked off his many reasons.

"Actually, it wasn't to everyone. It was a family matter."

He let out a huge sigh of relief. "Odessa. Right?"

I nodded.

"Then that's one worry I can let float away. I'm sure she started it, hoping the captain would let her stage her big grand event in the theater. We must have a show or the guests would be highly disappointed."

"She wanted to turn the wedding into a stage production?"

Francis grinned at me. "Don't let Odessa fool you. She didn't want a small private wedding for her son and his partner. She wanted a huge Broadway-show-style wedding. Why do you think she picked the Mardi Gras sailing? The only thing stopping her was her son's insistence the wedding wouldn't take place if she tried pulling a stunt like that."

"How do you know?" Once the question was out of my mouth, I regretted it. I didn't want to offend the guy now that he was liking me again and chatting away.

Francis laughed. "Odessa told everyone. She fretted and fumed for all to hear. Her son not agreeing to her plans. The captain not canceling a show for her, so the wedding couldn't take place on the stage. Wrong crystals being delivered. Then someone stealing her replacement ones. Quinn swapping them. Complaint after complaint. I think the captain wished he quit when he found out Odessa booked the Presidential and Honeymoon suites, and also two other rooms."

Where did Odessa get that kind of money?

A strand of hair escaped the twist I put it in and floated in front of my eyes. I twisted my head, hoping it moved on its own. No such luck. The wayward strand dipped itself into the champagne. I titled my head to the side, swiping the errant hair back into place. A movement above caught my attention. I looked up. On the stern, a lone figure stood bathed in moonlight, a pure white gown giving her a glowing appearance. Pale locks flowed out behind her as if her hair was a trail on the wind. The woman was barefoot. I couldn't see her features as the large light above washed out her face. Her build reminded me of Ronnie. I blinked. The image vanished.

"Are you all right?" Francis took the half-full glass of champagne from my hand and placed it on the table.

I was standing with my mouth open and felt myself sway. "I'm fine."

Concern blossomed on his face. "You don't look fine. Maybe you've had—"

"I didn't drink too much," I said, doubting my own words immediately. Barely ate anything all day. Champagne. Pain medication. Horrible combination.

"I was going to say a rough day. You and Ronnie were inseparable for the last few days. This has to be as much a shock to you as anyone else."

"And to you," I said.

A deep sadness overtook his concern for me. "Sadly, no. I knew one day Ronnie would end it. I just figured she'd have made a bigger production out of it."

"Did Ronnie say something to you?" Had she reached out to someone?

"No. Ronnie had always been a little eccentric, but over the last year, since her parents died, she started losing her grip on reality. Talking to herself. Hanging off the deck. Forgetting entire conversations she had with people and making other ones up. Some days she was sullen and angry. She was like someone else."

NINETEEN

The next morning, I shifted from foot to foot, anxious to get off the ship and spend ten hours on land. I was out of my room in record time as I had planned my outfit out last night. Now, if the people in front of me would follow the simple instructions—ID and keycard in hand—instead of digging for the items once they reached the metal detectors and security guard, we'd all be out in the sun instead of only seeing glimpses of it.

A couple exited the ship. I took a step forward.

"This isn't your card," the security guard said.

Great. Drama. Just what we needed. I held in my sigh. I was sure the guard didn't want my commentary.

"My apologies." William's voice drifted to me.

I bent to the side and stretched my neck out. This might be worth a delay.

"I must've forgotten to give Lucinda back her keycard."

"The captain won't be happy about that. You shouldn't have that or be in her room."

"I know. With her stomach ailment, I figured it was best I take care of her rather than have any other crew member get sick."

The woman behind William backed up a bit. The other guests in line followed suit. Straightening myself, I quickly copied them so no one tripped over me. I didn't want William catching me eavesdropping.

"What's going on up there?" a man shouted. "We're going to be late for our excursion."

"I'll keep it here and make sure she gets it back. If you don't have your card, you need to step out of line."

"Here it is."

The line moved forward. Before long, it was my turn. I held out the required items.

"Sunglasses up. I need to make sure this is you." He tapped my ID card.

I settled the glasses onto my head.

He scanned me out. "Have a lovely time in St. Thomas."

That I would. Hoisting my tote onto my shoulder, I walked down the gangplank and onto the dock and soaked in the scenery. The water lapped at the hulls of the ships in port. There were four other cruise liners docked at St. Thomas. The *Serenade* had been the last one. A lot of cruisers were worried that the best spots on the beach were already taken. Everyone seemed to have a preferred shop for renting beach chairs and umbrellas. The newcomers looked anxious, trying to decide if shopping before or after a quick romp on the beach was a better choice. My day was planned for me. Odessa had bought our party tickets for an excursion to Coral World Marine Park.

I shaded my face and looked around. No sign of the rest of my party. I glanced at the note I jotted down. At the end of the pier. This was it. Where were they? I felt my stomach do a roller-coaster dip action. Had I been stood up again? It was one thing to ditch me for a dinner on the ship, quite another on a dock. I pulled in a deep breath. Think happy thoughts. At least you'd have the day to explore alone, I thought. No worry about hissy fits.

Unless I threw one. The sun beat down on my head. If a member of the Roget clan didn't appear soon, I'd abandon them and search for my own fun. First stop, buying a large beach hat. Preferably pink. I took a few steps over to a large wooden map. I plucked a brochure which doubled as a map from an acrylic pocket. There was plenty of shopping places. My eye was drawn to a vendor's area showcasing arts and crafts made by the locals. My kind of place.

There was grumbling from Lucinda's tour group, who were waiting a few feet away from the giant map. "She better not have given us the Norovirus."

I heard the Rogets before I saw them. Once again, a battle was brewing among them. I tucked the brochure in my tote and forced out a smile. This was my first time in the Caribbean and I'd make this day happy.

Claire skipped next to her mother. Odessa walked a few feet in front of them, heading straight for me. Garrison and Bob followed after the ladies. Even from a distance, I spotted the tension in their shoulders. A scowling Ted was the straggler of the pack.

"We have a slight issue." Odessa glided up to me.

I kept the pleasant smile on my face. I had a feeling my plans were about to change. "And what would that be?"

"Well, we've come up short a ticket." Odessa blushed. "I had all of them the other day, but this morning one is gone. We searched the whole cabin. That's why we're late. I tried getting another one, but the tour is booked."

Ted glared at his mother. "And as I said, numerous times, we'll tell the tour guide what happened. When no one else comes with a ticket, he'll know the spot is Faith's. There's no reason to leave her behind."

Gee, I wondered how it got lost. I fought the urge to send a glance in Claire's direction. I had a feeling the girl had something to do with it.

"Or he might think we're trying to sneak someone onboard," Odessa said. "This isn't a tour just for our cruise ship. The guides know the number of people on the tour so they can have adequate size transportation, but not who specifically."

"It doesn't hurt to try," Ted said.

I loved the fact he was sticking up for me, but I wanted it to end. People were staring at us. While I had looked forward to the trip to see the coral and sea life, I'd rather not tag along on a trip where someone didn't want me.

"I didn't want to see the coral anyway," I lied. "There are some shops I wanted to visit." I hurried off before Ted spotted my tears.

Keeping my eyes on the map, I continued forward, ignoring Ted calling my name. I walked faster. The more distance between me and his family the better. I slammed into someone. I looked up. "I'm so sorry."

It was John. He offered me a sympathetic smile. "I'd appreciate your company. What do you say?"

I folded the map and dropped it into my bag. "I say you're investigating a hunch and need a woman with you to have the proper cover."

He grinned. "And you'd be right. Come on, partner. Let's go see what Ruth plans on buying today."

"How are we going to find them?" I swept my arm wide. "There are thousands of people coming off the ships."

"It won't be that hard, since we know what William is in the market for…" He trailed off, looking at me expectantly.

"Diamonds."

"So we go where the biggest selection is offered." He held out a small box wrapped in a magazine advertisement. "Gift for you. Sorry about the presentation. It's all I could find."

I ripped off the wrapping. It was a small velvet box. I didn't like this. I flipped open the top. One-carat diamond earrings sparkled at me. I hated it now. The earrings had to have cost at least a thousand dollars. "I can't accept these."

"You can. First, my granddaughter has treated you horribly. And my plan won't work if you don't have some jewelry on."

"So the earrings are bait?"

"More like part of your cover."

"I'll wear them now and give them back before we head back to the ship." I put them on, dropping the box into my tote.

"You can keep them."

I fingered one of the diamond studs John had given me as bait. "It's better I don't. I don't want to explain to your ex-wife and sons where I got them."

John opened up a water of bottle and poured some into his

hands. He slicked back his hair, making it look thinner. He donned a pair of expensive sunglasses and handed me a matching pair. "Let's get you a hat, then it's off to find our man."

I stood in the center of the diamond store and tried to appear unfazed by all the bling in the room. The jewelry shop specialized in diamonds and millions of dollars of the gem sparkled underneath glass that stretched for miles. Or at least it seemed that way. Hundreds of cruisers circled the cases, jostling for position, pressing them right into the structure. The room was sectioned off into the type of piece a shopper wanted: rings, earrings, bracelets, necklaces, and a separate area for wedding sets.

"What do you think she's in the market for?" I whispered.

"We'll do a quick canvas of the room together and then split up if we don't spot them." John cupped my elbow in his hand and led me around the room. "Make sure to point and ooh and ahh over stuff. We're shoppers."

So far, this wasn't hard. We wandered around the room. I exclaimed over a few pieces and averted my gaze away from wedding sets. I was getting the impression people thought John and I were a couple. It was kind of disturbing. I stepped away from him, giving us a few inches of personal space.

He closed the distance, wrapping an arm around my waist.

I tensed.

"I see them in the necklace section. We need closer to the case. Just play along."

Placing his hand on the small of my back, John guided me toward the front of the crowd.

My purpose smacked me upside the head. We were a couple. He was my sugar daddy. I held in a groan. Next time, I should find out his plan before I agreed. I can't believe how easily I got myself into this situation. Though considering the other things I'd wedged myself into, this was on the tame side—minus the whole creepy factor since John was Ted's dad. I shivered.

"Chilly, my sweet?" He pulled me toward him and rubbed his hand up and down my arm.

I elbowed him in the side. "Don't call me that, and stop with all the touching."

A gaze slid in our direction.

"I know, honey, I know. Not in public. You're a shy one," John said.

I narrowed my eyes. He grinned and shrugged. "We have a large audience," he whispered.

He was enjoying this way too much.

A couple in front of us was huddled over the case. Every other spot was at least three people deep. This was the closest I'd get.

I stood on my toes, craning my neck for a better view. The young lady in front of me had a fantastic coloring job. At the top of her head, the color started as bright red and faded into a dark brown. Lovely, but not what I needed to see. I braced my hand on John's shoulder and rose to the very tips of my toes.

"Anything you like, darling?" John drawled loudly. "I really want you to have something to match your earrings."

"Maybe we should come back later. It's too crowded in here," I said.

"Sir, please bring your lovely lady over her," a voice cajoled us at the end of the counter. "I have a spot over here where there are some lovely pieces."

John ushered me over. "My friend told me there was great service here. I'm glad I took his advice."

"Everyone is treated like royalty here." The young man beamed at us. "Would you care for a cool beverage while you browse? Beer, champagne, water?"

John opted for water and I followed suit.

"Have whatever you like, darling," John said. "You know this old ticker of mine can't handle anything harder than water out in this heat."

"Water is fine," I said.

"Fine?" John widened his eyes and faced the clerk. "My gal

here is settling for fine. Does she look like she should accept fine when perfect is offered?"

"Of course not, sir. I'll bring a water and a champagne for your miss." He skedaddled to the back.

"It's a little early for champagne," I said.

"Consider it part of the story we're creating. I have to be the overly indulgent rich guy wanting to impress you with the world he can offer you."

"Don't you mean buy?"

He grinned at me. "That a girl. Now you're getting it. Pick out a couple of pieces you'd like him to show us."

"Should I start with something cheap and work my way up?"

"It's up to you. Go straight for giving the gold-digger impression, or let the salesperson sway you into some more expensive."

"I'll go with mid-range. I have discerning taste, yet don't not want to take advantage of you."

"Perfect," John said.

There sure were a lot of diamonds in the world, and half of them were in this store. Diamond necklaces were nestled in velvet. There was a two-carat solitaire in a simple setting paired with a herringbone gold chain. The stone was dazzling. Next to it was a layered heart pendant. The small heart had diamonds all around, while the outside heart had diamonds on one side. The pendant dangled from a delicate white gold rope chain. Beside it was a necklace with twenty large diamonds, forming a V. A small chain with diamonds trailing down dangled from the center of the V. My breath stuck in my throat. I smacked my chest a few times. It was the price of a house in Eden—okay, actually two. Maybe three if you wanted a quaint three-bedroom house in the old part of town.

The sales clerk placed our drinks on the counter. "Sorry for the delay. Another couple asked for some help. I let them know I was with a customer, but the elderly woman needed water."

"I'm not in a rush." I glanced down the row, raising my glass to hide my face a bit. William and Ruth. William wore khaki shorts and a light blue shirt, the outfit complementing the pale blue and white sundress Ruth wore. Tiny anchors decorated the fabric. Ruth fanned herself with a wide-brimmed hat and pressed a bottle of water to her cheek. William was tapping away on his phone. "You can go help that lady and her grandson first. I'm having so much trouble deciding. Everything is so lovely. We're working out our budget." I ran my fingers over the solitaire diamond necklace, drifting a little over to the hearts.

"Give me a little time to convince her to go with her heart's desire," John winked at the guy. "She's so budget conscious."

"If she's looking for hearts, we have more styles down this way." The clerk walked over a few feet and spread his arm to the showcase section of the case. "If you're a pink fan, we have some pink diamonds down here."

Closer to William and Ruth. There was a hulk of a man between William and where I'd stand. Perfect. "Do you mind, honey?" I batted my lashes.

"Of course not. I'll stay here and guard this one," John said.

"Aren't you a dear?" I slid over a few feet and pretended to ponder the choices before me. I was close enough to hear William and Ruth's conversation and still be blocked from their view.

"My other couple is still deciding, madam. What has caught your eye?"

Ruth sighed. "I'm torn between these two pieces. What do you think, William?"

Tap. Tap. Tap. William sure was interested in his phone. "Whichever you'd like. They'd both look lovely on you."

She let out a strained laugh. "I know that, silly boy. Which would go better with my cocktail dress? The gold one with the beaded black jacket."

"White gold wouldn't blend in as much," William said.

"Do you still have a picture of my bracelet? I'd like to get something similar."

"Of course."

"I can't believe I lost it. I might have to pick up another one."

"I'm sure it'll turn up. That happened the last time we cruised. Remember? You found it in your suitcase. It was tucked in with your unmentionables."

Ruth giggled. "That's right, silly me."

"Here are your choices, madam. The white gold in this piece gives off a little bit of a blue shimmer."

"No, that won't do," Ruth said. "Now this one would be magnificent."

I glanced over. Ruth was holding up an exquisite necklace. The chain was substantial, chain links separated by large circles. In the middle of the piece were two pink diamonds surrounded by smaller white diamonds to create a flower shape. The necklace cost as much as the town of Eden.

The man beside me shifted, giving me a clear view of William.

William flipped his phone around, showing the screen to Ruth. "The gold will match your dress, but not your bracelet. I'm not sure that style suits your classic beauty. The other necklace would drape beautifully on your neck." He trailed a finger down her throat.

She blushed and giggled like a schoolgirl. "But the hint of blue doesn't go with my gown."

"It will match your pale blue gown. You'll look like the ice queen Elsa," William said. He shoved the phone into his pocket. "It's a simpler design that will go with more of your wardrobe. It'll work with gowns or everyday wear. You did say you wanted a piece that wasn't so flashy it'll look out of place at the movies or a dinner out with friends."

She patted his cheek. Her eyes crinkled and she tilted her head, suddenly facing me. "You're absolutely right. Can you box this one up for me?"

Had she seen me? I scooted back toward John, taking extreme interest in the jewelry. My face was almost pressed into the glass. "I think we should go. Ruth might be on to us."

"Does she know you?"

"Yes."

TWENTY

"Now what?" I asked as we rushed out of the diamond store.

"I'd love to know how much the necklace cost." John pushed me forward. "Start walking. I'll catch up."

I saw what he saw: William and Ruth stepping outside. John gazed at the window display, head tucked low. I yanked out the map and stepped into the middle of the walkway, pondering choices. I pointed at one place, shook my head, and then flicked my hand towards another spot. Not the best acting in the world, but I hoped it worked.

"Over there," Ruth said. "Isn't she on our cruise?"

"Yes. She's a friend of Ronnie's," William said, a mix of curiosity and anger in his voice.

I tightened my grip on the map. Play it cool.

"Poor thing looks all alone. Let's have her join us for lunch."

I felt a touch on my elbow. I acted startled, crunching the corners of the map. "Hi. Can I help you? William, I didn't see you there." I smiled brightly.

Ruth looked from William to me and back again. Her eyes twinkled. "We're going for lunch. Care to join us?"

"I don't want to intrude."

"You won't be." Ruth batted her lashes at William. "Will she, dear one?'

"Of course not. Why don't you two settle in and I'll be along shortly. I have a quick errand."

"We'll be at our place." Ruth hooked her arm with mine. "It's a lovely spot with a beach view. They have the best burgers and margaritas there."

Perfect way to witness interactions between the couple. "Thanks. It'll be nice having lunch companions."

"On your own for the whole day?" Ruth tapped the cobblestones, her cane making a rhythmic sound. There was a bounce to her step I hadn't seen the other day in the theater. Then again, whose mood wouldn't improve with the sun shining down and the hint of the ocean in the air?

"Yes. There was a slight misunderstanding about purchasing tickets for an excursion. I missed out." I shrugged. "What can you do but make the best of a beautiful day?"

Ruth tsked. "I'm surprised your man didn't stay with you."

"His young daughter is on the cruise as well. He doesn't spend as much time with her as he'd like. They live about two hours from each other."

"Being a father is more important than being a boyfriend."

Yes. It was. Even though I agreed with that truth, it still stung.

"Let's walk along the boardwalk. It's a lovelier view."

Ruth was right. The stores facing the ocean had a very tropical appearance. Quaint. The shops were restaurants and mom-and-pop stores filled with handmade wares. Weaved blankets hung from the awnings. An old woman sat outside, braiding a young girl's blond hair. Her gnarled, tanned fingers moved fast and furious, over and under, creating intricate braids. Young men walking up and down the sidewalk held up posters offering deals on renting beach chairs and umbrellas. The guy giving away a bucket of beer with each rental was getting the most business, even with a higher price. There was something eye-catching about free.

"We'll keep you company." Ruth pointed at a restaurant with a large deck facing the beach. "We're here. Our favorite spot is in the corner. It has the best view. It's a lucky day because it's empty."

I took a seat at the table. Ruth was right. The view was spectacular. The turquoise blue water gleamed, a lovely contrast to the pale beige sand. The waves whooshed in the background, accompanying the sounds of laughter. A cool breeze drifted over us. It felt refreshing.

A waiter arrived with a large pitcher of water. "Ms. Ruth, it's nice to see you. Your usual?"

"Yes, and for William. He'll be along shortly. Would you like a menu, Faith?" Ruth lifted an eyebrow. "Or shall I order for you?"

"I'll have what you're having," I smiled at her. "I trust your taste."

She beamed. "I'm happy to hear that. So tell me, why did you run out of the diamond shop so quickly?"

Drat. She had spotted me. I spread the napkin on my lap and fussed with it. "I'd rather not say."

"You can tell me." Her eyes twinkled. "I know what's going on."

"You do?" I doubted it as she seemed very happy about the situation. Unless she was the one who hired John.

"William." She wagged her finger. "I know when a girl is trying to catch a boy's eye."

She thought I was after William? It was better than the truth. I dipped my head down. "I'm in a relationship."

"Have you been dating long?"

"A few months. We've been friends for a while."

"A cruise is a big test for a relationship, especially when a child is brought along."

The waiter dropped off our order.

"We're on the cruise to attend a wedding. It's a great way to meet his family."

"And yet, you're here alone while they're off, together I'm presuming, on a tour."

I shoved a fry in my mouth. I didn't like the feelings the conversation stirred in me. Loneliness. Anger. Bitterness. The worst one of all.

"I'm here, ladies." William bounded up the steps and rubbed his hands together. "Just in time for food."

"Faith and I were having a lovely time chatting. She's a delightful girl."

"I'm sure she is." William slid a smile in my direction. "Ronnie took to her right away. She usually has a hard time opening up with people."

"Your sister was vibrant and adventurous. I'm happy I met her." My voice caught. I hadn't known her long, but I knew her loss was great for those who knew and loved her.

"Where do you live, Faith?" Ruth asked, a little too brightly. I don't know if the talk of Ronnie troubled her or she wanted a pleasant topic for matchmaking purposes. Pick-ups didn't usually occur when talking about relatives who recently passed away.

"West Virginia. How about you, William?"

I cupped my chin in my hand and stared at him, hoping I seemed a little starry eyed.

"East coast." William took a bite of his sandwich. When he was done chewing, William switched the conversation. "What are your plans for tomorrow?"

"I haven't made any," I said, remembering Ruth's request to join William for the excursion being a surprise. "Probably lay out on the beach and read."

"Nonsense," Ruth said. "A young lady like you should take in the sights." She clapped her hands. "I have the perfect idea. Faith can go on the ATV tour tomorrow."

"It's a couple's tour," William said. "It's all booked."

Ruth pouted. "We'll double check when we get back to the ship. It's a tour of some scenic spots on the island and includes a stop at the beach. It'll be lovely."

"I'm sure she can arrange her own entertainment." William adjusted his position. His hardened gaze met mine. "Am I right?"

For some reason, the guy didn't want me on the tour. Which made me want to go ever so much. "It sounds fun."

"It's for couples. It won't be fun if you're by yourself." William's smile was strained. "I'm sure there are plenty of other tours available for tomorrow. I've heard the catamarans are wonderful."

"I have a lovelier idea," Ruth said. "Faith can go with you. I'm not really up to sitting on the back of an ATV for so long." She drummed her cane on the ground. "It's settled. Faith will take my place on the tour."

William's eyes narrowed. Instead of arguing with Ruth, he shoved the remainder of his sandwich into his mouth. The guy was not happy at all.

"Thank you for walking me back." Ruth hooked her cane onto her arm and removed her ID and keycard from her wallet as we approached the ship. "My leg is throbbing and I must get off it."

William bowed. "I'd never forgive myself if you didn't make it back."

She patted his cheek lovingly. "You're such a dear. I wish you hadn't cut your day short."

"I was told port days are the best times to snag a deal at the spa." I rummaged around in my purse. "Besides, I thought I was going to be indoors most of the day and I forgot my sunscreen. I'll get burned if I shop for much longer."

"That is true," William said. "A bad burn can ruin a vacation. I'll see you lovely ladies later."

"Coming?" Ruth inched toward the security checkpoint.

"My goodness, I think my ID is at the bottom." My head was practically in the bag. "I'll see you later."

"Enjoy your afternoon at the spa."

When I no longer heard the *tip-tap* of her cane, I removed my head from the bag and went after William. He couldn't have gotten far. Re-boarding the ship was the perfect cover. William thought I was on the ship, so he was roaming free. I'd find out what he did away from Ruth.

Since William wasn't expecting a tail, he was moseying his way down the sidewalk. I remained a few people back, staying behind someone taller than me. The bright colors of the shops were so inviting, it was hard passing them all by.

"Come see our hats. Many designs." A woman called out to me. Many of the stores had a worker outside personally inviting shoppers into the stores, while others held up signs offering deals. I continued forward, weaving out of the way of the workers on the sidewalk.

Ahead of us were colorful tents. The Vendors Plaza was in front of me. William was a man on a mission. He pushed through the crowd, not looking at any of the shops. He knew exactly the store he wanted, and that was where I wanted to go as well. I picked up my pace, pushing down the wiggle of regret for all the items I bypassed. I loved handmade items and so wanted to bring home something from St. Thomas. But sleuthing came first.

William paused at a blue and white tent. A heavy rope attached to a pole kept the tent open. Scarves dangled from wire hooks and fluttered in the breeze. He excused himself around a group of women. A row of costume necklaces caught his attention. He picked one out and placed it into a basket. He chose another, glanced at his phone, and then discarded it.

I edged closer, examining the scarves. Again, he repeated the process. Picked out a necklace, checked his phone, and either placed it back on the rack or dropped it into the basket. I wanted a closer look at the necklaces. I plucked two scarves from the hangers and draped them over my head, making my way into the booth. It wasn't much of a disguise, but the best I could do under the circumstances. He moved on to the other side of the tent, where wooden bead necklaces were displayed. He grabbed a handful and dropped them into his basket. Not particular about those.

The necklaces William had perused reminded me of the necklace Ruth had bought. I picked one up. It was a close match, if my memory was good. If only I had a photo. My eyes widened. Photos. I bet William was consulting a photograph he took at the diamond store. He hadn't been texting. I picked out the two necklaces that most matched the image in my memory.

William slipped out of the side of the tent. Fury raced through me. The guy couldn't even be bothered to buy the necklaces. I dropped the ones I held and started after him.

"Miss? Are you buying those?" The woman stared at my head.

The scarves. My cheeks flamed. "Yes. I wanted the silver one also."

"I get it for you. You stand in line."

I did as told, taking off my disguise. I snagged the necklaces I'd put down and also grabbed one that reminded me of the heart necklace I admired earlier. After a few minutes, I was at the front of the line and paid for my items. My grandmothers were getting scarves.

The plastic basket was discarded a few feet from the booth. I scanned the area. The crowd was large. Where was he? William was wearing what pretty much all the men wore, a light-colored t-shirt, shorts, and a baseball cap.

Since my height didn't give much of a vantage point for spotting William, I strained my ears and listened. He had a very distinctive voice.

"Are these the only blue crystals you have?"

William. I carefully made my way toward him, using tent poles and people as hiding spots. One man evil-eyed me.

I smiled. "Spying on my boyfriend. It's my birthday soon. He's getting me a surprise."

"Wait for the surprise." The man moved away from me. I shouldn't promote myself to super spy anytime soon.

The man shook his head and handed William a sandwich-size baggie full of crystals of different sizes and colors.

"Nothing lighter? I'm trying to match a dress."

A group of rowdy teens walked into the shop, laughing and jostling each other. One of them knocked into a display near me. It clattered to the ground.

William started to turn. I ducked down and scurried out. I inserted myself into middle of a boisterous party.

I glanced over my shoulder. William was walking in the opposite direction of me. I peeled away from the group. Two hours left. Plenty of time for visiting a shop or two. My grandmothers would love a rum cake.

Tugging out my map, I wandered down the street, alternating

between what was in front of me and the map. Looked like there was a place off the main road. If I had the map oriented correctly, it was on the left. I veered off the main walkway and into the small alley. Brick stones lined the path. Drat. The map was flipped.

Feet scuffled behind me. I started to turn. Pain exploded in my head. My knees gave out. Everything turned dark.

My head and cheek throbbed. The pain felt different. The ache in my head pulsed, like a bad headache trying to decide if it wanted to turn into a migraine. My cheek had a sensation of pins poking into it or tiny bugs biting at my flesh. I scrambled into a sitting position, dusting off my cheek. Pebbles pinged on the rough ground. The air smelled musty. It was dark. I crab-walked backwards, stopping when my back hit a cold wall. Where was I? What happened?

The what I figured out easily. Someone hit me on the head and ditched me in—that was where the ideas ran out. Slowly, I stood and peered around. Looked like a cellar of some type. I patted my pockets. Still had my cell phone, so my assailant wasn't robbery-motivated. I ran my finger across the screen. Dread and fear wrangled for control. Thirty minutes. I had a half hour to find my way back to the ship or be left behind. Tears waved the image on my phone. I lost an hour of my life and I didn't know where I was. Or how to get out.

Don't give up. Think. Settle down, I thought. I drew in some breaths, regretting the deep inhale as the musty air filled my lungs. I got myself into this; I surely was capable of getting out. I turned on the flashlight app and took in my surroundings. Stairs. I made my way up and pushed on the wooden door. It didn't budge. Either it was locked or someone put something on top of it.

I moved the light around the room. The cellar was empty. That was a plus. No creepy crawlies. No torture devices. Nothing indicating someone came here regularly. Maybe that was a negative. If no one came down here, who knew how long I'd be stuck. I had a phone. This was definitely a time to call Ted. The roaming warning popped up and the bars for service flickered between none and barely any service. I shuffled around the room, hoping for a service spot.

A scratching sound drifted down. A thump followed. My heart pounded, matching the beat in my head. There was nowhere to hide. I turned off the light and shoved the phone into my pocket. I scrambled for the shadows in the back of the cellar. I nearly tripped over an item in the corner. I picked it up. My tote bag. I draped the strap of the bag crosswise over my shoulder and shoved my hand inside. The silky material of the scarves slipped through my fingers. I dug deeper. My fingers bumped against my wallet. No jewelry. Why were the costume jewelry pieces worth stealing and not my phone and money?

The trap door opened. I shuffled through the dark patches, angling for the best spot to get the jump on my captor. I'd knock him down, then get out of there and find a police officer. Anyone. I wasn't picky.

A foot touched the first step. "Faith?" John leaned over.

He'd work. "I'm here." I went up the stairs. The sunlight blinded me. I squeezed my eyes and turned my head.

John grabbed hold of my hand and ran, dragging me with him. I blinked, trying to adjust to the light. I stumbled. My brain and feet were not quite coordinated at his pace.

"Thank God I found you," John said.

I seconded the sentiment. I looked over my shoulder. No one was following us. Escape was too easy. They hadn't wanted me, just the items I purchased. "I bought some costume jewelry pieces from a shop William was at and whoever attacked me stole them. The necklaces are a good match to the one he convinced Ruth to buy at the jewelry store."

"That doesn't matter now. Let's get out of here."

"How did you find me?"

"I'll explain later. Save your breath for running. We have a long way back to the dock. Time is ticking away."

"The ship won't leave us."

The quick look he threw over his shoulder said, "In a heartbeat."

A stitch was already developing in my side and every footfall echoed in my aching head. I lost my footing and almost crashed to the ground.

John tucked me into his side, keeping a strong hold around my shoulders. His features were pinched and worry blazed in his green eyes. I was getting the impression we weren't going to make it back in time. If John went ahead, he'd be able to stop the cruise with a quick word to Odessa. I was sure she wouldn't want me left on St. Thomas. Her granddaughter, on the other hand, probably wished it.

"Go. I'm holding us up. I'll get there. Ask them to wait a little bit."

"I'm not leaving you. It's not safe."

"They got what they wanted. Jewelry I bought at the Vendors Plaza." I tugged up a corner of the strap of the tote.

"I'm not leaving you behind." He had a strong hold around my shoulders. "So don't get any ideas of ditching me. I never leave a partner behind."

"We'll both end up stuck on the island."

"It's a beautiful island. We can catch the ship at the next port." He slowed our pace. "Do you have your passport?"

"On the ship."

John grimaced. "Second rule of cruising, always bring your passport when you get off at a port."

"I'm not much of a traveler. What's the first rule?"

"Don't miss the ship."

"You have to go. Stop the ship from leaving." I heard the panic in my voice. "I don't want to stay here." An extra day on a beautiful island wasn't too awful, but someone here hurt me. Or they were back on the ship. William's name emblazoned in my mind like a neon sign. He knew my plans. Matter of fact, he prompted Ruth to start the interrogation and acted like he wasn't interested in my answers.

"That's not an option." John stopped us. "I think I found our answer."

A few feet away from us, a young man was strapping a package onto the back of a moped.

"I don't think stealing transportation is a good solution."

"I'm renting it. Wait here." John squeezed my shoulder and ran over to the young man. He took out his wallet and pointed at me, then the moped. The young man looked thoughtfully at me. He answered John. John flashed some dollar bills. The young man shook his head. More bills came out. The guy's mouth twisted. The negotiations were intense. John shoved the money back into his wallet and pulled two crumbled bills from his pocket. He smoothed the bills out, presenting them to the young man. The guy's eyes widened. Quickly, he untied his package and motioned for John to take it.

We had a ride.

"Hop on. We have just enough time." John turned the key.

I climbed on.

John took off, weaving through the crowd. I held onto his waist for dear life. People shouted at us. Or rather, at him. He was the driver. I was just a passenger on the bat-out-of-hell race to the dock. My bag slapped against my leg. I hoisted it up so it didn't interfere with John's driving and pitch us both to the road. I was in enough pain. The pounding in my head settled down into a dull ache. A few aspirins and I'd feel better.

The road changed into a white concrete walkway. Soon after, I spotted the cruise ships. The *Serenade* was the last one at the end. Crew members from various ships stood on the walkway, beckoning for stranglers—including John and me—to hurry.

"Seven minutes. Seven minutes," voices with various accents bellowed toward us.

John stopped near a small guard shack. "Go. I'll see you later on the boat."

"What about not leaving anyone behind?" I slid off the moped.

"You're not."

"We're in this together."

"Not after today. You're fired."

"I'm what?"

"I no longer need your help. I got this. Go. I want to make sure the guy I borrowed this from gets it back." John patted the bars. "And it won't be good if we walk onboard at the same time."

"You think the security personnel are going to tattle to Odessa?"

"No, but you have about six minutes to get yourself onboard. When passengers haven't returned, announcements are made to see if maybe their cards didn't register correctly."

I cringed. I understood. Now. "Ted has heard my name. He'll be waiting for me."

"Get on the ship so I can."

I ran for the *Serenade*, knowing John was walking a few yards behind me. I had to get Ted away from the security area so his father could re-board without any problems. The first guard glanced at my ID and keycard before shooing me to the second security guard that was on the ship. "Hope you enjoyed your shopping."

I rushed up the ramp, breathing a little easier now that I was officially on the boat. I handed over my keycard and ID card.

"Made it in time," the woman said, scanning my keycard. "I'd advise you not to cut it so close tomorrow."

"She won't." Ted's tone held a deep rumble. I knew it well. His emotions had been all over the place and he was holding them in. I hurried toward him, wanting nothing more than his arms around me.

"What kept you?" Ted asked, tilting my chin up.

I went with a partial truth. "I slipped and banged my head. It gave me a massive headache, so I had to rest for a bit."

"Are you all right, sweetheart?" Ted drew me into his arms.

The security guard was at our side. "Are you feeling all okay? The infirmary is down the hall. The doctor can take a look at your injury."

John peered into the ship.

I leaned heavily against Ted. "Maybe I should. I'd like to get an ice pack."

"I can call for a wheelchair."

Ted scooped me up. "I'll take her."

I rested my head on his shoulder and snuggled into his chest. His heart thumped against my cheek. Heaven. Sadly, it was a short walk. Ted set me on my feet and tipped my face up. His eyes were troubled.

"I'm fine." I stood on my toes and kissed his lips, letting the pressure linger for a few seconds. "I'm sure all the running to get on the ship rattled my brain some. I'm much better now."

"Don't trust him." Ted tucked my hair behind my ears. His hands lingered on my ears, turning one of the studs. Worry shone in his green eyes.

"What?"

"My father. I saw him. Whatever delayed you had to do with him."

I didn't bother to argue. "I was lost and your father found me. He made sure I got back here."

"Why do I have a feeling that truth is covering up some other truth?"

"Please don't worry about me. I don't trust your dad. But you should trust me."

"I do...to find a heck load of trouble." Ted held my hand. "You should change for dinner. Your clothes are a little dirty."

"I fell. The ground is dirty." I pulled away from him. "I can find my way back. I won't get lost."

"Not lost, sidetracked."

"What do you think I have planned?"

"Finding out why Ronnie jumped."

I remained silent. The man was right. I wasn't going to agree or argue with him. I used the stairs, hoping along the way Ted decided I'd make him late and leave for his room. It didn't work. Halfway up, I was glad Ted stayed with me as I was feeling a little light-headed. Two floors until my destination, I wrapped my arm around his waist, needing the support and comfort his body provided.

We reached my floor. High-pitched wails greeted us. Two little boys stood in the middle of the hallway, near what had been Ronnie's room, and cried as their mom tugged on their hands.

"We'll be late for the show," the mom said. "I have candy."

The boys screeched and turned themselves into limp rag dolls.

"Can I be some assistance?" Ted asked, offering the mom a sympathetic smile. "It seems the floor is a little too hot for their feet."

The mother brushed back strands of hair from her forehead. "They think there's a ghost in that room. We've heard some noises. Scuffling sounds and faint singing have come from there. Poor woman."

"She's coming back to eat us!" one of the boys bellowed, laying on the floor, one arm raised as his mother still held that hand.

"There isn't a ghost in there," Ted said.

"Besides," I added, "ghosts don't eat people. Zombies do."

The mother threw a you're-not-helping look at me.

"Maybe she's a zombie," the littler one said.

"Can't be," I said. "Zombies don't sing. They groan."

The boys nodded and pushed themselves off the floor. "Zombies would be better. We could light it on fire to kill it."

"No fires," Ted said. "The captain won't like it."

"He wouldn't like zombies on his ship either," the oldest one said, defending their plan.

"There are no ghosts or zombies on the ship." The mom's exasperation was coming through loud and clear. Our help wasn't quite so helpful.

"The captain is having her stuff packed up. That's what you heard," Ted said.

The boys weren't buying it. "We hear it all the time. Even at night. Real dark at night."

I squatted down. Two pairs of blue eyes stared into mine.

"Ted...my guy here...is a detective. What you heard is someone cleaning out the room. That's all."

The little boys were still skeptical.

"I promise. He knows his stuff."

"I'll patrol the floor tonight if that would make you feel better," Ted said.

"You can stop ghosts?" the oldest boy asked.

Ted smiled. "Sure can. I have a special zapper. I'll bring it down and have it set up."

The youngest grinned and bounced up and down on the balls of his feet. "Can we have one? You can't be out here all night. You need sleep."

"Sure. But it'll look like a small flashlight," Ted winked at the boys. "To fool the ghosts."

Excitedly, the little boys ran toward their cabin. The mother followed after her offspring. "Thank you."

"What do you make of that?" I touched Ronnie's door.

"That there's something going on I need to find out about, and you should keep sticking your nose in my father's business. He's up to something."

"I thought you said stay away from him."

"I said don't trust him. He trusts you, so your job is to keep throwing a wrench in his plans."

My heart pitter-pattered. Ted knew what I was doing. And he approved. Kind of. But I was sure he'd prefer I not find myself coming to in dark cellars after getting hit in the head by an object. "You know."

"I saw my dad buy diamond earrings yesterday, and now you're wearing some."

I should've remembered to take them off.

"And I know you well, Miss Hunter." Ted raised my chin and brushed his lips across mine. My body tingled. I clung to his shoulders. Ted deepened the kiss and pulled back after a few moments. I felt his reluctance.

"You better go get them a flashlight."

My words came out throaty. I headed for my room.

"Can you remember that for me?" Ted's lips twitched.

"What?" I unlocked my door.

"That I know my stuff. It'll save me aggravation down the road."

I grinned and slipped into my room. "And where's the fun in that?"

TWENTY-ONE

My poor travel journal was becoming a case book. Instead of being sung a lullaby to fall asleep last night, I had scribbled down all my thoughts. After all the worries were out, I could finally fall into a light, untroubled sleep. The morning looked beautiful and I hoped it stayed that way. I was ready for a new day and port to explore.

The line to leave the ship moved quickly and soon I stepped off the gangplank onto a long stretch of white asphalt. A sign promised plenty of beach and shopping awaited cruisers at the end of the long walk. There were two other ships in port and clusters of people set off to enjoy St. Maarten. Off on the side, tour guides held signs in the air, awaiting their charges.

Anxiety finally grabbed onto me. I had wondered when it planned on showing up. This morning, I was proud of myself for remaining calm and not allowing my overactive imagination to take control. Usually upon waking, I'd have filled my brain with a dozen scenarios of why going on this excursion with William was a horrible idea. Taking in a deep breath, I raised my head and let the sun warm my cheeks.

"Faith," Ted called out to me.

My mood dipped. I knew he had plans with his daughter today, and I had wanted to avoid witnessing a tantrum—and explaining my adventure for the day. Conjuring up a smile, I turned.

His green eyes sparkled and a bright smile stretched out his cheeks. His happiness at seeing me transformed my smile into a real one, and it had nothing to do with Ted being alone. He tossed a beach towel casually over his shoulder. The man looked good in a tight fitting t-shirt and blue board shorts. He took me in and a slight frown developed. Scrap it all. Gave myself away. It was clear there was no way I planned on spending time on the beach since I wore jeans, sneakers, and a long-sleeve cotton t-shirt.

"How's your head this morning? I've been worrying about you. I mentioned it to Garrison so don't be surprised if he wants to examine you." Ted's concern gaze traveled over my body.

"No lingering effects. I actually slept okay last night. I can't wait to take on this day." I grinned at him. "I have big plans."

Ted slung an arm around my shoulders. "You shouldn't have to spend the day alone."

"I'm not," I said. "I have plans."

Disappointment flickered in his eyes. "I was hoping we could all spend some time together."

"Your daughter has been looking forward to her first beach experience with her dad. I don't want to ruin it."

"You wouldn't ruin it."

I sent him a sidelong glance and pursed my lips at him.

"Okay, it wouldn't thrill my daughter to have you along, but she wouldn't complain."

I repeated the look.

Ted grinned bashfully. "Not too much. Her mother and I had a long talk with Claire. We apologized for telling her that we had news to share with her on the cruise. It's understandable she thought it meant we were getting back together, especially since Grandma had us all rooming together. My news was introducing her to you, and Elizabeth's news was her engagement to Neal."

Poor kid. Her parents set her up for a big fall. "Promise me no surprises. You're not very good at them."

He crossed his heart. "I promise. I guess I'm not good at any kind of deception. Spend the day with us. Elizabeth wants to get to know you better."

"I appreciate the invite, but I'm okay. Truly, I am." I cuddled into his side for a moment, showing him I meant what I said. "This vacation has been hard on everyone. I'm sure Claire senses something horrible happened and isn't sure how to deal with it. I'm going on an excursion to see the island." I patted my tote. "Take some pictures. Write in my travel journal. I want to experience everything I can. I'm looking forward to scrapbooking this trip."

"I hope I'm in it," he said.

"Daddy, wait up!" Claire raced for us.

So did I.

"You're welcome to join us when your tour is over." Ted placed a hand on Claire's shoulder and looked down at her. "Right?"

Claire, who was out of breath after her mad dash, nodded.

"It'll be hard to find you. I'll see you guys back on the ship tonight at dinner. It's steak and lobster night." I grinned. "I've been looking forward to tonight's menu."

Claire's eyes twinkled. She was a smart kid. She already figured me finding them on a crowded beach would be a Herculean task, so she knew it was safe to agree with her dad. I had to admit I liked that about Claire. She was quick and had a small amount of deviousness in her. I just wished she didn't use it all on me.

Elizabeth joined us. "Your mom told me about a wonderful café where we can get a picnic lunch to take with us to the beach. They also rent beach chairs there."

"Daddy invited Faith to come with us. I hope that's okay, Mommy." Claire's voice was all breathlessness and innocence as she beamed up at her mother. Ted smiled proudly, sharing an I-told-you-it'd-work-out look with Elizabeth.

What neither of them spotted was Claire's crossed fingers hidden behind her back. So much for the talk swaying Claire to give me a chance. She was hoping for a resounding no from her mother. I'd give the girl her wish.

"As I told Ted, I'd love to, but I have plans," I said. "The excursion won't end until right before it's time to board the ship. I'll have just enough time to get a present for my grandmothers. I have to go. I'm holding up the group."

The tour guide for the ATV excursion was glancing around the area, waving a sign frantically over his head. Most people were paired up two by two, the exception being William and Francis. An older couple stared at the ATVs with a mix of excitement and horror. I hoped Ted didn't figure out this was a couples' trip and I was the second half of William's pair.

Fortunately, Claire was eager to drag her dad away from me, so no explanation needed. And there would've been. I hated ATV's and always found a way out of going ATVing with friends. Ted knew this. While it would've been nice to picnic on the beach with Ted, I had a feeling I'd have better luck with sharp turns and steep inclines than I would of having a pleasant and enjoyable lunch with Claire around.

William shifted from foot to foot, glancing at his watch in random intervals. I never knew anyone who was so interested in the time when on a vacation. This was a working vacation for William. I walked over to him. "I hope you don't mind I'm filling in for Ruth."

"Does it matter if I do?" William shoved his hands in his pockets. No Mr. Charming this morning. "This little switch was concocted without any input from me."

His sister just died; of course he wasn't in a good mood. I implanted the thought in the forefront of my brain. "Ruth was so upset about you being alone and I spontaneously offered to go in her place." And thereby getting a free trip. Heat raced across my cheeks. "I'll reimburse you for the ticket. I was a little scatterbrained yesterday and forgot to offer. I'm sorry."

William heaved out a sigh. "It's fine. The money isn't an issue. I told Ruth it was okay for her not to come, that I'd be fine on my own, but she said she found a replacement and it wasn't nice to disappoint you."

"I guess you're stuck with me." I smiled at him.

"That I am."

Spending the day with Claire suddenly sounded more appealing. I figured company was preferable on a trip where the rest of the people paired up like they were going on Noah's Ark.

Unless there was a reason besides seeing the island to go on the excursion.

The tour guide counted the group. "Wonderful, everyone is now here. My assistant will be passing out sustenance bags to every couple. You'll have snacks and water. I also advise to put any valuables into the bag as it can get bumpy and the packs are designed to attach to hooks in the back of the ATV."

I went to put my small tote inside and William stopped me.

"Keep your ID and room card with you. You'll have a heck of a time getting back on the ship if you lose those." William stared at the guide.

The man draped his arms around Paul and Glenda, the old couple from our muster drill. The couple beamed at everyone. "My friends here will set the pace for the tour. We might not get to do everything, but what we do experience are memories of a lifetime."

Paul hiked up his knee-length khaki shorts and grinned at us. His bright blue shirt with pineapples made him the perfect person to follow. "Been dying for this trip. I can't believe me and the missus are here."

Glenda smiled shyly and dipped her head. The missus wore an outfit matching her spouse's, topped off with a sunbonnet and huge Jackie O style sunglasses shielding her eyes and face. A scarf dangled down from her shoulder. Tears filled my eyes.

William drew in a shaky breath.

Ronnie's lifetime had ended.

This wasn't what I signed on for. The helmet felt heavy on my head, but I was thankful for it. No wonder Ruth bailed on this trip after watching the video. This wasn't a relaxing drive along the beach or on a trail. We were zipping down the highway, cars merging in and out of our pack.

Our excursion group was fifteen deep, with William and me toward the end, driving down a very busy road in St. Maarten. Cars zoomed past us. If I was stupid enough to reach out, I could touch one. A car veered toward us—or did William veer toward it?—and honked. The blare worked its way into my body, tightening my muscles. This was a bad idea. Very bad. I wasn't this desperate to learn William's true plan for this outing. I wanted out. But it was too late. No way was I jumping off. I gripped the bar on the back of the ATV and squeezed my eyes shut. Almost as soon as I closed them, I opened them back up. I'd rather know what I was facing. It might be the only way to survive.

Plus, missing all the sights was silly. I couldn't write in my journal about the tour if I closed my eyes, ignoring the world around me. I soaked everything in, paying attention to the details that made these buildings different than the ones in Eden. The colors were softer. More pastel than the neutrals I often saw in my hometown. People ambled along the sidewalks, gazing into windows rather than walking with a purpose. Life seemed slower. Of course, most of the people I watched were likely vacationers and in no hurry. We passed an apartment complex. The large gate and guard in front of the complex contradicted the serene and inviting environment the pale pink and cream colors radiated.

I hoped we left the paved road soon. I yearned for a scenic view of the lush trees I caught a glimpse of and the ocean I smelled. I leaned forward, keeping hold of the bar. The helmet shifted forward. "Why are we using the main road? This is kind of dangerous."

"Lunch. Beach. Scenic route on the way back. This is the quickest way and allows more time at the beach."

I didn't bring a suit. At least I had the option of rolling up my shirt sleeves. My jeans were another story. "So no tour of the entire island? The favorite spots of the residents. The most scenic places. None of that?"

"Didn't you listen to the guide? Change of plans. Now keep quiet. I'm driving."

I swallowed hard, pushing down my panic. A roundabout loomed before us. I hated them when driving in a car. I was hating them even more being a passenger in an ATV with cars whipping by on the other side. If I lived through this, I'd never, ever get on an ATV again.

Okay, if I didn't live through it, I wouldn't be doing it again either.

The first ATV in our group, driven by one of our guides, entered the roundabout and our line of vehicles followed like a bunch of ducklings following their mama. It wasn't so bad. Not too fast. Not too slow. The cars around us slowed down, allowing us plenty of space. My nerves settled down. Time to enjoy the experience instead of fearing it. I wanted to tell Ted I had a fabulous time and mean it.

The group exited the roundabout and merged onto a sandy path. The beach was before us. I regretted leaving my cell in my tote. The white sand glistened and twinkled like glitter, a perfect complement to the blue waters stretching out from it. My hands tingled, eager for a touch. Small white caps broke the surface. The moment William parked, I sprang from the ATV, ready to enjoy the beach even though I had forgotten my suit. I'd roll my jeans up as much as possible and frolic in the water. No way was I missing the opportunity.

Our main guide pointed at a section of beach between two large blue flags. The breeze from the ocean tickled the fabric, making the flags sway ever so gently. The rest of the beach was crowded with vacationers and local women walking up and down the sand, selling handcrafted items. "Right over there is our area. Beach chairs will be brought over after lunch. It's picnic style, and your sandwiches and drinks are in your bags."

The second guide handed out a beach blanket per couple. William snagged ours and tossed it to me. "I need to use the restroom. Start without me. Might take a while."

I wasn't sure what he meant by that and didn't want to ask. Some things I was better off not knowing. I fluttered the towel. The blue terrycloth material drifted down, staking our claim on a small section of sand. I plopped down and opened up our bag. There were two sandwiches, an ice pack, bags of chip, two bottles of water, and apples. I arranged the items in the middle of the towel and waited out of politeness.

"Mind if I join you?" Francis asked, placing his towel beside me.

"Not at all." I shaded my eyes. Where was William?

Francis dropped onto the towel, sending small puffs of sand into the air toward me. "I should mind my own business, but you seem like a nice person so I feel like I should warn you."

"About what?"

"William. He's not a nice guy. He's friendly and all, but it's for a purpose. The only reason he talks to someone is because he wants something from them. It's the same way he treated his sister."

I was actually the one with a hidden agenda. William had rather I found another activity to join. "How did Ronnie feel about him?"

"Adored him. He was the only family she had left." Francis glanced around before pulling out two beers from his backpack. "Want one? I only brought two, but I'm willing to give one up."

"No thanks."

"Don't pin any hopes on William. You're not his type."

"What do you mean by that?"

A tight smile stretched Francis's lips. "Let's just say William likes his women old. Real old. Like ready-to-die old. I swear that guy is a beneficiary in the will of half the senior citizen ladies who cruise on the *Serenade*."

Francis shoved a quarter of a sandwich into his mouth and scooted away from me. A shadow fell across me. William had returned, and he was unhappier than ever.

TWENTY-TWO

My breath caught in my throat. I raised myself a little off the ATV seat, wanting a better view of the beautiful scenery before me. The curvy road led us to a spot that showed off the island and ocean to perfection. A section of the land jutted out into the ocean. The waves lapped at the rocky terrain. I removed one hand and raised my cell phone, snapping quick shots. The dirt road made it impossible to hold the camera steady with one hand. Our group was traveling at a slow speed. I removed my other hand from the bar and steadied my phone with both hands. Excitement flowed through me as I envisioned my cruise scrapbook.

"Hold on."

Those were the first words William had said since we left the beach. I wasn't sure if he'd heard what Francis said, and I sure wasn't asking.

I continued snapping pictures. The ATV picked up speed and the back tire hit a largish rock. I bounced up into the air, nearly losing my grip on my phone—and my place on the back of the seat.

"You should listen."

Quickly, I shoved my phone into my front pocket and grabbed on with both hands. By the time the excursion ended, I'd need pain medication, as my left hand was getting stiff. Clamping onto the bar for so long was aggravating the injury.

We drove over another rock. One by one, the vehicles in front of us pulled over onto a large expanse of grass. William brought us to a stop.

"Brief picture stop," the lead guide said. "This is the best place for a panoramic view of this side of the island."

I hopped off and took some pictures. William wandered along the side of the road. Besides Paul and Glenda, everyone else stood near the ledge, snapping away. The elderly woman remained on the back of the ATV adjusting to secure her beach hat. Her husband placed his hands behind his back and stretched. He winked saucily at his wife.

William was at the edge. There wasn't a barrier between the shoulder and the ledge. One wrong step and you'd take the tumble of your lifetime down a rocky hill and land on some pretty ominous-looking boulders. The tops of them resembled little knives, ready to stab a person in the back and any other body parts that touched them.

"I wouldn't get so close," I said.

"Plan on pushing me off?" William asked.

"There's no reason for me to do that."

William stormed over, grabbing my shoulders. His fingers dug into my skin. I struggled against his grasp. Pebbles skittered down the side of the hill. Remain calm. There are too many witnesses around, I thought. My pep talk did little to settle my pounding heart. I planted my feet, not wanting sudden movements sending me over.

"No reason for you? But others have one and you know it." William's eyes seemed crazed.

With every word, William squeezed tighter and pushed me backwards. My heel found the edge. "That's not what I meant."

"What did you mean?"

I glanced behind me. It was a long drop down. "Nothing."

"Mount up," the tour guide called out. Paul and Glenda elected to go next to last, the rear tour guide promised he'd have them back to the ship on time.

"Be careful what you insinuate about people." William whirled me away from the ledge and let go. "Any more commentary from you, and you'll have a long walk back."

* * *

I prayed for the main road. I'd even go around the roundabout a few times. Mountain roads didn't bother me. I'd driven them all my life. What scared me was the speed William took the turns at and our vehicle of choice had no top. If we overturned, it wouldn't bode well for either of us.

"Can you slow down?" I asked, gripping the bar as tight as my sore hand allowed.

"Don't want to get behind."

"You're passing people."

"I'm done with this trip."

So was I, though I preferred a safer way for it to end.

Paul and Glenda flew past us. Glenda screamed.

"Can't slow down!" Paul cried out.

The rear guide raced past us, hunched over the steering wheel.

The lead guide was waving everyone to the side. The other ATVs were parking on what was barely a shoulder. Paul and Glenda hurtled down the hill, weaving close to the edge. My heart jammed in my throat. "Can we do something?"

"Get ready to bail." William slowed.

"What?"

A flat clearing came into view and he shoved me off the ATV. "Jump."

My body launched sideways. I screamed. Doing my best, I tucked and rolled. The moment of impact knocked the breath out of me. I flailed my good hand around, desperate for a handhold on anything. All I grabbed was grass. The blades slipped through my fingers. I continued snatching for a handhold, moving my legs like I was running. I wasn't sure how far I'd roll before the end of the world arrived and would rather not find out the hard way.

My body hit something solid. Hard and a little yielding. Arms wrapped around me.

"Are you okay?"

I turned my head. No pain. Good. I was wrapped in Francis's

arms. He had thrown himself in my path to save me. "Thanks."

"You're lucky you didn't slip off later," Francis said. "A few feet more and I couldn't have made it to you in time."

"I didn't slip," I said.

A long, terrified screech blanketed the area. A crash silenced the sound. "Oh my God." I pushed away from Francis and sprang to my feet. I started running down the road. The helmet shifted forward. I pushed it back up. The couple. They were hurt.

Francis held my hand, keeping me upright as we ran toward the accident. Pebbles skittered under our feet. The sound of rumbling was a few yards in front of us. As we neared, the buzz of the conversation slowed us down.

"Did you watch? Saved their lives."

"A superhero in action."

"Good thing he knew that shortcut."

"Hope he's not in trouble for wrecking the four-wheeler."

We reached the couples, who were talking excitedly. I glanced down. An ATV was at the bottom of the ravine. One tire spun lazily. There was no repairing it.

No wonder the guide zoomed past us. I doubted his employers would fault him for ditching the ATV. Lives over property. Half of the group huddled around the elderly couple. Glenda sobbed in her husband's arms. He stroked her back, face ashen. The remainder of our group was slapping the back of the rescuer. The guy was hidden among his fan club.

The lead guide stood behind Paul, bracing him up.

"Orlando went ahead to get a van. Those who no longer wish to ride, or no longer have a ride, may take it home. We shall collect the ATVs later."

If Orlando, guide number two, went for the replacement transportation, who was the group congratulating?

The sea of fans parted. William was in the middle. William saved the couple. The elation I felt evaporated. What was he up to?

William excused himself and approached me slowly. He offered me a half-smile. "I'm glad to see you're okay."

"You could've pulled over and explained." I wasn't letting him off the hook that easily. Or maybe at all. Not for one second did I believe the choice was made for pure altruistic reasons.

"Time was of the essence."

"You could've killed her." Francis clenched his hands, glaring at William. It was nice having a protector, not necessary, but nice. I squeezed his arm, letting him know I had the situation under control. I'd learned how to tell people off.

"I slowed down. I knew she'd land safe," William said.

"You just didn't care," I said.

"Of course I did." There was an evil glint in his blue eyes. "I slowed down."

TWENTY-THREE

The gold engraved invitation on my bed mocked me. I had forgotten. Tonight was the beginning of the Mardi Gras celebration on the ship, starting with a masked ball and continuing into tomorrow with lots of activities. The cruise line arranged a later start date for their official celebration to not interfere with ports of calls. Now I was at a loss. My wedding/fairy dress had been ruined and I needed a costume. The stain never came out and I didn't want to show up as a stabbed fairy.

I stared at the contents in my closet. I had limited choices. My gaze fell on my black cocktail dress. I had worn it the other night to the memorial service. The cardigan I paired with it made it more demure and less flashy, as the small sequins only covered the bodice of the dress. I had two hours. I was a crafter. I had an overactive imagination, as everyone liked reminding me. I'd come up with something. I had wings and a tiara.

I tossed those items onto the bed. It was a start.

An image popped into my head. I took out the black dress and placed it on the bed, tucking the fairy wings underneath and adjusting them so the tips showed. Not bad. A little Maleficent instead of a good fairy. Even the tiara worked, kind of.

I picked it up and turned it over. With a few alterations, I could go full-blown evil fairy. Add some black horns. Use a safety pin to dip the cleavage a little more. If I tied the cardigan at my waist and fluffed out the collar, I'd have the cloak effect. For the horns, I'd just need a pair of long black socks stuffed with tissue. I could grab some stir sticks from the buffet and use those to straighten out the socks so my horns weren't floppy. A brilliant plan was coming together.

The stateroom phone rang. "Hello?"

"In case you hadn't heard," Garrison said, "the wedding is tonight. Odessa thought it'd be perfect because the atrium is decorated from top to bottom and the show tonight is a big band playing dance music."

"When was this decided?" My face flamed. I was getting close to an epic fit. Being kept out of the loop was getting really old.

"While the rest of us were off on excursions. Odessa just told me fifteen minutes ago. I've been trying to calm Bob down."

"At least you guys have your wedding attire, which doubles as a costume," I said. "My only option will make Odessa's head explode."

"Do tell." There was a lilt in his voice.

"The cranberry juice ruined my wedding outfit. I was planning on wearing a black gown and that's not appropriate for your wedding."

"It's a formal affair now, so it's totally appropriate," Garrison said.

"You might not think so when I tell you my whole plan for my costume."

"I'll probably love it more."

"Do you have a pair of black socks I can have?"

"Yes."

"I'm going to be Maleficent tonight."

"I love you."

I had no problems finding the Roget clan in the dining room line. I followed the sound of bickering.

"What are you wearing?" Odessa screeched, her fairy wings quivering.

"A tux." Bob and Garrison looked magnificent in their black tuxedos with deep purple bow ties.

"White. For weddings one wears white."

"Mom, it's their wedding. They can wear what they want." Ted sounded a little envious of his brother. I bet he'd rather wear a black suit than the white one his mother forced him into.

I stayed in the background, waiting for the tantrum to end before I entered into the picture. If she didn't like the matching elegant black tuxedos Garrison and Bob wore, she'd hate my converted cocktail dress.

"And where's your mask?" Odessa asked.

"We left them in the room. I'll get them after dinner," Bob said. "I didn't want to ruin my hair and insisted Garrison match."

"You have a crew cut," Odessa continued ranting. "You can't ruin your hair."

"I'm being vain today," Bob said.

"Today? Today you go against me? I wonder why that—" She stopped talking, her gaze on me. "I see the reason."

"I have no sway over them." I approached the group.

Ted's eyes widened. I wasn't sure if it was because he found my getup alluring or if he was amazed at my audacity.

"Why is Faith wearing black to the wedding?" Claire asked.

Bob looked at his niece. "Because there's a horrible strain on her dress. Faith asked me and Garrison if it'd be all right if she wore her black gown."

"She must have another option," Odessa said.

"You know—" I began.

Ted cut me off. "Faith is standing here, Mother. You can address her directly. I've had about enough of the rudeness."

He might have had *about* enough; I had had enough. "I wanted to enjoy the costume ball, and this was the only dress I have that I could turn into a costume with such last-minute notice."

Odessa at least had the humility to blush.

"I like it." I adjusted a flopping horn.

"I do too." Elizabeth smiled. "I think you did a fabulous job at pulling together a great looking outfit. I look like a bloated fairy." She patted her stomach.

"You look beautiful," I said, before turning to Bob and Garrison. "I appreciate you guys matching me, but I'd be fine being the only one in black."

"I wouldn't," Bob said. "You're part of our family. I won't have you excluded anymore."

Claire's attention snapped to her uncle.

"How was your excursion, Faith?" Elizabeth spoke so loud her voice echoed off the walls.

"Interesting," I said.

Ted's attention swiveled toward me. Bad choice of word. "Interesting how?"

"I hate roundabouts even more when merging on and off of them sitting on the back of an ATV."

"Who was driving?" Ted tilted his head, angry eyes on me.

Ugh. I walked into that one. "A friend."

"Why are you being so evasive?"

Claire clutched onto his arm. "That guy over there."

Ted looked down at his daughter. "What guy?"

For a child who disliked me so much, she sure was interested in what I was doing when I was leaving her alone with her dad.

"The one who gave her the bracelet.'"

"He didn't give it to me," I said. "He nodded hello. I just happened to sit at the right seat."

"She's—"

Dripping in jewels, Ruth limped over to us, the tip of her cane plinking on the marble part of the walkway. "Hello, Faith. Thank you so much for keeping William company for me today. It was so nice of you to help him rescue my friends."

"Rescue?" Ted's expression was a cross between concern and what-are-you-up-to-now. "What happened?"

"An older couple had a runaway ATV, so Faith hopped off so my William could rush to their aid. They invited him to join them at the Captain's table."

"The Captain's table, how nice." Odessa's tone indicated an entirely different feeling.

"Yes, so I was going to ask if you mind dining with me, Faith. I hate eating alone."

Ted opened his mouth to decline for me.

I rushed out an acceptance. "I'd be delighted."

The waiter led us to a quiet table in the back of the restaurant. We had a lovely view of the ocean. The moon shone off the waters, highlighting the random white caps breaking through. For stretches of time, it appeared we sailed on smooth glass. I was glad Ruth asked me to join her. This was more enjoyable than dealing with Claire's attitude.

"Looks like we'll have a smooth ride to our last port," Ruth said. "Have any exciting plans for our last sea day tomorrow?"

I nudged the menu to the corner of the table. I knew my choice. Steak and lobster, tonight's special. "No. I plan on relaxing by the pool, taking a specialty class or two. There's a mask-making class in the morning."

She cupped her chin in her hands, eyes wide and a grin breaking across her face. "I've heard bits and pieces of what happened today. Sounds like my dear one was a true hero today. I'd love to hear the whole story."

"I didn't see much of it because I was peeling myself off the ground since he knocked me off the ATV before he went to save the day."

Ruth's eyes widened. "Oh my. That wasn't very nice. I'm sure he had a good reason for it. William is a gentle soul."

A snort escaped.

"You're not overly fond of my William anymore." There was a hint of steel in her voice. "May I ask why? Is it because of ungentlemanly behavior or rumors?"

"I don't want anyone getting the wrong impression about us," I said. "I'm in a relationship. I went with him today as a favor to you."

Our conversation paused as the waiter came and took our orders. Bread was delivered along with a bottle of wine Ruth pre-ordered.

"William and I have a bottle every evening. This one pairs well with lobster." Ruth had a glass poured for us and raised hers. "Thank you so much for joining me. Let us toast to new friends. I do hope I didn't put you in an uncomfortable position."

"You didn't." We clinked glasses. "I like helping people."

"I could tell that about you." She smiled brightly at me, all forgiven in a second.

And yet she didn't have a clue about William. Her sweetness and inclusiveness reminded me of my grandmother Hope. Ruth had the same laugh lines at the corners of her mouth.

The waiter dropped off our dinner. She smiled thanks. Her nose crinkled up just like Hope.

"He's using you," I blurted out the truth. I hated knowing this kind, gentle woman was being taken for an expensive ride. "William's stealing your expensive jewelry."

"No, he's not."

"I won a bracelet that looks like your costume piece."

Her eyebrows rose. "And that makes him a thief? You have quite the imagination."

"William wanted me to sit there. My room is near his sister's and we were becoming friends. Easy for him to get mine and switch them." Or send Ronnie to get it by traveling from one veranda to the other.

She waved off my concerns. "Don't be silly. That's not how the drawing is usually done. Tickets are handed out by Lucinda and then an audience member draws one out. Usually a child. It was switched up. And how is replacing my fake with a real one using me?"

"You're smuggling stolen jewels in your luggage or on your body. Once you get home, he switches them back."

"I'm sure you've heard many unflattering stories about him." Ruth waved off the waiter, who came to take our dinner plates. "He's told me that Ronnie's friends dislike him. It's why William has been spending much of his time in Lucinda's room this trip. He isn't as likely to run into Garrison. He's usually always by my side."

"What about your missing bracelet? I heard you ask him about it the other morning."

Her hands shook and she placed them on her lap. "William found it for me. It was in a different location. Absentmindedness is one of the drawbacks of aging."

"Does that happen often? Especially with your jewelry?"

The mix of anger and alarm that crossed her face said everything. It had. Numerous times. "Items get lost and I can't take it with me when I die so it doesn't matter. How about we enjoy dinner and speak of something more pleasant? Like our plans for tomorrow."

Her attitude confused me. "He's stealing from you. You're not upset about that?"

"You're a tenacious woman."

"I prefer the truth, and something's not adding up to me."

"That, my dear, is because you only have two categories to place William. Good or bad. There are so many more options."

"We're talking about criminal activity. There is only one place to file it. The man is using you."

Ruth heaved out a sigh. "At least he's honest about it, unlike my children. I know they're only interested in my money. So I'm spending some and letting William get away with some. It's mine to do with as I wish."

Her confession rendered me speechless.

"My candor surprises you." She patted my hand like a doting grandma. "You're such a lovely girl. An innocent. I'm so sorry William accidentally dragged you into this game."

"I've had my share of rough experiences."

"Have you?" Interest flared in her gaze.

"I'd rather not talk about it. It'll ruin the evening."

"We can't have that." Ruth refilled our wineglasses.

"Your children aren't concerned about you and William?" I sipped the wine.

"They're concerned about William and my money." Ruth settled back into the chair. She swirled the wine in her glass, watching the liquid trail down the side before taking a long drink. "They've been to a judge to get power of attorney over my finances. Unfortunately for them, dear old Mother is sharp as a tack and had the foresight to drop hints to William about becoming certified as a home health aide. William received his certification, and everything he does for me appears legitimate. It doesn't bother me if he exchanges an expensive necklace or bracelet for a bauble. I'd rather let William have it than my greedy children."

"Why not just give it to him?"

Ruth laughed. "Where's the fun in that? Besides, if William knew I was on to him, he'd move on. The boy is a con man at heart. He needs a thrill to feel alive."

"Why not will it to him?"

Ruth shook her head, once again patting my hand. "Oh, sweetheart, there's so much you don't know about my type of life. There would be lawyers, judges, meddling children, and a long, drawn-out court battle where all my money and assets would end up as the lawyers' once they tallied up the bill for their services. My children wouldn't have my money, but I don't want the lawyers having it either. Consider what I'm doing charity."

"What if I told you that you're just making him bolder? He's moving on and has another target in mind. Your friends he saved this afternoon."

Tipping her head back, she laughed. The sound tinkled through the restaurant, one of those contagious types of laugh causing everyone around to smile. "You are such a dear. Now don't you fret about Paul and Glenda. They have always wanted to travel and waited until he retired. Now their health isn't so good. Their children are too busy to vacation with them. We found a way for William to meet them that'll take away some of the suspicion off William's intentions. Their children will be so grateful to him." A hint of sadness faded the brightness in her eyes. "As I won't need William's services much longer, he can help them, and they'll be able to make sure greedy family members don't get their hands on it."

"They weren't in danger." A pressure built inside of me, like a mini explosion. I gripped the edge of the table, trying to keep under control.

"Paul competed in motocross events until he was fifty. It was a ruse. They need a young and able-bodied man to travel with them. William will soon need an additional source of gems. I played matchmaker."

"Why not sell their jewelry and hire an aide to travel with them?"

"Unfortunately, Paul's son was able to convince a judge to give him power of attorney over their money. I figured William would charge them a minimal fee knowing he'd have access to Glenda's jewelry. Paul and Glenda's allowance will stretch further for more trips, and their family members won't get the pieces after their deaths. We hoped William rescuing them would quiet any concerns from the family members."

"What if the plan didn't work?"

Ruth blushed. "We never considered that."

Ruth and her friends had created a game without assessing any of the risks they were accepting. "Why involve me?"

Ruth blushed.

"William seemed to take a liking to you. I thought it would be better if he was spotted enjoying time with someone his own age. Quiet down some of the gossip. I didn't realize he'd behave so ungentlemanly for the rescue attempt."

"You arranged all of this so William can think he's some great con man?"

"While I'm disappointed in my children's behavior toward me, I have no one to really blame but myself. I don't want them to benefit from my death, yet I don't want to hurt my son and daughter's feelings once I'm gone. It's better they believe I was a fool than have them know I knew they hated me. Besides, these employment opportunities I arrange for William don't hurt anyone."

"It hurt Ronnie. It's likely she died trying to protect him."

If that's all there was to it, why had Ronnie and William been interested in the tiara?

Ruth excused herself, bowing out on the masquerade ball that had taken over the atrium and the decks.

I joined the party outside. It was a lovely night for the dance. Clear skies. Little wind. Warm night. I slipped my mask out of my beaded purse and put it on, adjusting the fit so the eye holes didn't slip down to my cheeks. I had added the small crystals Ronnie gifted me to the outside so the corners of my eyes were framed by sparkles.

Waiters and waitresses carried around trays with sparkling apple cider and champagne. I took a flute, pushing down the déjà vu feeling. This reminded me so much of Ronnie's memorial service. I spotted Garrison, slinging back a champagne and then reaching for another one. His mask was pushed onto the top of his head, giving him the appearance of having grown a horn.

"How are you doing?" I waved off the approaching waiter before Garrison grabbed another.

"I hate this. It reminds me..." He trailed off, a shudder running through his body.

I hugged him with one arm. "I know. Let's think happy thoughts. Is your wedding taking place in the atrium or theater? Or on a deck? It's a nice night."

"Nowhere. We're not having a wedding tonight. Bob went to tell Odessa. I just can't. This takes me back to Ronnie's death." Garrison swallowed hard. "I need a drink."

"Water or sparkling cider? I'll get you one."

"Forget it." Garrison rubbed his eyes. "I'm going back to my room. I can't do this. I thought I could."

"Maybe if you go into the atrium or deck nine. It's set up like a ballroom. You don't have to get married tonight, but it'll be good for you and Bob to have a relaxing time together."

"I can't relax. Ronnie died. She was killed. I know it, and nothing is being done. We know the same thing we did two days ago."

"I know a little more." I snagged Garrison's hand and led him toward the small alcove where Ted and I breakfasted three days ago, which now felt like a lifetime ago.

It was hard getting through the crowd as some of the women wore elaborate costumes with hoop skirts. There was one woman dressed in a black outfit from head to toe. A heavy netting covered her face. Was she pretending to be a mourner? My stomach turned over. Considering two people had died, it seemed tacky and inappropriate. The woman probably had her outfit all planned out and didn't have anything else to wear. She was left with the option to participate or stay in her room.

"Yes. It was just like on a movie," an elderly woman talking to the mourner said.

"Yep, the young man zoomed down and stopped our ATV."

"It sounds exciting." The woman's voice was gruff and scratchy.

"I'm glad you're feeling better," Paul, the man who William saved, said. "We had really wanted to take your class the other day. My wife got a kick out of having her jewelry appraised."

"I hadn't realized my Christmas and birthday presents were worth so much." Glenda playfully swatted her husband. "This old lug told me he got them from a sidewalk vendor."

"I must say, that's an interesting costume you're wearing," Paul said.

"I'm positive I'm not contagious anymore, but just in case..." Lucinda moved her hand up and down to showcase the heavy veil. "I went with this getup."

The spot where Ted and I had breakfast was empty. "I found out some information tonight at dinner." I filled him in on my conversation with Ruth.

"But William doesn't know Ruth is on to him?"

"More like Ruth is arranging everything for him. She's kind of scamming the scammer."

"Ronnie died because of that?"

"We don't know why Ronnie died. William believes he's

stealing from his clients. He doesn't know they are allowing it."

"But what if someone else figured out he was stealing and confronted him?"

"Like Ronnie?"

Garrison nodded. "Like Ronnie."

TWENTY-FOUR

Masquerade balls were not fun when you were trying to find someone. The crowd was dwindling down, but I was still having a hard time locating either Bob, Ted, or John. It was hard to tell who was who when most people wore a mask. With Ted wearing a white suit, I thought he'd stand out like a beacon. Either he ditched the party or had changed clothes. There had only been two men wearing white tuxedos and neither of them had been Ted. One was a given considering he was six inches shorter than Ted; the other I found out the hard way. I was so glad I chose my second option of greeting rather than the first. The wife wasn't too thrilled with me hugging her man; she'd have been less so if I kissed him.

There were a few couples dancing on the deck. At night, the retractable floor closed the pool up and the entire deck was used as a dance floor for parties. The moon shone just right to highlight the couples. I found the almost grooms. Garrison and Bob had pushed their masks onto their heads and looked into each other's eyes as they slowly moved in a circle on the dance floor. The love radiating from them strummed the tender places in my heart. I'd leave them in peace.

Other couples danced near them, each pair seemingly lost in their partner. One couple wore elaborate pirate costumes, another were Iron Man and Black Widow, and one had pieced together a costume from everyday clothes. The cruisers' masks were two large anchor patches with white ropes attaching the anchors together and tied around the back of their heads.

"Would you care to dance?" Blue eyes shone from behind a black mask. I knew the voice. William. He held out a hand, waiting for me to place mine on top.

"No." I placed my hands behind my back.

"I think we should talk." His smile was brittle and he continued holding out his hand.

I guess he wasn't taking no for an answer. What could go wrong with all of these people around? And if I wasn't mistaken, the older gentleman sitting on a lounge chair, dressed as a police officer, was John. He had stood up the moment William approached me and was now taking an undue interest in the life preservers on the starboard side of the ship. I slipped my hand into William's and was led onto the dance floor that had been the family swimming pool this morning.

"I heard you've been telling people your own version of what happened on the excursion." He waltzed me into the center of the floor.

He didn't waste any time getting to the point. "I'm telling the truth. It's not my fault you told a tale."

"Your recollection isn't quite accurate. Though I'm sure you think so. It was a very scary moment. Understandable you'd forget."

"That's not what happened. You're wrong and I'm right. You pushed me off."

"I did no such thing. I'm not a violent person." His grasp tightened around my waist, nearly squeezing the breath out of me.

I dug my nails into his wrist. "I don't feel like dancing anymore."

"I do." He squeezed my sore hand.

Tears stung my eyes. I held in a breath, waiting for the pain washing over me to fade. "You're hurting me."

"I'm just holding your hand."

There was no more charm in William. The guy was dangerous. Scary. I wanted away from him. "Let me go."

"We have a few more things to chat about."

"No, we don't." At first, I wasn't sure if William was capable of hurting his sister, but now I knew he was. I also feared for Ruth and her friends. Even though her plan was to help him, I doubted he'd be pleased she'd figured out what he was up to. The trio was in trouble. I jerked away from him, scrambling back a few feet.

Surprise flashed across William's face.

The floor moved beneath my feet. I flailed my arms, trying to maintain my precarious balance. What was going on? Before I knew it, there was nothing underneath me and I smacked into the cool water. I went under. My dress tangled around my legs, making it difficult to surface. I pulled the skirt up to my waist and waited to touch the bottom. I sprang up. My dress slipped from my hand, and I turned to gather it back up. My back hit a solid surface.

Panic welled up in me. What was going on? I heard screaming. I had to be near the surface. I sunk down and looked. The floor was closing back over the pool. The moon hit the water, highlighting my escape route. I gathered my skirt and tucked it down my bodice, modesty no longer any importance to me. I swam for the exit. The spot grew smaller and smaller.

Sputtering, I broke the surface. I was away from the pool edge. I tried pulling myself up onto the floor, but it was too slippery.

"Grab my hand. We'll pull you out." A crew member had walked into the water, a life preserver around his waist. Another crew member standing on the concrete pool side held onto a rope attached to the preserver. I wasn't sure if I had enough time.

"Float." John flattened himself on the floor. "I'm going to push you."

I flipped over to my back. Using my feet, John launched me toward the guy in the water. The moments our fingers touched, he snagged my waist and practically threw me onto the deck. Garrison and Bob were there. Taking a hold of me, they helped me stagger away from the pool. I motioned them away. I need a breather and a seat.

"What happened?" Ted dropped beside me.

"No one knows. The floor opened, then started closing." Bob draped a towel around me.

The ends of the floor met each other. The pool was gone. I shivered.

Ted pulled me against his side, rubbing his arm up and down mine. "Faith's freezing. Can I get another towel?"

I let him think it was because I was cold.

Garrison handed over another towel and knelt beside me. "Are you okay?"

"I'm fine," I said, coughing a few times. I glanced around. The couples looked more bewildered than worried. Everyone was back on the surface. Where was William? I jumped to my feet, striking my shin into the neighboring deck chair. I ignored the pain. "Where's William? I was dancing with him."

Bob and Ted scanned the area. "Don't see him."

I shook off the towels and ran over to a crew member standing by a set of controls. "He's in there. I think my dance partner is still in the pool."

The crew member slammed his hands on the button. "It's not working. I need maintenance. Get the skimmers. See if we can jam it open."

Crew members scattered for tools.

The maintenance woman ran over, puffing for breath.

"The floor malfunctioned. Someone's trapped underneath."

The woman unscrewed the panel and got to work. There was a split wire in the panel unit. The crew member frowned and tossed a concerned look at a security guard who had arrived. He silenced her with a sharp nod of his head. She stripped the wires and then connected them. The floor started retracting. Two crew members, one wearing a breathing apparatus, slipped into the pool. The diver went under the water. The other crew member shined a flashlight into the water, traveling the beam back and forth.

The area was silent. I held my breath, hoping for a miracle for William, but already knowing the outcome.

"Need some help here." The crew member in the water waved his hand in the air.

The cruise director, Garrison, and the Roget brothers ran over.

Black Widow walked over to me and wrapped her arms around me. "Come on, honey. Let's go over to the bar."

A spot farther away from the pool. I shook my head. I wanted to know. Had to know. "I want to stay here."

"Sweetie, nothing you can do will help him."

And she was right.

William's lifeless body was brought to the surface, then laid out on the deck. The ship's doctor began CPR. William remained motionless.

The doctor placed his fingers at Williams' neck then sat back on his heels and motioned for a towel. With a sharp snap, the towel fluttered down to cocoon the top half of William's body.

Ted held out his arm, stepping into my room first and turning on the light. After a few moments, he waved me inside.

"Is something wrong?" I peered around him, nothing seemed out of place.

"Just a precaution. Every time I turn around, you're in some kind of unpleasant situation."

That was one way to put it. "I can handle myself."

"It's not you I'm worried about. It's the unsavory people my father has gotten you involved with."

I stared at Ted.

He crossed his arms and gave one sharp nod. "I know. It wasn't too hard to figure out since I know my dad was on this ship for some reason. And it wasn't to see Bob and Garrison get married. It's not his style to cause trouble to hurt people, no matter what my mom believes. It's time for you to tell me what's going on. Like if you know who might have been the ghost in Ronnie's room the night she jumped."

I glanced down at the floor, my wet feet creating a damp spot on the carpet.

Ted groaned. "Please don't tell me my dad sent you in there."

"No." I rubbed my foot back and forth across the carpet.

"Garrison and I did it on our own."

"You dragged Garrison into this?" Ted sounded incredulous.

My head shot up. "I did not. Garrison didn't believe...doesn't believe...Ronnie killed herself. He was sure we'd find an answer in her room. I had dropped my purse in there. Right after Ronnie fell. Jumped."

"He broke in?"

"He had a key to her room." I wasn't sure if Garrison still did, but I didn't want to completely rat him out. Besides, we might want that key tomorrow. I shivered.

"I'm sorry. Here I am giving a lecture while I should be encouraging you to get out of that wet dress."

I stink-eyed him.

"Not for nefarious reasons. You're getting cold. You've experienced a traumatic event tonight. You should be resting." Ted opened up the drawers in the dresser and pulled out my Mickey Mouse pajama set. He handed over the shirt and short set. "Get changed and I'll tuck you in. I promise to turn around and cover my eyes."

I wished I brought something a little more adult like as Disney graphics weren't the way to remind Ted I was a woman. Unfortunately, my other nightwear had the Little Mermaid.

"Were you in Ronnie's room any of the other times those children mentioned hearing a ghost?"

"It wasn't us."

"There's one other possible suspect. My father. I need you to keep him away from this floor tomorrow."

"How? Besides creating a cage match between him and Odessa. If I tell him to stay away from Ronnie's room, he'll be there before I finish the sentence."

"With misinformation."

"You want me to lie to your father? Send him off on a quest he'll never finish?"

"Yes."

"He'll catch on."

"Then there's another option. I just don't know how I'll pull it off."

I was intrigued. "What?"

"Have Claire ask him to spend time with her. He won't say no to her."

I didn't see that happening. Claire was determined to stay close to her father so I'd stay away. Unless I made other plans. What possible activity could I do that let Claire know her family was safe from my clutches? I picked up the activity guide left on the bed and scanned it. There had to be something of interest.

I tapped the paper. "There's a gumbo-making class that's adults only and at the same time, there's a class for adult and kids about treasure seeking. It's to help learn techniques for a big treasure hunt on the island Friday. The buried prizes include *Serenade* merchandise, game systems, iPhones, two hundred cash, free drink coupons, and also one for twenty percent off a cruise. I'll go to the cooking class. John will follow to see what I'm up to."

"This cruise line must be raking in some cash with all these high-priced gifts," Ted said.

"Maybe they don't offer these for every cruise. They might be special for the Mardi Gras cruise."

"True. But..." Ted trailed off, worry crossing his face. He nudged me off the bed and peeled back the cover. "Let's get you into bed. Big day tomorrow."

I crossed my arms and gave him a haughty look. "Really, Detective Roget, is that anyway to sweep a lady off her feet?"

"I'm not trying to get you into bed for my sake." He paused and looked up at the ceiling thoughtfully. "Okay, I'm trying for my sake, in a way. It's the only way to keep you away from trouble for a few hours so I can sleep."

"Really? What are you going to do? Tie me to the bed?"

Ted's gaze brightened with a wicked gleam.

Blushing, I scrambled into the bed. It was better to pretend I didn't utter those words. Something was troubling Ted and he wasn't sharing with me.

Ted tucked me. "I'll see you later. Get some rest."

I sat up, shoving the blankets to my waist. "How can I? Someone just died. I was with William when it happened. It could've been me."

"I know that." His voice was rough. He sat on the edge of the bed and gathered me into his arms. "It'll keep me up all night."

"I don't think it was an accident."

"Neither do I. That's why it'll help me do my job knowing you're tucked in bed safe and sound."

"Your job?"

Ted stood. "The captain asked me to help him search William's room. Three deaths during a cruise are three too many. He's scheduled to have some FBI agents meet the ship at the island on Friday."

"Are you going to be guarding the room?"

"I'm helping him document what's in the room and collecting anything that might prove William's death wasn't an accident. Now get some sleep. Don't worry about the ghosts or other creepy things wandering the halls. The captain will have security guards and the room hosts patrolling the areas tonight. Bob and I are taking an early morning shift."

"My hero." I slid underneath the covers.

"I'm trying to be."

TWENTY-FIVE

I was blow-drying my hair when a thump filtered past the whirl of the dryer. I shut it off. I heard it again. It was a loud rap on the door. "Rise and shine. I have coffee and pastries."

I bolted out of the bathroom and let Ted in the room. The scent of caffeine weaved around me. "What did you find out last night?'

"Here I thought you were excited to see me."

"I am." I took one of the cups of coffee. "And this."

"Admit it. You only want me for my coffee."

I walked onto the veranda, hoping Ted followed with the pastries. I had dreamed of having breakfast out here with him while the sun rose. The sun had been out for an hour, but it was better than nothing. The seas were a little rougher than the previous day. I carefully placed my coffee down before sitting in one of the deck chairs.

"I'm taking your non-answer as me being right." He lowered into the deck chair beside me.

"Any and everything means you're right." I sipped my coffee, the perfect amount of sweetener and creamer. The man knew how I loved my coffee.

Reggae music floated down to us. It was a heck of a party upstairs. The sun bounced off the water. I averted my gaze as it was a little blinding.

"This is the nicest my morning has been so far." Ted's voice drew me back to the present. "I hate it's about to end."

"It doesn't have to. We can just stay here all day." Even as I said it, I knew it wasn't possible for me or Ted. We both needed answers. The sooner the better for all of us.

"No, we can't. It's not in us." Ted let out a huge sigh. "Word about William's death is spreading. People are freaking out. Naturally, they're worried about the deaths. There's a rumor circulating that William actually killed Ronnie, that it wasn't suicide, and the guilt got to him. That he killed himself."

"We can throw out that theory. There's no way he could've retracted the floor while he was on it."

Ted shrugged, eyes still focused on the horizon.

"He wasn't the only one on the dance floor. There were so many innocent people. He'd be killing all—" I shut up. Me. Garrison. And Bob. With him. Maybe that's why he invited me onto the floor and maneuvered us to the center of the dance floor. We'd have less of a chance of getting out.

"People have done stranger things."

"How would he have access to the panel?"

"He traveled on this ship frequently and was friendly with a lot of the crew members. He might have watched someone. Plus, we found some tools in his room, but they don't look strong enough to handle what needed to be done on the panel."

"I bet they're Ronnie's jewelry-making tools. She loaned me a set to fix my tiara."

"Do you still have them?"

"They're in my safe." I picked up my coffee and went back inside. I opened it and handed the items over to Ted.

He examined them. "These seem about the same size. I'm going to have to take them."

"Fine with me. Did you happen to find a diamond bracelet in there?"

"We found a lot of jewelry."

I filled him in on what Ruth told me.

Ted rubbed his forehead. My heart went out to him. This vacation wasn't very relaxing for him either. "Let's stop by the captain's office and see if you can identity your bracelet."

*   *   *

Laid out on a desk in Captain Henderson's office were diamonds, rubies, sapphires, and other stones. William had been a busy thief. My fingers itched to touch the bling, but I kept my hands behind my back. No way did I want my fingerprints on them. Off to one side were a couple of costume pieces, one a match to the necklace I saw Ruth buy.

"Do you see the bracelet you won?" Ted asked.

"No." If William didn't have the bracelet, who did? Was that person responsible for his murder?

"You can pick any of them up to get a closer look," the captain said.

"I don't think getting my prints on them is a good idea."

The captain handed me a set of plastic gloves. "The detective and I used a pair of these."

Did John know his case was about to get busted wide open by his son? I slipped on the pair of gloves and moved the pieces of jewelry around. "It's not here. I won it at the seminar Sunday morning."

"Did you attend the seminar on Monday?"

"Lucinda didn't show up that day. She was sick," I said. "From what I heard, she also bailed out on the shopping trip on St. Thomas because she was still unwell."

The captain frowned, stroking his chin. "Then where did she go? If Lucinda had not scanned off the ship, I would've been told. No one told me she did not fulfill her obligations. I do not like surprises like this on my ship."

"Crew members also have to be scanned on and off the ship at the ports?" Ted asked.

"Yes, even if they are going off the ship for work related purposes. If Lucinda went off the ship and didn't come back on, I'd have been alerted."

A memory slipped into my head. "Maybe she didn't leave the ship."

Ted and the captain gave me an odd look.

"William had accidentally handed the security guard Lucinda's keycard instead of his own. William had been taking care of her while she was sick."

Captain Henderson jotted down my words. "I'll take a look at the time stamps and also speak with the guard."

There were a whole lot of other surprises on the *Serenade* he should be concerned about. Like two employees, current and prior, and a guest dying under mysterious circumstances during the cruise.

"I'll ask to speak to this Ruth and also Lucinda. Detective, do you mind being present while I talk with them? Make sure I'm asking the correct questions. Since Lucinda and William have spent much time together, she might have typed the message."

"I'll be there."

"What message?" I asked.

"We found Ronnie's phone in William's room," Ted said. "The night she died, he posted on an internet message board."

"Or Lucinda did," I said.

"We shall find out from her." The captain stood.

"Make sure you take plenty of vitamins and wear a mask. From what William said, Lucinda has a pretty awful stomach bug."

"Then she'll be moved to the infirmary. Keep an eye on her and ensure she doesn't infect the passengers." The captain flipped through a large planner-style book. "How about in one hour? Maybe your brother can attend also. We should search Lucinda's cabin. Again. The bracelet must be in there. Lucinda's behavior is most suspicious."

"It could be in Ronnie's room. Zombies," I said.

The captain sent a concerned look in Ted's direction. Fortunately for me, Ted knew where I was going with the comment.

"A family on that floor mentioned hearing noises coming from the room the night Ronnie died," Ted said. "The little boys thought it was zombies."

"More than likely they heard your father," the captain said. "I had asked him to search Ronnie's room. He had found nothing."

"What if William or Lucinda put it in Ronnie's room since it had already been searched?" I said.

"Faith has a good point," Ted said.

"Then I'd like you and your brother to look in Ronnie and Lucinda's rooms."

"We can do that." Ted hooked an arm around my waist and ushered me out of the office. "Please keep Garrison away from Ronnie's room today. I don't want to upset him or have him put himself on the captain's radar. Somehow my dad will be blamed if Garrison becomes a suspect."

"A suspect? How in the world can your dad tie Garrison into this jewelry theft ring?"

"He can't for the jewel heist stuff, but it's possible for William's death. It wasn't an accident. Someone tampered with the retracting floor over the pool. FBI agents will be boarding at the next port, and I'm sure they're doing background checks on the victims and the passengers right now. Garrison will come up on their radar. He's never liked William."

"Come on, that can't be common knowledge."

"If Garrison's coworkers are asked about his relationship with Ronnie and William, it'll be said that he adored Ronnie and hated William. He believed William used Ronnie's mental illness to his benefit."

Ronnie had mentioned being on a prescription. "How could William use her illness against her?"

"I'm not sure as Garrison kept her actual diagnosis quiet, but not his feelings about William. He'd rant about specific incidents, but not how he was using her."

"What do you think? You didn't seem to like Ronnie much."

Ted scrubbed his hand over his face. "No. I thought she was playing Garrison and using her illness as a way to explain her flightiness. She was always asking to borrow money. Now come to find out she had a pretty hefty stash hidden away under a different name."

"She what?"

"Opened an account using a slight variation of her nickname."

"How did you find out?"

"I have my sources."

"Who?"

He zippered his lips.

I narrowed my eyes. Gee, the excuse sounded very familiar. "Ronnie's tied into the diamond scam."

"It appears that way."

"Garrison isn't going to like hearing that. It still doesn't mean the FBI is going to put him on a suspect list."

"I've participated in this type of rodeo a time or two," Ted said. "If I didn't know Garrison, I'd put him on my list. He had motive. He had means. He had opportunity."

"No, he didn't. He was dancing with Bob. On that dance floor."

"Right near the edge of the pool where they could easily get to safety. They made sure to get you out, but he didn't make a move to see about William."

I had to agree with Ted's assessment. It was suspicious. If I was nosing around in the matter and didn't adore the man, I'd slap Garrison's name on my list too. "I'll get Garrison to take the gumbo-cooking class with me."

"Let's go fill in the family in on the plan. They're waiting for us in the atrium. This morning my mom decided we should all attend the seminar on treasure hunting so we can participate as a family in the hunt tomorrow. I'll have her take notes for us."

"Sounds like fun." Not. I forced out a chipper smile.

The seminar didn't bother me, but having a day of being labeled as part of the group yet not being part of it sounded like torture. Of course, if things went as they had before, there would be some reason to exclude me from the treasure hunt and I could enjoy the island on my own.

Tomorrow was my last day of vacation, and I planned on having some beach time. So far, all my attempts had been thwarted. Not that I tried all too hard.

"There you two are," Odessa greeted us. "We've been standing here waiting."

"All the good seats will be gone." Claire pouted, directing a glare at me.

"Faith was ready to go, but I had to make a side trip." Ted placed an arm around me, which caused Claire's anger to grow. Ted wasn't very good at figuring out how not to make his daughter mad at me. "And I hate to say it, but I won't be able to attend the seminar."

"Why not?" Odessa straightened her spine and tipped her chin up, doing her best to look down on Ted, who was taller than her.

"Because," Ted said. "Bob has to come with me too."

"Why?" Odessa's eyes blazed.

"Because." Bob grinned, enjoying the fury pouring from his mom. "Take notes for me, Jelly Bean." Bob ruffled Claire's hair.

"'Because' is not a reason," Odessa called out after them.

In the corner, I spotted John in a lounge chair near the bar, his face half-buried in a leather menu. I elbowed Garrison, doing the shifty eyes toward John. "Garrison and I have to leave as well."

"Why?" Odessa stretched the word out.

I so wanted to say because. I smiled innocently. "I wasn't aware of this morning's plan and already paid to attend the gumbo-cooking class."

"I signed up also," Garrison said. "Ted thinks I should keep an eye on Faith."

"Sounds reasonable," Odessa said.

Gee, glad to know she thought so highly of me. I hooked my arm through Garrison's and hightailed it out of there.

I drew him toward the art gallery, which was a hallway between the atrium and the theater. Paintings were hung on the wall and a bored-looking crew member sat at a desk, waiting for someone to pay the, in my opinion, exorbitant prices for the artwork and the cost to mail them home. The area was empty except for the one crew member and an elderly couple shuffling down a row of Thomas Kinkade paintings.

I stopped in a corner. A cubicle wall hid us from view.

"So what are we going to really do?" Garrison asked.

"We're going to figure out who could've taken my bracelet." I explained about the captain benefitting from Ted and Bob's investigative skills. "We know it's not in Ronnie's room."

"Someone could've put it in there now. There have been noises heard in there," Garrison said.

"I think someone's been searching for my bracelet. It's either worth more than we believe, or something on the bracelet will prove who the killer is."

"How?"

"I dropped my purse after Ronnie died. The killer returned to take any evidence out of the room. Remember, Ronnie's scarves and her jewelry tools were taken. They had been in her room when I talked with Ronnie before I went to the portrait session."

"You just said those items were found in William's room."

"It doesn't mean he took them. He didn't know I'd lost the bracelet. He asked me about it the next day."

"So who put them in William's room? That leaves the suspect as Odessa." John came around from the temporary wall.

"I was wondering when you'd show yourself," I said. "Or it's Lucinda, who's been hiding out most of the cruise. From what I've heard, William has been taking care of her. The only way to prove Odessa is guilty is to see if she has the bracelet." It was time to take Odessa off the culprit list once and for all. Odessa had been with her family when Ronnie died, surrounded by us. There was no way she had taken the bracelet, and the only way to solve the case and make sure no one else was killed was to get John onboard with the rest of us. We needed him to help find the real murderer, not chase after a phantom.

"And just how are we going to do that?" Worry shone on Garrison's face.

"With this." John held up a keycard. "With Odessa occupied, now's the perfect time to take a quick look in her suite."

There was an itch in my gut. Call it woman's intuition or bad memories taking root, but I didn't trust John Roget for one second. There was a reason he wanted us with him. Witnesses. I had a feeling we were being set up to find the evidence.

And I'd make sure John paid for the deception.

TWENTY-SIX

The Presidential suite was like a mini apartment at sea. There were two separate bedrooms, a mini kitchen minus a stove, and a large living room with a small dining table tucked in the corner. No wonder John suspected his ex-wife. The room had to have cost the amount of a small car, and this was only one of the rooms Odessa booked for the week. I bet Garrison and Bob's room was about the same size with identical amenities.

"We'll have to split up," John said. "This is a large space. We don't know how long Odessa will be gone. I'll take her room, Faith the main living area, and Garrison can handle the other bedroom where Elizabeth and Claire are staying."

"Okay," I said, almost a little too eagerly. I held my breath, waiting for the guys' reaction. Either my ears heard a tone no one else did, or they weren't concerned about my joy in rifling through Ted's belongings and the main area. I had a strong hunch John was finding incriminating evidence in Odessa's space.

I got busy in the main room, putting on a good act of really believing I'd find something in there. I wanted John to think I wanted Odessa pegged as the guilty party so his guard was down. It was the only way to stop him.

"My goodness, these girls travel with a lot of stuff. How many outfits does one child need?" Garrison's voice carried from the other room. "I don't see any jewelry in here."

"Look for a safe," I said. "There might be one in every room. Ted is living out of his suitcase." I unzipped the suitcase quickly. The teeth made a loud whizzing sound. It was really quiet in

Odessa's room. After a few seconds, I slowly zipped it back up, taking care so there was no sound. "I need to make sure I don't move things around too much. Ted will notice. Everything is in a particular order."

"Fortunately, I don't have that problem. Claire and Elizabeth like things haphazard."

I snuck over to the door to Odessa's bedroom. It was cracked open. I touched it with my fingertip, creating a little more space. I peered in. John was on the floor, the upper part of his body under the bed. The large honeycomb quilt hung to the floor on all sides. Quietly, I tiptoed over to the opposite side of the bed and flattened myself on the floor.

Grabbing the end of the quilt, I yanked it up. John's eyes widened. His right arm was outstretched toward the corner of the bed. An object glittered at his fingertips. Was he shoving it in the small spot between the bed and nightstand or had he found it?

I felt sick. "What are you doing?" I practically yelled.

"Finding evidence." He seized the item, yanking it out.

I scrambled to my feet and ran over to him. In his haste, John dropped the item. I grabbed for it. John leaned down at the same time. We clunked heads together. I blinked away the pain and closed my fingers around the bracelet. My bracelet. I was right. The delicious feeling of vindication didn't last long. I was furious.

"How can you do this to your ex-wife? Your sons' mother. You loved her at one time." The bracelet shook in my hand. If I was any angrier, I'd crush the diamonds into dust.

"Why are you yelling at me?" John fired back. "Odessa is the one that took your bracelet."

"That's a lie. You planted it here."

John backed away from me, surprise and hurt splashed across his face. "That's where I found it."

"She never had an opportunity to take it," I said. "It was in my purse. I dropped it in Ronnie's room. There was no way she was able to make it to Ronnie's room before Garrison retrieved it."

"The captain spotted your purse on Ronnie's veranda, Faith.

That's why he decided to get Ted and have him help search the room and collect the evidence. He knew Ted had experience with criminal investigations and was still in law enforcement. Captain Henderson wanted everything done by the book."

"So, you're saying…"

"No one went into the room before you and Garrison returned. I was watching," John said. "I told Captain Henderson that I knew it was your purse so I grabbed it and gave it back to you. It wasn't evidence."

"And he was okay with that?"

"No, but it was too late. I didn't want you or Garrison getting in trouble for going into the room."

"The bracelet was stolen before I dropped my purse."

John nodded. "Odessa made you take it off."

I scowled, not sure who I was angry with at the moment. "You sure do know a lot of things you weren't around to witness."

"The captain witnessed Odessa's tantrum and relayed it to me."

"What's with all the yelling?" Garrison entered into the room.

I pointed at the bracelet. "John found it under the bed." I let the sarcasm flow when I said found.

"Someone put it there." Garrison reached for the bracelet. "It wasn't Odessa."

"That's what I've been saying."

"I sure didn't place it under her bed." John wrapped it in a handkerchief and tucked it into his pocket.

"I'd believe that before I'd believe Odessa stole Faith's bracelet."

So would I.

"She was the one who threw a fit and had Faith take it off for the pictures." John pulled out his cell phone and texted a message. "We'll just let the captain decide."

An idea took root. "The captain gave you a copy of Odessa's key. Right?"

John's expression answered the question for me—affirmative.

"The captain heard Odessa asking me to put the bracelet in the purse. So..." I trailed off. John's complexion worried me a little. Was the man about ready to have a heart attack? I tilted my head toward John, hoping Garrison understood what I was trying to say with the spastic movement of my neck.

"Are you all right, John?" Garrison asked begrudgingly.

"Are you kidding me?" John pushed out the words. "You're accusing the captain? Have you lost your mind?"

"All the pieces of the puzzle point to him."

"Except he hired me. The fact was the bracelet wasn't found in Ronnie, William, or Lucinda's room. The other person the captain suspected of being involved was Odessa."

He had a point. Scrap it all.

There was a gasp by the door. We turned. We'd been so involved in blaming, we hadn't heard the door open.

Claire stood in the doorway, her eyes wide. "Grandma. Daddy. Faith is in Grandma's bedroom."

"Faith, what..." Ted stopped talking. His gaze traveled over us a few times, like he'd run us over and was backing up and repeating the drive-over a few times.

John, Garrison, and I closed ranks, picking the plan of "safety in numbers" as our defense.

"What in the world? Why are the three of you in my room? I'm calling the captain on you." Odessa pointed her middle finger at John.

"Don't bother." John smiled. "I've alerted him to the situation."

"What situation?" Ted side-eyed his father.

"The stolen bracelet being in Odessa's room." John pulled my bracelet from his pocket and held it up.

"Stolen bracelet?" Odessa's brows drew down. "Why in the world would I take someone's bracelet? I have enough jewelry of my own."

"Not someone's. Faith's bracelet. The one you didn't want her wearing."

Slowly, Odessa turned and faced me. She crossed her arms, raising one hand to cup her chin.

Ted, Garrison, and John backed away. I was in trouble. Huge.

"You think I took your bracelet." Odessa paused, holding up her index finger. "Excuse me, you think I stole your bracelet, so you had John and Garrison come help you search for it?"

Claire bit her lip, sliding behind her father.

"No." Denial squeaked out of me. "The bracelet was stolen the night Ronnie went overboard. John told me he was coming to look in your room because the bracelet wasn't found in the other rooms searched. I was afraid he had it and was trying to plant evidence against you. I was here to stop him. I just didn't do a very good job."

"I didn't plant it." John's face purpled. "It was here."

There was a loud rap on the door.

"We'll see what the captain has to say."

Odessa walked out of the bedroom. We trailed behind her, like a gaggle of paparazzi following the next big story.

John brought up the rear. "Go right ahead. The captain hired me. He's been trying to find out who's been stealing jewelry from passengers and replacing them with high-quality costume pieces."

Trembling, Odessa turned. "Captain thinks I'm involved?"

"Your name came up."

Tears shone in Claire's eyes.

"We should discuss this later," I said, hitting my foot into John's shin.

"We don't have a choice." John opened the door. "Come on in, Captain Henderson."

Odessa hustled over to Ted, standing slightly behind her son.

The captain placed one foot into the room.

"I did it," Claire whispered. Her scared voice sounded like a gunshot. "I took Faith's bracelet. She didn't deserve to have it."

Claire had been standing by the photographer that night while our group played "move Faith around to get the proper portrait."

"This seems more like a family matter. I'll take my leave." Captain Henderson reversed out of the room.

"Why would you say Faith didn't deserve her bracelet?" Garrison asked.

"Because she cheated."

"I didn't cheat." Once again, I found myself explaining the situation to Ted's daughter.

"That guy did this with his head when we were going to sit." Claire tilted her head to the side. "You moved over and the seat you were in was the one to get the prize."

"I see," Odessa said. "Claire had been very distraught the day Faith watched her. Claire mentioned something about not winning a bracelet and I told her we'd pick out something at one of the ports."

"Is that why you didn't want me to wear it?" I asked. I wasn't sure how to take the men's silence, but decided not to inquire about it.

"Yes. I didn't want Claire to have a sour expression on her face for the portraits. It was hurtful enough that she couldn't stand by her father and mother. Since my arrangement for the picture was vetoed, the least I could do was have Faith take off the bracelet."

"I didn't ask for anyone to move," I said.

"Mother, you're not being fair to Faith." Ted looked at his daughter. "And neither are you, Claire. I'm sorry your mother and I didn't veto this room arrangement immediately. It's given you hope for us getting back together. We aren't."

"Here you all are." Bob and Elizabeth walked into the room. "We were wondering where everyone ran off to hide."

Claire burst into tears and threw herself at her mom.

"What is going on?" Elizabeth gathered her child into her arms.

"It's not true. Tell Daddy you changed your mind." Claire lifted her tearstained face to stare into her mother's eyes. "Please? I want you with Daddy. Not anyone else."

"Oh dear. This again." Elizabeth sent a look of pure pleading at Ted. "Can you take care of this for me?"

"I've tried and this is the result."

"Claire being worried about the captain also brought out some of the dramatics," Garrison said.

"The captain? Why in the world is she worried about the captain?"

"I found Faith's stolen—"

"Lost," I interrupted. "Refer to it as lost."

"No," Ted said. "Let's keep to the truth and call it what it is. Someone stole Faith's bracelet from her purse and it was found in Odessa's room."

Elizabeth held Claire's chin firmly in her hand. "Did you take it?"

"Yes. I was going to give it to the captain." The tears had left Claire's voice. Now it was full of defiance. "She shouldn't have it."

"Claire thinks the guy who was helping at the seminar cheated by telling me where the bracelet was. He was nodding hello to someone else and I thought he was hinting I should move a chair over. I did and won the diamond bracelet."

"Why would he do that?" Elizabeth asked.

Good question. "Better view for both of us if I moved over." Okay, I did think the guy was up to something, but letting Elizabeth and Claire know about the jewel thievery going on wasn't a good idea. There was no reason to bring a child into this mess, not more so than we had unwittingly done.

"But what about Faith fighting with Grandpa? She broke into our room." Claire crinkled up her nose. She thought she had me.

"Actually, I invited Faith and Garrison into the room. I have a key."

"That won't be happening again." Odessa shot out her hand. John handed over the keycard.

"Is there anything else I should be aware of?" Elizabeth asked.

"No. Whatever else needs to be discussed is between my mother, father, and me," Ted said.

"I should probably be involved," I said.

"You are too involved in this already," Ted said. "That's the problem."

"I think this is where Garrison and I take our leave." Bob wrapped an arm around Garrison's waist. "We'll leave you guys to your argument. I sure am glad we got married before this cruise."

"What?" Odessa screeched.

"You're married? Already?" Hurt wound through Ted's voice.

Claire's lip trembled.

"You said we weren't going to say anything." Garrison swatted his husband in the arm.

"It seemed the time," Bob said. "Too much bad has happened on this ship. I don't want my mom trying to plan anything else."

"I can't believe you got married without inviting your own mother." Odessa's lips quivered.

"I warned you, Mom. If you started controlling all the decisions, Garrison and I would do our own thing. You kept it up and I was tired of talking to you about it."

"Did your parents attend?" Odessa fixed a hurt look on Garrison.

Garrison started to speak.

Bob shook his head. "You don't have to answer her question, love. Garrison and I made the decision together, Mom. We went to the courthouse. It was the wedding we wanted. Simple. Beautiful. No fanfare. We made this decision because of your behavior."

"I'm not really a bridesmaid?" Claire's expression was a mix of pout and rage. I wasn't sure which would win out and would rather not stick around to find out.

"You are," Garrison said. "We're still having a second wedding with attendants and a party, but not on the cruise. It hasn't been a happy time, so Uncle Bob and I would rather wait."

"Everyone will be there?" Claire flicked her gaze in my direction.

Silently, I walked to the door, head held high. The last thing I wanted to do was show Claire her attitude was hurting my feelings.

"If you keep acting ugly, Claire, you won't be coming," Bob said.

Elizabeth and Claire gasped.

"You can't be serious." Odessa wrapped her arms around Claire. "What a horrible thing to say to your niece."

"Garrison and I want to share the moment with everyone we love. That includes Faith."

"And Neal," Garrison chimed.

Claire stomped her feet, one foot after each word. "My family is Daddy, Mommy, my uncles, and my grandparents. No one else. Ever. I don't like her. I don't like Neal. Stop trying to make me." Claire fled to the bedroom and slammed the door.

"You're going to have a heck of a road ahead of you, Elizabeth." Garrison said.

"I know." Elizabeth tenderly rubbed her slightly rounded stomach.

"Honey, waiting isn't going to help the situation. You should tell her tonight," Odessa said.

I left the room. My plan for the evening was room service for one.

TWENTY-SEVEN

I sat sideways on the small couch in my stateroom, looking out the open balcony door while I ate dinner. While I missed ordering from the fancier choices in the main dining room, I was enjoying the peace and quiet in my room. There was a cool breeze coming off the ocean tonight joined by a light mist, so I decided against the veranda. I had enough of getting wet yesterday.

I wanted to watch the aerial performance and had already fixed myself up. There was still an hour before the show, and I wanted to go down before all the good seats were taken in the atrium. From the pictures in the activity guide, I surmised the large chandelier was replaced with swings and a bar.

There was a knock at the door.

Leaving the security chain on, I opened the door. It was Ted. A not-very-happy-looking Ted.

"Can I help you?" I asked through the small space.

"I need to ask you a question." Ted smiled at me, the emotion not making it into his eyes.

Whatever it was, I had a feeling he knew the answer and it annoyed him. "Do you now?"

He drummed his fingers on the door. "One of your neighbors is giving me the evil eye. I think she's about to call security on me. I'd rather talk to you in your room. My father told me something rather interesting about your shopping trip in St. Thomas."

Was it about John using me to spy on William and Ruth, or that he found me in a cellar? Reluctantly, I allowed Ted in. "I'm planning on going to the show tonight so we have to wrap this talk up quick."

"Fine. Why did you tell me you tripped instead of the truth?" Ted worked his jaw back and forth. Every muscle in his body was tight.

Maybe I shouldn't have wanted to rush this.

"Faith—"

"I didn't want you to worry, or know that I was helping your father investigate a case."

"He shouldn't have asked you."

I'd had that similar thought, but wasn't admitting it to Ted. Besides, if I wasn't involved, his mom would've been thrown in the brig. Or at least I believed so. "Maybe not, but he did and I agreed. He told me your mom was one the suspects and I wanted to make sure your dad didn't railroad her."

"My father has many faults, but making up evidence to arrest someone isn't one of them. He takes the law seriously."

"How was I supposed to know that?"

Ted fought back a smile.

"John had asked me to keep an eye on Ronnie as he was concerned William was trying to involve her in the diamond scheme, and it would hurt Garrison if Ronnie was tangled up in the mess."

His smile slipped. "A lot worse happened, which is what I've come to talk to you about."

I felt a pressure in my chest, like a small rock was grinding against my breastbone. "Please don't tell me someone else has died."

"No, but Lucinda has found a way to make herself vanish. She's been in her room, but no one has spotted her since the costume ball."

"The night William was killed, I saw Lucinda talking to Paul and Glenda."

Lucinda was out and about. She knew the ship. Because of her illness, crew members were staying away from her so they didn't catch whatever she had. Had William confessed something to Lucinda, or had Lucinda feared William was trying to set her up?

While I knew Ruth was allowing William to steal her jewels, neither William nor Lucinda knew that.

Ted wandered out to the veranda.

I was getting wet after all. The moon was hidden behind the clouds. The water appeared darker and menacing tonight. Every movement of the boat had my body on high alert. I stood beside Ted.

He braced his arms on the railing, peering down. "This vacation hasn't been what either of us planned."

"No. Life is rude like that. Comes along and changes things up without our permission or asking us for input."

Ted turned, back pressing into the rail. "That's happened to you a lot. Your first marriage. Having to leave the Army and change your career from working in law to clerking at a scrapbooking store."

"At least I'm back at home with my grandmothers. And I'm assistant manager at Scrap This. I get to order scrapbooking items. Make layouts for classes. I love crafting and get to do it for a living. It could be worse." I smiled at him. "I also met you."

"Am I a negative or a positive in your life?" A smile played at his lips.

I kissed his cheek. "A positive. Most of the time. There were times you were the last person I wanted to speak to, and look how we get along now."

"I need a little closer look." Ted wound his arms around me and dipped his head. I met his lips halfway. I felt the scorching kiss down to my painted toenails. Ted's hands roamed up and down my back. I wanted to ditch my plans for the one Ted's touch promised, but there was enough emotional upheaval in our worlds right now.

"Save those thoughts for later." I reluctantly bobbed and weaved out of his touch. Heading back into the room, I snagged the handle of my small tote and my Canon Rebel. "There's a show I want to catch."

*   *   *

When I reached the atrium, there were a few front-row seats left. I brought my camera, hoping to get some amazing pictures of the aerialists for my scrapbook. I heard a sniffle. Six chairs down the makeshift row consisting of lounge chairs and a couch was Ruth. She dabbed at her pale cheeks with an embroidered handkerchief. She had cared about William. He wasn't a villain to her.

I walked over to her. "Is this chair taken?"

"No." Ruth's voice was monotone. She gazed off at nothing, not bothering to see who asked.

I sat down, adjusting the chair so she had personal space and I had a clear shot of the lowered bars.

Her shoulder shook, tears running down her wrinkled cheeks. "I'm sorry, but I'd like to leave."

"Of course."

Ruth used her cane to push herself out of the deep chair. "Thank you." Our eyes met. She dropped back into the chair, adjusting the grip on her cane as if she was holding a bat.

I scooted my chair farther from hers.

"Why did you tell a detective what I told you?"

"Once William died, it seemed important that they know."

"They questioned me all morning." She swiped at her cheeks. "Wanted me to describe what I knew William took and give them names of my friends. There was no need to drag me into that sordid mess." Her hand shook so hard, the cane slipped from her grip.

I was a horrible person. I had wanted to comfort her, not cause her more anguish. "I'm sorry for your loss. The only way the captain can find out who was responsible for what happened is by having the truth."

The lights flickered. Ruth cradled her cane in her hand. "I'd prefer if you leave me be. William had wanted to watch this performance as a final farewell to his sister. Instead of saying goodbye to her tonight, he said hello to her yesterday."

The performers came out in simple black outfits, carrying

pastel scarves. The performers were somber. The music piped through the sound system was subdued.

Bernard stepped onto the stage. "Tonight's performance is dedicated to our coworker, friend, and family member Veronica Hastings, whose life was cut short by a tragic accident at sea. The dance tonight was choreographed by her fellow aerialists, showcasing the routines Veronica performed which wowed all and made her the grande dame of the *Serenade*." He blew a kiss toward the ceiling. "We can go on, dear Ronnie, knowing you are somewhere spectacular where you are finally happy and free."

When some of the pain ebbed from Ronnie's death, I'd gift Garrison an album with these pictures. It might offer him some comfort knowing her fellow performers cherished her. I zoomed in to get pictures of each individual aerialist, holding my finger down to capture multiple images in seconds. With the low lighting and the distance from my front-row seat to the stage, I'd get some duds. I wanted plenty of choices.

The first aerialist secured the scarf to the bar. My mind urged me to remember something about Ronnie's death. It was there. If only I could grab onto it. My journal. I wrote everything down that night in case it was important later. I pulled the journal from my bag.

I hadn't revisited the words of that day, not wanting the reminder, especially after my mind conjured up Ronnie's ghost. Using my cell as a light, I read what I wrote. The scarf had been tied to the rail, like in movies when a kidnapped victim was escaping using sheets tied together. It wasn't doubled over and threaded through itself like the aerialist's was.

There was no way Ronnie would've been able to pull herself back up to the rail. She'd have known that. Ronnie took pride in being a performer. She loved it. And Garrison. She wanted to be there for his wedding. I had also heard her fighting with a man moments before I entered her room, which Ronnie denied and said was her arguing with herself. Had it been William? But if so, why would he be killed?

The security camera pointing toward Ronnie's veranda had been broken. The retracting floor of the swimming pool was tampered with. A crew member fiddling with those items wouldn't raise suspicion. For all his faults, William had cared about Ronnie. She was his family. What if he suspected someone and confronted them?

Like the hard-to-find Lucinda. The other night, her voice had been gravelly. I could've easily mistaken her for a man the night Ronnie died. It was possible Lucinda had gotten her keycard back from the security guard and disembarked from the ship in St. Thomas, but hadn't conducted the tour. Had she followed William and Ruth instead? Maybe she wanted a cut of the money or was the brains behind the operation. Ronnie was tough physically, but emotionally fragile. Had Lucinda grown concerned that the captain or John would break Ronnie, so she silenced her forever?

I sent Ted a text. "Has anyone found Lucinda?"

He replied with one word: "Negative."

My fingers flew over the keyboard. "I don't trust her."

"Neither do I."

TWENTY-EIGHT

Today was our last day on the ship. I stood on my veranda, watching us dock at the last port. I rested against the railing, cell in one hand, coffee mug in the other. Tomorrow, we'd return home and go about our lives. Or at least most of us. There had been so much loss on this ship. I wasn't sure I'd ever want to cruise again. If a person felt threatened, there was nowhere to escape, except for the watery depths. I glanced down at my cell. Still no update from Ted. Did that mean Lucinda had been found?

Closing my eyes, I tilted my head back, smoothing my hair from my face and trying to get rid of the melancholy mood settling over me. The ship made a grinding noise and pivoted. I opened my eyes.

A group of waving crew members stood on the wooden dock held up by concrete columns. We were at our last port, Haiku, the cruise line's private side of the island. The sand was smooth, unmarred by footprints. The turquoise waters gently lapped at the shore. It was a breathtaking sight. The walk to the beach wasn't very far. Small huts, private cabanas rented out to cruise guests, were situated on the left-hand side.

There was a knock on the door. I stepped back into the room, closing the sliding door. No need to air condition the outside.

"Room service."

My Spidey senses tingled. My coffee had already been delivered. "Wrong room."

"I have the hang tag. It is for your room."

"Leave it by the door." I wanted to argue with the delivery

person, should have, but I was curious about my breakfast. I heard the guy leaving, grumbling under his breath. He thought I was trying to get out of tipping him. Before I removed the security chain, I cracked open the door and looked down. There was a room service tray. The scent of coffee wafted up to me.

I unfastened the chain and retrieved the tray. Quickly, I secured myself back in my room. I had read—and involved myself in—enough mysteries not to take the breakfast at face value. I lifted the lid. The plate was filled with a variety of pastries and in a small bowl was an assortment of jellies and butters. My stomach rumbled. No way was I touching any of it. Underneath the plate, I spotted the edge of a small beige envelope.

I opened it up. It was a request from the captain for a private meeting. He'd like to meet by the morgue. Going off to meet someone near a morgue screamed *bad idea* and potential victim in the making. There was no way for me to know if the captain actually wrote the invitation, or if someone like Lucinda had written it and slipped it under the plate. If it really was a meeting that needed kept on the down low, I understood the clandestine efforts for it, though a phone call would've worked as well. Better actually, as I wasn't buying what the note was selling.

But I was intrigued. I knew John hadn't arranged this. He'd have used his magical key and waltzed into my room. I drummed the card on my fingertips. I couldn't stay here all morning and contemplate all the evil-doing scenarios in my head. Time was ticking. According to the note, the meeting started in twenty minutes. I picked up my cell and called Ted. If he didn't answer, I'd send him an SOS text. He'd respond immediately. I wasn't looking forward to my phone bill at the end of the month. I was racking up a nice amount of roaming charges.

"I'm so proud of you," Ted said.

"You're proud of me for calling you?" Gee, he sure had lowered the bar when it came to my behavior.

"Yes. I was afraid you'd just go meet with the captain. I figured I received the same notice as you. I was coming to your room."

I opened up the door. Ted was walking down the hallway. He looked horrible. I didn't think the poor guy got much sleep last night. His clothes were wrinkled and he was unshaven. The scruffy look didn't do a thing for him.

Ted held up his hands in surrender, slowing down to a shuffle. "The captain thought it was the only way to get a message to us without alerting anyone else. He's hoping Lucinda will get nervous if she doesn't hear anything and will pop out of hiding."

"She's still gone? The ship isn't that large."

"She's found a great spot to hide, or someone is helping her."

"Has every room been checked?"

"Yes."

"Have you and the captain checked the morgue? Maybe she's taking up residence with Quinn and William." I quickly asked for forgiveness for my tasteless suggestion. I prayed lightning didn't strike me down.

"You don't want to help search it?"

I shivered. "Nope."

"I'm sure it's been checked. And if she got into the unit with Quinn or William, she isn't getting out without help."

"I'll grab my beach bag and go with you." I slipped back inside, retrieving my bag. The morgue was on the same floor where we disembarked. I didn't want to have to backtrack, especially since I'd be on the correct floor. I might be able to make it to the front of the pack and not have to wait in a Black Friday cheap-TV-for-sale-length line.

I linked my arm through Ted's. "Couldn't he have picked a nicer meeting place? The morgue is creepy."

"It's where he's meeting the FBI agents. Two agents are boarding the ship, one to look into Quinn's death and the other to handle William's murder investigation. There's also talk about taking a closer look at Ronnie's death as the agents aren't quite ready to believe it was a suicide. Bob, my dad, and I will fill them in on what we've learned. The captain will be handing over all evidence. I'll be glad to be done with this matter."

"Word is going to spread quickly."

"That's why agents are coming onboard after most of the guests have disembarked onto the island."

"What if Lucinda escapes?"

"It'll be hard. The police have been notified and are keeping an eye on the fence that separates the cruise line's side of the island from the locals. Her only option will be to swim for it. She'll be stopped by the Coast Guard cruiser stationed a few miles from shore."

"Your mom will ask where you are."

"I've taken care of that. I told my family I'm sick. I'm going to rest."

I looked him up and down. "I can see why they believed you. You look awful."

"Thanks."

Since Ted had already explained the situation to me, which irritated the captain as Ted stole his thunder, he dismissed me after a few minutes. I was at the front of the line. The Roget clan—minus the law enforcement contingent of the bunch—weaved their way up front to take advantage of my place in line. People started grumbling, but Odessa silenced them with one look.

"We don't want to lose you in the crowd," Odessa said. "We need to make more of an effort to stick with you."

Her act of inclusion seemed a little like a threat to me because of the deep pout on Claire's face. She was determined not to like me. This had been a stressful week, so I was giving myself and Claire a break. I'd work on becoming friends with the tween during her visits with Ted.

She'd see that I was fun to be around.

"I just want off this ship," Garrison said.

The few passengers in front of me moved forward.

"Adults to the left, children to the right," the cruise director announced through a megaphone as we stepped onto the dock. A group of cruise photographers snapped away.

"In twenty minutes, we'll start the family hunt. Please stay in your proper group so you can win age-appropriate prizes. The tickets that are buried describe the prize and the age it's intended for."

"Claire and I will wait for the family hunt to begin." Elizabeth tried holding her daughter's hand. Immediately, Claire took large steps away from her mother. Elizabeth's mouth trembled, the hurt clear on her face.

"I'd like to go with the other kids," Claire said. "They're splitting us up into age groups. I bet all the family prizes are for parents of younger kids. I'd really like to win something cool. Please, Mom? It's not that I don't want to hang out with you." She tried very hard not to shift her gaze in my direction.

There was a lone towel cart parked underneath a palm tree. A crew member was practically inside of it, legs dangled out while their head was deep down in the towels. Why was the crew member reaching so far down when there were plenty of towels on top? The person straightened, walking away with a stack of towels. The towels were blocking the person's face. The gait was familiar. I believed Lucinda managed to sneak off the boat by hiding in the towel cart.

"I have my spot all staked out." I shook out my treasure map. "While you guys work out what you're doing, I'm going treasure hunting. I'll see you back on the ship." I walked away like I knew where I was going, not like I was desperate to catch up with someone, even though I was.

When Lucinda turned the corner, she dropped the towels near a golf cart the employees used to transport those with disabilities. This particular cart had its innards on the ground. It wasn't going to be used anytime soon.

Lucinda hurried along the pathway, neck twisting to the left and right. Instead of her usual outfit of a little black dress, she wore the standard crew-member garb: white shirt, khaki pants, and a cap. One hand was hidden under her shirt, a bar-like object pressed against her chest. The sun glinted off the tip of the object peeking out from the hem of her shirt. A small shovel. Was Lucinda preparing to bury evidence or dig something up? She paused and turned around, a frown developing as she scanned the area. Her cap was pulled down low on her forehead and large aviator style sunglasses hid half her face. She paused, shaded eyes focused in my general direction.

I smacked the map and hurried off to a spot on the side and dug crazily, stopping and consulting my map every few minutes. I knew when someone was up to something. I watched Lucinda's feet. She strolled forward a few yards, then her feet disappeared. Quickly, I glanced up. The leaves of a palm tree quivered. Lucinda had gone for the path not traveled. She was approaching the gate that separated the private part of the island the cruise rented from the main part where the locals lived. Lucinda was making a run for it. The only other place that road led to was a cliff. I doubted Lucinda was planning on jumping off and swimming to the mainland. I followed.

She turned sharply and disappeared. I quickened my pace.

The area where Lucinda vanished was dense in tropical foliage. A small palm tree shaded a sign hung from an iron rod usually used for hanging plants. "No Trespassing. Employees only." Which was it? No trespassing or employees only? If caught, I'd feign confusion or claim I missed the sign. Carefully, I parted some large leaves and walked through the underbrush, making sure I didn't step on any dry leaves or twigs. Between the dense foliage, I spotted a bit of sky and heard the ocean crashing. My cover was ending soon.

I heard the sound of metal striking rock. I dropped on all fours and crawled toward the spot where the plant covering ended. Lucinda was digging near the end of a drop-off. She sure wasn't looking for the loot the cruise director buried. The leaves moved behind me. I spun around. Two green eyes peered at me before disappearing. Claire. Please let her run off to tell her family I was hiding out in the tropical plants.

Instead of leaving, Claire stood beside me, looking down on me with triumph shining in her eyes.

"Go back," I said between clenched teeth. "You don't belong here."

"Neither do you. Guests aren't allowed here."

"You're right. I'm doing something wrong. Go let your dad know."

"You're up to something." Her tone was more smug than accusing. She wanted me to be up to no good so that her dad would leave me. "I want to know what."

I'd use her dislike of me to my advantage. "You're right. I'm meeting someone. Don't go tattling to your dad."

An arm shot through the foliage and snagged onto Claire's. She screamed as she was hauled out.

"Close your eyes!" I scrambled out after her, reaching for Claire. Her best chance of getting out of this situation safely was not seeing Lucinda, so she wouldn't be a witness. Her hands flailed around, searching for mine. I grabbed onto one for dear life. Claire went limp, eyes squeezed shut and screaming for all she was worth.

I fisted my hand and slammed it onto the bend of Lucinda's arm. "Let her go."

Claire used her feet to scramble backwards, eyes still closed. Tears streamed down her face.

Again and again, I hit Lucinda. With a strangled howl, she released Claire and stumbled backwards. I hoisted Claire to her feet and shoved her behind me. I swept Lucinda's feet out from under her.

She crashed to the ground. The sunglasses slipped off.

I gasped and froze. Scowling up at me wasn't Lucinda, but Ronnie. The shock running through my brain gave Ronnie enough time to scramble to her feet.

"You were safe. Until now." Her voice was rough, lower. Almost sounded like a man's voice. Her blue eyes had a hazy appearance and darted left and right. She stepped forward. "You should've left all of this alone. I helped you, and this is how you thank someone for doing you a favor?"

"A favor? You've never helped me." I kept myself between

Ronnie and Claire. The cliff was close behind Ronnie. "Keep going backwards. Eyes closed or on the ground. Don't look up."

"William saw you following him and attacked you. I paid a little boy to go tell your boyfriend's father that he saw an American woman go down into a cellar and hasn't come out. So he went to see if it was you since no one had seen you get back on the ship. If not for me, you'd have been left in St. Thomas. It was all settled. Almost all over with," Ronnie said in her new voice. "She was almost free with no more harm."

"You don't have to hurt anyone else."

"You've given me no choice. You know she didn't die."

She was alive and killed someone else. "You threw Lucinda off the boat that night and tried to make it look like you—Ronnie died."

The other Ronnie tsked. "She didn't do that. He did. William. Always scheming. Always with a plan. Lucy girl asked for a bigger cut. William thought it was because she swiped some of the jewelry from his biggest score two months ago. I took it for Ronnie. Of course, Lucinda denied it and it made William furious, so it was bye-bye to her. I told him we should pretend it was Ronnie who went overboard. No one would know. Let her start over in St. Thomas or St. Maarten. He agreed. Then he said he'd tell the captain Ronnie killed Lucinda if she didn't tell him where the jewels were. People were asking a lot of questions about the death. She swore she didn't know. He called her a liar." Ronnie tapped her—his?—chest. "She wasn't a liar. I hid them. Me. Ronald. Veronica needed money to get away from everyone who wanted me gone from her life." The wildness in her eyes increased and an evil smile curled her lips. "He'd have killed Ronnie. She was already dead. No one would've known or cared."

"Tell the police it was self-defense. You don't have to hurt anyone else. She won't tell anyone. She's just a little girl."

"Only I protect Ronnie. Others use her." Ronnie jabbed a finger into her chest with each word.

"That's not true. Garrison does. He loves her. He wanted to prove William was responsible for all of it."

Something flickered in Ronnie's eyes. The haze cleared up for a moment before settling back in. I had to get through to her.

"Say goodbye to the girl." Ronnie tried reaching around me.

I punched her hand. She drew back, sizing me and the terrain up. It was a long way down, and I believed she was figuring out a way for me to test just how far down.

"Keep your eyes covered, Claire. Uncle Garrison will come and get you." I dropped the names, hoping one brought the Ronnie I knew and liked back long enough for Claire to escape.

Ronnie's glazed over eyes darted back and forth. She inched toward me, hands balled. "I can't let you leave."

"I won't. I promise." I remained between Ronnie and Claire. Every move she made, I matched with a small change of my body position. I wouldn't let her see Claire, especially since the child might peek. Claire scooted on her rear, hands feeling the ground around her. There was a small trail near the cliff. If Claire reached it, she'd have an easier time of running away.

"I can't let anyone leave. She knows." Ronnie pointed at Claire. The little girl froze, a strangled sob shaking her body.

"All the child knows is that her dad's girlfriend snuck away from the family to meet up with some guy. I'm meeting a guy. She doesn't like me. She followed me to prove that I'm not good enough for her dad. Right?"

Claire sobbed out a yes.

"See? I haven't said your name. She's no threat to you. You'll be long gone before she can get back to the ship and get her dad. He stayed on the *Serenade*. He's not out here."

"You're lying."

"No, I'm not. If he was here, she'd have brought him along to prove I was sneaking around behind his back. Even better than snitching on me."

Claire continued to sob, drawing farther back. Her hand was on the dirt.

"Run!" I rammed into Ronnie, knocking us both to the ground. "Go now!"

Ronnie cursed. She clawed at my face. I grabbed at her hands, trying to pin her to the ground. The woman was strong.

"He's not my uncle. He's not my uncle," Claire screamed over and over again. "Help me!"

Good girl. That should get her a cavalry. I continued to wrestle Ronnie, locking my arms around her upper body. She wedged her shoulder under my chin and pushed. I heard the skittering of Claire's sneakers on the pebbled path. She was close to the edge of the cliff. It was a long way down to an extremely rocky bottom. Claire let out a startled cry. I looked over. She teetered, pinwheeling her arms.

"Fall to the left! The left." I scrambled to my feet, preparing to grab onto Claire or push her to the side, even if it meant I went over instead.

Ronnie knocked me aside, running over my splayed legs to get to Claire.

I snagged her ankle. She spun and stepped on my hand with her other foot. Even through the pain, I held on tight. I wouldn't let her hurt Claire. "Veronica, you don't want to do this."

"Stop calling me that." The gruff voice had a hint of a softer tone. Ronnie. I was getting through to her.

"She's a child. I know you wouldn't want to hurt a child. You don't want to do this. You put the message on that cruise message board. You wanted us to save you from Ronald."

"You don't know what I'd want!" Ronnie kicked me in the face.

Crying out, I instinctively let go, my arms going to protect my face as she went for another attack. As she kicked out, her other leg flew out from under her. The end of a cane had hooked around it. Ronnie tipped backwards. A desperate scream tore from Ronnie as she toppled off the cliff.

"No!" I leapt forward and grabbed at her—snatching only a handful of air. My feet landed on the edge. The ground crumbled underneath me. I twisted, snagging the ledge. Pain shot down my arms. I tried bringing my leg up, but the movement sent small pieces of the cliff I clung to falling into my hair. I found a small foothold and planted my left foot on it. That gave me some time.

A frail hand clamped onto me and a cane lowered down. Ruth's gaze meet mine. Regret shone in her eyes. "Grab onto it and hold on."

"You didn't mean to."

"I think I did," Ruth said. "William didn't deserve to die. Not like that. Now take hold of the cane."

I had a stranglehold on the edge of the cliff and shook my head. I was afraid I'd pull Ruth over.

"Don't let go, Faith." Claire's small hand covered mine. Her green eyes were filled with hope and fear. "They'll be here soon. I'm sorry."

"It's not your fault, Claire. You don't have anything to apologize for."

"I was mean to you." Tears clogged her voice, garbling her words together. "I stole your bracelet."

The earth under my left hand pulled away from the rock. Quickly, I found a new handhold.

"I don't want you to fall!" Claire sobbed, inching toward the edge.

"Go back, Claire. I'll be fine," I lied. The ground I clung to with my right hand was also loosening.

"I like you. My dad really likes you. Don't fall."

The small ledge underneath my left foot crumbled. I jerked down. My nails scraped farther down the rock. I fought the urge to look down, not wanting to see the rocks below—or Ronnie's body.

"I got it from here, Jelly Bean." Bob appeared in my view. "How the heck did you wind up there?" He latched onto my wrists. "Let go, Faith."

"I'm losing my footing. I'll pull you over."

Bob rolled his eyes. "Darling, there's no way you've gained that much weight on the cruise."

I glared up at him, planting my feet onto the cliff as I walked up. "Gained *that* much?" What the scrap was wrong with him? If he went over with me, it kind of served him right. I inched upwards.

Actually, I didn't want Claire seeing that. Or even just watching me falling to the rocks below. She might not like me very much, but it sure wasn't a vision a child should have stored in their memory. My feet landed on solid ground, and I smacked him in the shoulder. "A man should never comment on a woman's weight."

Bob pulled me into a tight hug. "Thank God you're all right. I knew if I riled you up, you'd get your butt up here."

I was up there. On the ground. My knees grew wobbly. Claire wrapped her arms around my waist, trembling from head to toe. Taking in deep breaths, I promised myself I could fall apart when I was alone in my room. Not now. Not in front of Claire.

Ted ran toward us. Sobbing, Claire ran for her dad. I stayed put. A few feet from him, Claire paused and looked back. She ran back to me—for me. She held my hand, taking off for her father. Bringing me with her. Ted knelt and caught us both in his arms.

TWENTY-NINE

The female agent handed me a stack of papers. "Please read over your statement and let me know if anything has been left out."

Local police officers, and more FBI agents, were boarding the ship to take custody of Quinn, William, and Ronnie's bodies. Ruth had told me she planned on claiming William and making sure he had a proper burial—after the authorities decided what to do regarding her role in the matter. Paul and Glenda were let go after some stern warnings since they hadn't allowed William to steal from them.

Signing my statement was the last item to complete, then I could start putting the incident behind me. As the *Serenade* had headed back to Port Canaveral last night, instead of partaking in the farewell events I talked to two different FBI agents about what had happened. It had been a long day and I promised the agents I'd see them first thing in the morning to sign my official statement if I could get a few hours of sleep. They had agreed as there wasn't anywhere for me to go and the fact I wasn't a suspect.

The captain's voice came over the loudspeaker, thanking everyone for cruising on the *Serenade* and wishing them a pleasant and uneventful trip home.

I read through my statement. "Everything is in there."

"Sign at the bottom." She placed a business card on the table and pushed it toward me. "If you do remember anything else, give me a call. It's likely you won't get the diamond bracelet back even after the investigation is over."

"Fine by me. I don't want it." I pocketed her card and headed out the door.

Bob was standing right outside.

"Your turn?" I asked.

"I completed my statement last night. I was hoping to speak with you before Ted hustled you off the ship."

I glanced down the hallway. Ted was there waiting for me. If I wasn't mistaken, the annoyed look on his face was directed at his brother and not me.

"Thanks for saving me." I hadn't had much time to speak to Bob, Garrison, or Odessa after Ronnie fell to her death. I wished there had been a way a save her also. She was a troubled soul who needed help.

"No need to thank me." Bob tried to force out a smile but it seemed to get stuck and looked more like he was trying to hold back a grimace. "I'm glad you're all right. Garrison feels so guilty about everything that's happened. He doesn't want to see anyone right now. He's ashamed."

"That's ridiculous." I squeezed Bob's hand. "It's not his fault. Do you think he'd talk to me?"

Bob shook his head. "I'd wait a few weeks. You and Ted can visit for a weekend. He kept Ronnie's mental illness a secret because he didn't want anyone to judge her unfairly. He didn't know she was dangerous."

"Ronnie wasn't dangerous," I said. "It was Ronald. And Ronald being on the ship was solely on William."

"Hopefully, Garrison will realize that soon. I hate seeing him burdened by this. He had planned on taking her to a treatment facility after the cruise. My mom had talked to the captain about Ronnie's strange behavior but never connected it to a deeper issue."

"How's your mom doing?"

"She's feeling just as guilty as Garrison. She wonders if her attitude toward Ronnie also brought out Ronald." Bob rubbed his eyes. "I invited her to spend a few weeks with us but she doesn't think her presence will help Garrison. Instead, she's going to take a few months off and stay with Claire and Elizabeth."

"It'll do her good to be with her granddaughter."

"I'm glad my mom isn't going right back to work on the *Serenade.*" Bob narrowed his eyes then raised his hands in a gesture of surrender. "My brother wants me to wrap this up. My question is likely to send Ted on the warpath, but I don't have a choice. You're one of the few people I trust who can actually help me."

"Then Ted will have to get over it. I consider you a friend and I won't abandon you." I had no idea where Bob's request would take me, but there were times to ignore caution signs blinking in your head. This was one of them. I trusted Bob.

"Garrison needs me right now. If I had some help with some of my administrative and research tasks, I wouldn't have to spend so much time at the office. Nothing dangerous I promise." Bob crossed his heart.

"Are you done yet?" Ted's impatient voice carried down the hall. "We need to disembark."

"One more minute," Bob said.

"You said only one minute about six minutes ago," Ted said. "You need to work on your time management skills."

"You need to work on patience," Bob fired back.

"Waiting five extra minutes is being patient."

My eye stared getting twitchy. I decided to end their bickering. "I'd be happy to help. I'll need a few days to adjust my work schedule at Scrap This. I can't bail on my grandmothers."

"You don't even have to do that. I'll deliver a computer to your house with all the software you need for your tasks. Most of our work can be accomplished through emails. I'll make sure you're set up with a secure server..." Bob trailed off. "Go before Ted's head explodes. I'll explain everything later."

I walked over to Ted. "We were almost done with our conversation."

"Bob talks too much. I'd like to get off this ship but wanted to wait for you."

I understood that feeling. I was looking forward to being on land.

Or rather off the *Serenade*. I kind of liked cruising—except for the murders.

I linked my arm through his. "Good thing, since you're my ride to the airport."

"Actually, there's been a change of plans. We're not going to the airport today," Ted said as we walked down the gangplank.

I groaned. "Our flight was delayed? I just want out of here. I'm done with vacationing."

"Are you sure?" Ted gathered up our luggage and escorted me through customs.

Since we had nothing to declare, it was a short and painless process. Though it was sounding like getting back to Eden would be anything but easy.

"Yes, I'm sure."

"Even if the detour we're taking is a five-day stay at Disney World?"

I spun him to face me. "What?"

"You know, the place where Mickey Mouse and Tinker Bell live? Where dreams come true? That place. We're staying there for a few days before we head home. Just you and me."

"But...work. You and I have jobs. What will the chief say?"

"That some extra time off will be good. The gossip mill will have another story churning through it by then, so the station won't be overrun with reporters."

"My grandmothers."

"I called them. And I have a confirmation text. See?" Ted showed me his phone.

My grandmothers, Hope and Cheryl, wished me a magical time at Disney World. As a joint gift, they wanted a picture of me and Mickey. For individual presents, Cheryl wanted a Stitch plush and Hope a Mickey Mouse cookie jar. "What did you tell them?"

"That my family gave you a little bit of a hard time and I wanted to salvage the vacation by taking you on a side trip. That I need some quality time with you before I ask you an important question involving a ring."

"Are you serious or were you just manipulating my grandmothers? You know they've been trying to marry me off for the last two and half years."

"I knew they'd say yes, and I think it's better to give you a heads up on my plan." He grinned at me. "I know you need to agonize everything out before you make a decision on your personal life. If it was a crime, you'd jump right in."

"You're comparing the possibility of marrying me to a crime? I'm not sure if I should be flattered or insulted."

Ted herded me toward the employee parking lot. "I'm talking about your method of decision making. I've never seen anyone second guess themselves so much when it comes to mundane choices, yet charge ahead when it puts their life at risk."

"So now a proposal is mundane? Gee, Ted, you really know a way to a girl's heart."

He grinned at me and stopped beside a bright yellow Mustang convertible. "I do try. Here's our ride. My mom offered us her convertible for the week." He opened up the passenger door. "Let's get going. We're wasting daylight, and there are tons of rides and parks to explore."

"You're really taking me to Disney World?" I knew I had a sappy grin on my face as I slid onto the smooth leather seat.

"You've always wanted to go, so why not now? We're near Orlando. What better place to propose to you?"

"Are you asking me to marry you because I saved Claire?"

Ted pulled out from the spot and headed for the entrance ramp to the interstate.

"I will ask you because I love you, and life is rather boring and predictable without you around. I've accepted the fact you're a trouble seeker, and I know how to get you out of it."

I rolled my eyes. "I've always thought your intentions were to keep me out of it, Mr. Bossy Detective."

"I gave up on that a few months ago. Too much work."

"You know, I'm not trying to find it."

"I know. You're just good at your unique specialty."

"What's that? Wreaking havoc?"

"No, putting yourself second. So I'll put you first. I want no arguments from you."

I laughed.

He scowled. "I'm not joking."

"Of course it's a joke. If I don't argue with you, you'll think something is wrong."

"You do have a point." He slid a look toward me as he merged onto the highway. "No comments or suggestions?"

"How does Claire feel about it?"

"She said you'd be okay as a stepmom."

Stepmom. That worried me a little bit. I've never been a mom and didn't know if I was up to the task for an eleven-year-old.

"You saved her, Faith. You were willing to give your life for hers." Ted choked on the words. Tears filled his eyes.

"Don't you ever doubt yourself. Because I never have or ever will."

"I can deal with being okay. Gives me a good starting point and an opening for improvement."

"Just be you. Don't twist yourself into someone else. She'll love you. I'm sure of it."

Claire was at a rough age and there were already so many changes in her life. Her mother was having a baby. A stepdad on the horizon. And possibly a stepmom. I'd let Claire know I'd be a safe place for her. A friend. I'd work my way up from there.

Ted must've thought my silence was from insecurity and my possible role in Claire's life, because he started listing all my qualities a tween would love.

"And I'm sure once she sees how I can annoy you and ruffle up your well-smoothed-down feathers, she'll think I'm just the gal for you," I said.

"That's why Bob loves and adores you. He thinks I'm a little too impatient and you're helping me learn it. It'll be great for when Claire is a teenager, since I'll have had plenty of practice of keeping my cool with you. You are perfect for me. We mesh well together.

Our combined personalities keep the seesaw stable. No one is firmly planted on the ground or up in the air. It's a well-honed balancing act."

"The romance just oozes from your words." I placed my hand on my forehead. "I think I feel a swoon coming on."

"I haven't officially proposed yet. It'll be more romantic. I promise."

"Is that so?"

"When you're ready, just let me know you want to see the Hall of Presidents."

"The Hall of Presidents?" I loosened the seatbelt for a moment and twisted to face Ted. "That's quite an unusual place."

"I know. That's why I picked it. How many people have been dreaming about going to the Hall of Presidents? It's not usually on someone's must-do list of Disney attractions, so that's why it's the perfect spot. When you're ready to tell me yes, no, or let's hold off and date some more, just say you want to go to the Hall of Presidents. We'll be in Disney World for five days. I promise no hounding you for an answer. If you want more time, I'll revisit the question around Halloween. We're not conventional people, so no Valentine's Day or Christmas proposal." Ted glanced over at me and winked before returning his eyes to the road.

It was long enough for me to catch the emotion in his eyes. He loved me. For me. The headstrong part. The anxious part. The meddlesome gene that poked at his patience.

He knew me better than anyone had in a long time. He knew a surprise proposal would throw me off balance. He wanted to save me from making a rash decision or freezing up and later regretting my reaction. He was leaving the timing to me while making sure I knew what he wanted. No games. No guessing. Was I ready?

He rubbed my leg. "You've been put through the ringer in your past relationships. You might not be ready for a commitment yet, and I understand. Whatever your decision, it won't change anything between us. Okay, maybe a little if you say yes, as you'll have a ring, and my mother and your grandmothers will drive us crazy with planning, but my feelings won't change. I love you. In all probability, I have from the very moment we met."

"The very moment? You suspected I was withholding information on a murder. I seriously doubt you had loving feelings for me then."

He grinned. "Okay, I'm exaggerating a little. I liked your spunk, even though it annoyed the heck out of me. Most of all, I admired your loyalty to your friends and your determination to find justice. Those were likable qualities, so I hoped I wouldn't have to toss your cute butt into jail."

"What can I say, I grow on people."

"For the record, I was right. You were holding something back from me."

I rolled my eyes. "Must you always be right, Detective Roget?"

"Not always. I was wrong on who was the better guy for you. I've never been happier to be proven wrong." He twined his fingers with mine and gave a quick squeeze before he placed both hands back on the steering.

The way I preferred he drive. Warmth flooded through me.

I settled back against the seat. "So, who gets to pick the first attraction?"

"You."

"Great. Because I've always wanted to go to the Hall of Presidents."

Photo by KD Images

CHRISTINA FREEBURN

The Faith Hunter Scrap This Mystery series brings together Christina Freeburn's love of mysteries, scrapbooking, and West Virginia. When not writing or reading, she can be found in her scrapbook room or at a crop. Alas, none of the real-life crops have had a sexy male prosecutor or a handsome police officer attending.

Christina served in the JAG Corps of the US Army and also worked as a paralegal, librarian, and church secretary. She lives in West Virginia with her husband, children, a dog, and a rarely seen cat except by those who are afraid or allergic to felines.

The Faith Hunter Scrap This Mystery Series
by Christina Freeburn

CROPPED TO DEATH (#1)
DESIGNED TO DEATH (#2)
EMBELLISHED TO DEATH (#3)
FRAMED TO DEATH (#4)
MASKED TO DEATH (#5)

Available at booksellers nationwide and online

Visit www.henerypress.com for details

Henery Press Mystery Books

And finally, before you go...
Here are a few other mysteries
you might enjoy:

THE SEMESTER OF OUR DISCONTENT

Cynthia Kuhn

A Lila Maclean Academic Mystery (#1)

English professor Lila Maclean is thrilled about her new job at prestigious Stonedale University, until she finds one of her colleagues dead. She soon learns that everyone, from the chancellor to the detective working the case, believes Lila—or someone she is protecting—may be responsible for the horrific event, so she assigns herself the task of identifying the killer.

More attacks on professors follow, the only connection a curious symbol at each of the crime scenes. Putting her scholarly skills to the test, Lila gathers evidence, but her search is complicated by an unexpected nemesis, a suspicious investigator, and an ominous secret society. Rather than earning an "A" for effort, she receives a threat featuring the mysterious emblem and must act quickly to avoid failing her assignment...and becoming the next victim.

Available at booksellers nationwide and online

Visit www.henerypress.com for details

FINDING SKY

Susan O'Brien

A Nicki Valentine Mystery (#1)

Suburban widow and PI-in-training Nicki Valentine can barely keep track of her two kids, never mind anyone else. But when her best friend's adoption plan is jeopardized by the young birth mother's disappearance, Nicki is persuaded to help. Nearly everyone else believes the teenager ran away, but Nicki trusts her BFF's judgment, and the feeling is mutual.

The case leads where few moms go (teen parties, gang shootings) and places they can't avoid (preschool parties, OB-GYNs' offices). Nicki has everything to lose and much to gain—including the attention of her unnervingly hot PI instructor. Thankfully, Nicki is armed with her pesky conscience, occasional babysitters, a fully stocked minivan, and nature's best defense system: women's intuition.

Available at booksellers nationwide and online

Visit www.henerypress.com for details

NUN TOO SOON

Alice Loweecey

A Giulia Driscoll Mystery (#1)

Giulia Falcone-Driscoll has just taken on her first impossible client: The Silk Tie Killer. He's hired Driscoll Investigations to prove his innocence and they have only thirteen days to accomplish it. Talk about being tried in the media. Everyone in town is sure Roger Fitch strangled his girlfriend with one of his silk neckties. And then there's the local TMZ wannabes stalking Giulia and her client for sleazy sound bites.

On top of all that, her assistant's first baby is due any second, her scary smart admin still doesn't relate well to humans, and her police detective husband insists her client is guilty. About this marriage thing—it's unknown territory, but it sure beats ten years of living with 150 nuns.

Giulia's ownership of Driscoll Investigations hasn't changed her passion for justice from her convent years. But the more dirt she digs up, the more she's worried her efforts will help a murderer escape. As the client accuses DI of dragging its heels on purpose, Giulia thinks The Silk Tie Killer might be choosing one of his ties for her own neck.

Available at booksellers nationwide and online

Visit www.henerypress.com for details

Made in the USA
Las Vegas, NV
01 December 2022